THE BREAD AND BUTTER STORIES

The Bread and Butter Stories

Mary Norton

ISIS
LARGE PRINT
Oxford and Orlando

First published in Great Britain 1998
by Little, Brown & Co.

Published in Large Print 1999 by ISIS Publishing Ltd,
7 Centremead, Osney Mead, Oxford OX2 0ES, and
ISIS Publishing, PO Box 195758,
Winter Springs, Florida 32719-5758, USA
by arrangement with Little, Brown & Co. (UK)

The moral right of the author has been asserted

British Library Cataloguing in Publication Data
Norton, Mary
  The bread and butter stories. – Large print ed.
  1. Women – Social conditions – Fiction. 2. Upper class –
  Fiction 3. Large type books
  I.Title
  823.9'14 [F]

ISBN 0-7531-6067-6 (hb)
ISBN 0-7531-6113-3 (pb)

Printed and bound by Antony Rowe, Chippenham and Readin

CONTENTS

Introduction vii

The Girl in the Corner 1

The Blown-Glass Decanter 17

Talking of Television 35

Once upon a Time. 51

Take of Wormwood Seven Scruples . . . 63

Pauline and Bertha 72

Mr Sequeria 91

Supper in the Kitchen 106

Pleasure Cruise 120

The Lovely Evening 144

Lake Trout. 161

A House in Portugal 183

Sailing with Robert 201

The Fish Tank. 212

Beauty Bar 239

INTRODUCTION

My mother, Mary Norton, always called them *The Bread and Butter Stories*, because they earned our bread and butter. They were mostly written in the 1940s and 50s and drew heavily on her earlier life, so they are quite a mixture of fiction and nonfiction. She did have an idea of including the stories in an autobiography, with each one illustrating a particular part of her life. She'd very much enjoyed Jonathan Raban's book, *For Love & Money*, in which he did something similar. Mary did start writing an autobiography but never got very far. Somehow she needed the impetus of having to write to survive. In later years the pressure was off and she enjoyed her success, which brought her "playing time" and a lot of fun. Mary always said writing was a very lonely job; she'd far rather act or cook.

Mary Spencer-Pearson was born in 1903. She was brought up in a Georgian manor house in Leighton Buzzard which later became the model for Firbank Hall, home of the Borrowers. She was educated at a convent school and had a year in France. Arthur Rose, co-author of the lyrics to *Me and My Girl* and a great man of the theatre, happened to be in the house when Mary's parents were discussing her future. They were going to send her to an art school, when Mary burst out, "But I want to act!" She had never dared say it before.
"Why shouldn't she?" said Arthur.

He made her learn some Shakespeare and practise it from the stage of whatever theatre he was at, sometimes with a line of chorus girls behind her: "If you can do it here, you can do it anywhere," he said. He arranged an audition with Lilian Baylis, who took Mary on as a student at the Old Vic.

In 1925 Mary married my father, Robert Charles Norton. They moved to Quinta das Aguas Livres (Free Waters) in Portugal, the family seat of my father. The Nortons were one of the many English families domiciled in Portugal since the Peninsula Wars. Robert, better known as "Bob", was the head of the family and the eldest of ten. Many of his younger brothers and sisters still lived at the family home, so when he brought his shy young bride home she found an intimidating number of Nortons already ensconced. There had been great preparations for the arrival of the new Mistress, but when the manager saw her he exclaimed, "But it's just another girl!" However, Mary's arrival meant freedom for her young sisters-in-law who soon took off for a life in London and Lisbon.

Mummy, struggling to learn Portuguese, was very lonely to begin with and missed her family and friends at the Old Vic. So my father asked Lilian Baylis and the company to come and stay. Some of her fellow students remained friends all her life. Among them were Margaret Rutherford, who was much older than the rest, Esmond Knight, and Peter Watts who helped her in later years at the BBC. Mary needed friends like flowers need rain, and she had a great gift for friendship. At her memorial service Peregrine Worsthorne said: "Mary made each one of us feel that we were her only friend." She did take immense trouble over her friends. I remember once she bought a piano, because David Heneker, a pianist best known for writing the lyrics to the musical *Half a Sixpence*, was coming to stay.

There were four of us children: I, the eldest, closely followed by Robert (Bruv), Guy and Caroline — ten years between the lot of us. As a young girl I thought life in Quinta was heaven. There were seven springs that came up through our land, each one with a different taste — you could choose which water you drank at meals. I remember the smell of the pine forests, the fruit orchards, and all the animals and pets we had. It was a paradise for children. We left there when I was about seven years old, forced out by the great economic crash of the late 1920s and 30s. Bob lost everything trying to keep going: the family shipping business, the estates, his personal fortune, and even my mother's jewels. We moved to a small cottage clinging onto a mountain at Sintra, where the story "Mr Sequeria" (written years later) is set. Our mother was mostly alone with us children while father was working very hard trying to start a new business up in Setubal. When he did come home I noticed his hair was falling out in little circles like pennies. I used to put my fingers in them. I don't actually remember "Mr Sequeria", but I do remember his house, rather forbidding-looking, and I certainly remember "Luiz". We children thought that he was absolutely poisonous as well as totally unpredictable. I suppose nowadays one would say Luiz was a hyperactive child. We avoided him.

"Alfred", the French poet in the story, became our tutor. We thought he was old and very strict. He smacked our hands with a ruler if we didn't keep our closed hands on the table like good French children, and he wouldn't let us speak English, so we spoke Portuguese. When he forbade Portuguese we made up a language. We must have been fairly poisonous too. Although we called him Monsieur he could only have been in his late teens, falling for mummy, and following her about. She spoke excellent French, having lived there as a girl, and we could hear them both from the bottom of the garden, declaiming the great French plays in a stylised and extremely dramatic fashion.

The Spanish Civil War was raging close by at this time. In a cottage down the road lived three other friends, English boys — writers and poets — who'd just got out of Germany ahead of the Nazis, leaving one of their friends behind and in danger. They were communists. Mary persuaded daddy, who had some sway with the Embassy, to try and get the last boy out of Germany before he was interned. All this drama took place over polite tea parties. Ladies didn't entertain young men when their husbands were away except with a chaperone, so I, aged about eight, was mummy's chaperone on such visits. The talk went over my head, but I didn't mind because I played with Wystan's rabbits in the garden. Those young men were Stephen Spender, Christopher Isherwood and Wystan Auden. I don't know whether they ever got their friend out.

In 1939 my mother returned to London for an operation, bringing Bruv, baby Caroline and me with her. War broke out and the return trip back to our father and Guy in Portugal was now impossible. My father was first attached to the British Embassy, where he had the doubtful honour of heading the German blacklist. Then, wanting to see action but too old to rejoin his regiment (in 1914 he had fought as a regular gunnery officer, complete with his own horses and even his dog), he took some years off his age and joined the Royal Navy Volunteer Reserve. He used to say that he was the oldest and the largest second lieutenant in the navy at eighteen stone and 6ft 4in. In the autumn of 1940 my mother took us children to America where she worked for the war office. Mary had always scribbled stories as a girl but had always thought of herself principally as an artist. However, now money was short she began to write. Her first book, *The Magic Bedknob*, was written as a vehicle for the pictures of the American illustrator, Waldo Pearce. When it was re-published without any illustrations, the book was a great success. The sequel, *Bonfires and Broomsticks*, was written after we returned home.

We arrived back in London in early 1943, in time for the "little blitz" of buzz bombs and V2s. We lived in my grandmother's flat in Chelsea — at that time still a friendly bombed village of artists, writers and actors, nearly all impecunious. The street was struck a few times. During an air raid the people living upstairs would always come down to our flat, on the first floor. There would be a shy knock on the door and someone unknown to us, often in night clothes, and even curlers, would be standing there asking "Could we come in for the raid, please?", as if they were sheltering from the rain. We'd all sit in the hallway, with our backs against an inside wall, and feel a little safer. Over the following weeks more people joined us, even Jack, the porter, who lived in the basement. Tea would be made and because it was rationed, small presents of tea or flowers would appear later. I think our flat was popular because Mary always managed to make a home with a pleasant atmosphere. Put her in an igloo and it would somehow have been inviting.

Transport often stopped altogether during the bombing. I remember that Mary sometimes walked home in the blackout alone, through the broken glass, wondering, she said, if I'd got home from school all right. I, with the callowness of youth, would feel no qualms as to whether she was safe, unless she was *very* late. Mothers seem indestructible. Once however, Mary was in the blast when a V2 fell in the Chelsea Pensioners Royal Hospital at the bottom of Smith Street. Unlike the buzz bombs, when you heard the little bumbling engine cut out and waited for the crash, there was no warning. It was an odd explosion, not causing much damage to us because the windows were open, but I noticed that all the soup plates on the dresser had their middles blown out, leaving only the rims still standing in an orderly row. Mary seemed all right, but about a week later she read an article in *Readers Digest* called "My Eyes Have a Cold Nose". It was written by a blind man and in it, he described his first symptom of going blind: an inability to see out of the corners of his eyes. She had been suffering from the same problem for nearly a week so she went to her optician to be told that she had a detached retina. It wasn't an easy operation in those days. They gave her less than a fifty-fifty chance of success. Mummy, who always had a touch of the macabre in her, told me with a certain glee how they gave her a local anaesthetic, put the eye on her cheek, and operated on it while she could see! The recovery then was very drawn out. She had to remain absolutely still for about ten days. I used to go and visit her with her eyes completely bandaged in Moorfield Hospital, knowing that we were both wondering if she would ever see again. She'd ask me to wipe her face, which I did, terrified of jarring it. Then I'd read to her. When the bandages came off she could see — but very oddly.

The doctor advised blacked out glasses with just a tiny pin hole clear in the middle of each lens. We used to stumble about the Kings Road laughing, because her sight was so strange, like the distorting mirrors at fun fairs. By slightly shifting her face, she could make the person she was looking at have a minute head and huge body, or vice versa. Great if she was bored or didn't like someone, though the hastily stifled giggle might be hard to explain. The operation was a success and she returned to her normal myopia. But during the long recovery process, my mother had great pride in not showing her disability. This was the same in her old age, when she was nearly blind again with ripening cataracts in both eyes. Although she'd carry a stick it was more for show (it had a lovely handle), and she'd constantly stumble off kerbs and bump into furniture. So this was the blind girl's pride in the story "The Girl in the

Corner".

During the Second World War my mother took up acting again. She did a lot of radio, a season in Wolverhampton rep and character parts in London, including understudying Joan Hickson in *The Guinea Pig* at the Criterion Theatre. This was one of the happiest times of her life. There wasn't a great deal of acting to do as Joanie was hardly, if ever, ill; but it was the company that Mary so enjoyed. Rachel Gurney, who also lived off the King's Road, became a lifelong friend, as did Joanie (who appears as Miss Minnie Masters in the story "Talking of Television"). Denholm Elliot lived nearby too with his mother Nina, and Honor Blackman was the very young pretty *ingénue*. My mother said the company became a fascinating kind of family for her.

After the war we crossed the road and moved into a rented house at 41 Smith Street. It was a tall Georgian house with a long garden behind it, and was the favourite of all the homes Mary lived in. Acting work began to dry up as people came back into the profession. The bank manager was practically knocking down the door, so Mary settled down to write full time and Bob (who'd been de-mobbed) took over the shopping and cooking. She would shut herself in her room first thing in the morning, sometimes not even bothering to get dressed, living on trays of tea and tit bits brought up by daddy heaving his way up the stairs, or else some reluctant child, "Just take this up to your mother . . ." Bob found it difficult to get a regular job after the war, with so many younger men trying to restart their lives as well. He did get one job as a guide for some of the first holiday trips to Europe (he spoke seven languages) but it didn't work out. Being a generous man, and forgetting that he was no longer rich, he insisted on treating the punters, and would spend more money than he ever earned.

Mummy wrote mostly for the American magazine, *Woman's Day*, which gave her a thousand dollars a story-riches in those days, and far greater than what was paid in the UK. We lived on tick, with the kind co-operation of Mr Jones the grocer, Tarling the fishmonger, and many others. There were great celebrations when she was paid: our supporters would come round for drinks and bills were settled. Mr Jones was our principle benefactor. One day my father was sitting with him at his shop in the old Chelsea manor house and he happened to mention that Mr Jones's chair was very comfortable for his slipped disc. With the next grocery delivery the chair arrived. It was that sort of kindness that was a real help.

Our mother was a good cook, but when daddy took over he taught himself, primarily by working backwards, remembering what good food should taste and look like. Even scrambled eggs were presented as a chef's dish — rather a novelty in those days of austerity and rationing. Unfortunately his aesthetic sense didn't stretch to the kitchen. We children were press-ganged into clearing up the debris of what looked like the passage of a large tornado. One evening I came bursting into the kitchen and screamed as I felt something clammy, sticky and cold entangle in my long hair. When I put on the light, I saw wet spaghetti hanging everywhere from string washing lines. He'd found that he could buy cheap bags of newly made pasta in Soho. The trouble was getting it home and dried before it congealed into a great solid lump.

Mary would come down from her writing for dinner, and afterwards, if she was at a good place in her work, we'd sit by the fire and she'd read us some of it. I can't remember Bob ever making a remark about her writing. He would just sit at the table, playing endless games of patience; an occasional grunt would show he was listening. She was her own best critic, and it seemed that just reading the stories out loud was a help. She would write and rewrite and always get upset if a deadline came before she felt that there was nothing more to be done. Mary also got livid if publishers changed her words. It wasn't only the words, it was the rhythm, she said.

Her greatest friend and confidante was still old Arthur Rose. She said that he knew more about writing and the theatre than anyone she'd ever met. They used to talk on the telephone nearly every day for at least an hour. When he called, she'd ask for her cigarettes, get comfortable, and we'd know that the telephone would be out of commission for ages. The other great help in her writing was Margaret McElderry, the editor for children's books at Harcourt Brace in America.

Just after the war Mary sublet 41 Smith Street in order to pay some bills, and we lived first in Mevagissey and then in Polruan, Cornwall, just opposite Fowey. The house was perched almost directly on the water. There was our beloved "Edith", a rather heavy clinker built day boat, with a lug sail. Our father taught us to sail — he is the Robert of "Sailing with Robert" — without really explaining anything. It was more a case of "do this" or "do that" with various degrees of urgency. He must have done something right, because we children all grew up with a lifelong love, if not a passion, for sailing. We had no car. Edith was our only form of transport, used for shopping and lovely summer picnics to Ready Money Cove, Lantic Bay and Lantivet. Once, Daddy had been saving up for weeks to buy Mary a gold Cartier lighter, which he gave her at breakfast. We got in the boat, Mummy lit her cigarette, shook the lighter and threw it overboard. Daddy lunged but missed. "Oh," said Mummy, "I thought it was a match." Nothing more was ever said.

Back in London one day the telephone rang and I answered it. A gentle American voice asked, "Is that Mary Norton's residence?"

"Yes, who is it?"

"This is Walt Disney, can I speak with her please?"

I thought it was Bruv fooling around and said something rude, and teased him back in spite of the gentle noises coming down the line. It gradually and horrifyingly dawned on me that it really was Walt Disney. He came round and took Mary out to dinner. I have a feeling that they met several times when he was in London, I think he rather liked her. There is a letter in his own hand saying "I'll do anything you want Mary", signed Walt. His lawyers were a different matter. Mary sold them the rights of *The Magic Bedknob* and *Bonfires and Broomsticks* for a pathetically small sum, but every little bit of money counted in those days.

I don't quite know how *The Borrowers* started. Perhaps they were always somewhere in the back of her mind, with the constant moves and separations while her family were growing up, the scrimping and saving of the war years. Many years later a great friend John Cromwell asked Mary where the idea came from. Mary took a lot of trouble over a letter explaining the whole idea, and many years later she included it as a preface to *The Complete Borrowers* (Puffin 1992). This is the first part. It is early morning in this small whitewashed room, and I am sitting up in bed trying to answer this question of yours about what kind of events or circumstances led me first to think about the Borrowers.

Looking back, the idea seems to be part of an early fantasy in the life of a very shortsighted child, before it was known that she needed glasses. For her brothers, country walks with her must have been something of a trial: she was an inveterate lingerer, a gazer into banks and hedgerows, a rapt investigator of shallow pools, a lier-down by stream-like teeming ditches. Such walks were punctuated by loud, long-suffering cries: "Oh, come on . . . for goodness sake . . . we'll never get there . . . What on earth are you staring at now?"

It might only be a small toad, with striped eyes, trying to hoist himself up — on his bulging washerwoman's arms — from the dank depths of the ditch on to a piece of floating bark; or wood violets quivering on their massed roots from the passage of some sly, desperate creature pushing its way to safety. What would it be like, this child would wonder, lying prone upon the moss, to live among such creatures — human oneself to all intents and purposes, but as small and vulnerable as they? What would one live on? Where make one's home? Which would be one's enemies and which one's friends?

Buzzards, yes, they would be the enemies of her little people. Hawks too — and owls. She thought back to the gate which so easily the three human children had climbed. How would her small people manipulate it? They would go underneath of course — there was plenty of room — but, suddenly, she saw through their eyes the great lavalike (sometimes almost steaming) lakes of cattle dung, the pock-like craters in the mud — chasms of them, whether wet or dry. It would take them, she thought, almost half an hour of teetering on ridges, helping one another, calling out warnings, holding one another's hands before, exhausted, they reached the dry grass beyond. And then, she thought, how wickedly sharp, how dizzily high and rustling those thistle plants would seem! And suppose one of these creatures (Were they a little family? She thought perhaps they might be) called out as her brother had just done, "Look, there's a buzzard!" What a different intonation in the voice and a different implication in the fact. How still they would lie — under perhaps a dock leaf! All deathly still, except for their beating hearts!

The writing of *The Borrowers* in the early 1950s seemed rather a fun time. We were growing up. Although Guy was still at boarding school, Caroline was back home at a day school, and Bruv and I had started our first jobs. Richard Garnett, who'd been living next door, gradually moved in with us. He and Robert were working at Rupert Hart Davies, when it was a small distinguished publishing house. I think it was just Rupert, David Garnett (Richard's father), Teddy Young and the boys. We all got very involved in the Borrowers and their artefacts. Mary was insistent that everything worked. In fantasy you could have one thing that was magic or incredible, she said, but everything else had to be completely believable. Richard made a lovely model of the Clocks's under-the-floorboards home with the chess piece knight, Arietty's cigar box bed (from daddy) and the letters pasted sideways for wall paper, and stamps for pictures.

One day Richard came back to 41 Smith Street looking worried and was obviously sitting on something. He eventually told me that he'd found out that T. H. White, an old friend, was also writing a book about little people. He didn't know whether to tell Mummy, or T. H. White, or both. Very wisely he told neither. T. H. White's book was called *Mistress Masham's Repose*, and was quite different. It's strange how creative ideas seem to float about until picked up independently by different people in different places at about the same time. My mother was absolutely thrilled when *The Borrowers* was awarded the Carnegie Medal for the best children's book of the year in 1952. It gave her confidence a much needed boost and she rather enjoyed the kudos. After the Borrowers books my mother's writing slowed down. The bank manager no longer banged on the door and so there was time to relax and enjoy life. Mary and my father had been separated for almost twenty years by this time and finally decided on an amicable divorce. At sixty my mother married an old friend - Lionel Bonsey - and they moved to West Cork. They spent a happy time renovating a grand but dilapidated old house and entertaining their many friends.

My mother came across *The Bread and Butter Stories* again in her eighties. Only one box survived our many house moves. She thought there might be more, and used to talk about a missing suitcase full of her work, which somehow got left behind. Rather nervously Mary sent the story "Lake Trout" to her dear friend and agent Brian Stone. (This story was based on a trip my mother made with Margaret Rutherford, they had been friends since their student days at the Old Vic.) She was absolutely delighted when he loved it and asked for more. She was staying with me at the time and I remember the glorious bunch of flowers he sent her. We couldn't find anything big enough to hold them, and she definitely didn't want them split into smaller vases around the house. So they sat in her room, in a disguised bucket, looking beautiful. My mother wanted them re-published because she thought of herself as a storyteller, not only a children's writer. But she did want it understood that she was writing for a specific American market in the 1950s.

She did begin to update the stories but then decided they should be left as they were. The strength of them lies in the women characters' reactions to events, rather than the settings, and those emotions are universal, and timeless. I personally find something very touching about the stories because I can see her own little thread of inadequacy that ran through her life, borne of the cruelty she suffered at her convent boarding school. Even in old age she would have nightmares and wake up crying, "Please, Mummy and Daddy — come and take me away." I think the collection shows Mary's acute perception of human frailty and, how with a dash of humour, even a trifling incident can be turned into a good story.

Ann Brunsdon, London, 1998

CHAPTER
ONE

The Girl in the Corner

It was a longish journey from Cornwall. Seven hours. When the London-bound train rushes into the quiet country station and window seats pour smugly by, each with its glowering occupant, it evokes — even as it slows to a standstill — a suggestion of panic in the would-be passenger, and (in the hubbub of porters, luggage, hasty goodbyes), it is easy to ignore one of the major alleviations of travel: congenial choice of company. There is an element of fatal segregation about a British train (four a side and the door to the corridor kept shut) that justifies a moment of selection.

Pippa, when on her own, remembered this: she had a "railway role", by which she hoped to liven the tedious hours instead of merely bearing them. Travelling alone, she became no longer the harassed wife of an underpaid schoolmaster — and the mother of Mary, a role in itself — but a youngish, not unattractive woman in passably cut tweeds, with tidy luggage and a heightened sense of individuality.

But travelling with the family was different: and, on this occasion — the tail end of the long summer holidays, with Nigel already back at his desk in Oxford

— she had, besides Mary and the suitcases, one camp bed, three boiled crabs, a case of pilchards, and two cats.

There was a big cat and a little cat. Both white. Both strays. They were brothers, children of separate litters (and an unnamed village mother) — and they had only lately met. Hearts, in fact, were beating high in the cat basket. Big Bicho, highly nervous and temperamentally remote, had not taken kindly to the newcomer: he had scrambled to a safe height on the kitchen dresser and watched, with dilated eyes, the unsteady wanderings of Bicho No. 2 as he mewed, lost and motherless, across the flagstones. When lifted down and placed, with tender optimism, beside the infant brother at the milk saucer, he had squawked like a herring gull and fled — a streak of panic-stricken white — across the lamplit kitchen, into the salty night.

"He's gone," Mary had wailed, "and we're leaving tomorrow, and now he'll never come back."

But he had come back, warily, that very morning, pausing at every other footstep, starting at each sound, until — with a sudden dart from ambush — Mary had caught him and thrust him into the cat basket. Feline foreboding can seldom have been more justified: there, in the speckled darkness, crouched ultimate horror — white, wobbly, wavering, and hideously small.

So it was of the cats Pippa thought as she and Mary, curiously laden, ran along the platform behind the porter. "Jump in, Mary! There — just there!" she called, as the train slowed to a stop. "Quick, I'll take the basket." The emptiest compartment, that's what it had to be — for a moment of privacy in which to know the worst.

"Thank you. Yes, this'll do," Pippa assured the porter, fumbling in her purse for a tip. "Do sit down, Mary — here, by the window!"

But they were not alone. Two women sat across the compartment in corner seats beside the corridor. Pippa took the place by Mary, who sat beside the window; she placed the cat basket on the corner seat opposite.

"Could we open it?" Mary whispered.

Pippa threw a hasty glance towards the end of the compartment: both women were staring; the fat one, crocheting a glove, had stopped the needle in mid-flick; the red-haired girl, with uncleaned sandals and heavy, naked legs, sat with her mouth open and eyes swivelled as though arrested in the act of speech.

"Not until the train starts," Pippa whispered to Mary. "Animals are supposed to travel in the luggage van," she added under her breath.

The red-haired girl resumed her conversation; in the quiet of the country station, the London accent sounded particularly strident.

"Not that he did it on purpose. He was just made like that, if you see what I mean."

Her companion nodded. On her hat, odd sort of passion fruit made of leather nodded too; and the glove, as she crocheted, wobbled strangely.

"If I was Elsie," the red-haired girl insisted, "I would speak my mind."

"Would you?"

"Yes, I would. You can't let sleeping dogs lie."

"No, you can't, can you?" Placid and regular, the glove wobbled.

3

"They don't thank you for it," the red-haired girl summed up.

"That's right."

Pippa sighed. Seven hours . . . and longer it would seem for Mary . . . longer still for the cats. She felt for Mary's hand beside her on the seat; soft, boneless, a little sticky, and ardently responsive, it returned her squeeze. "I'll just listen through the lid?" Mary whispered. She got up and stooping laid her ear against the wickerwork. "They're very quiet," she said, as she sat down again. "You don't think a big cat might kill a little cat?"

"No, of course not."

"I know it's foolish," Mary went on, in a sudden clear, grown-up little voice, "but I love him so much."

"It isn't foolish," said Pippa, smiling. "Which one?"

"The little one. Though, mind you —" she turned and looked at Pippa with her slanting solemn eyes — "I'm still loyal to Bicho."

The compartment door rattled and swung open. It was their porter again with luggage. Good, thought Pippa, hopefully, new people . . . she felt in need of allies: the red-haired girl's views on "sleeping dogs" might, Pippa felt, equally apply to sleeping cats — and she was one who would not hesitate, on her own admission, to "speak her mind". Carefully, Pippa removed the cat basket, freeing the corner seat. A man and a woman climbed in.

"That okay, sir?" asked the porter, stowing the luggage on the rack.

"Yes, thank you." The man reached up to the heaviest case, adjusting it more securely. "Thank you very much," he said again; a tip was being offered; Pippa's eyes flicked away.

"That's all right, sir," said the porter, getting out.

"Oh, but you must," insisted the young man, "you can't —"

"That's all right, sir," repeated the porter, firmly. He slammed the door and peered in at them over the half-opened window. "Pleasant journey."

He refused a tip, Pippa thought wonderingly, that's odd. She stole a covert glance at the two people opposite. Both were about twenty-seven. The man was mousy-fair, bespectacled, neatly but inexpensively dressed; a dull face, but kind — gentlemen's outfitting, guessed Pippa, or possibly a junior bank clerk.

The girl was more interesting. She sat down beside the man, exactly opposite Mary, and next to the window. There was a certain self-consciousness about her movements; the swift, nervous smoothing of her skirt over her knees; the quick glance round the compartment — a defensive, independent glance which flickered swiftly, seeming to see without deigning to look; and, with the glance, went a secret little smile, as though what she saw had caused her amusement. She was hatless and slender, with thin fingers and long, fragile wrists. There was a nervous beauty about the sharply boned face, with its long, rather pointed nose and wide-open dark eyes. Her dark hair, uncurled, was simply cut, and as the train began to move, the draught from the open window caught it and blew it into feathery fronds about her wide forehead.

5

She seemed, without once having glanced at her, to be conscious of Pippa's far from obvious scrutiny. She would smooth back the blowing tendrils of hair with nervous fingers, lifting her face suddenly into the wind, then lean away again towards her companion, brushing his shoulder with her chin, whispering a little below the roar of the train, and laughing. He seemed, not embarrassed by this behaviour, but complaisant and shy, as if, though willing, he lacked the grace to compete.

A honeymoon couple, Pippa guessed: but the luggage was not new, nor were the clothes — very. The girl wore a blouse and skirt, extremely fresh and neat, and a separate jacket which, though well cut, did not match.

Why is she acting up? wondered Pippa. It can't be just for my benefit. Perhaps she, too, has a "railway role". Pippa glanced at the other women: they had just completed their stare and were about to look away: she caught its quality — leaden, phlegmatic, uncomprehending — before, once again, the needle flashed and the glove wobbled.

A gong rang. First dinner.

"Come along, Mary, let's go," whispered Pippa.

"Are we going to have late dinner on the train?" asked Mary in a loud voice.

"Yes, not late dinner. Early dinner. It's still daylight."

"Doesn't it cost a lot of money?"

"It does, rather," admitted Pippa. There was no one to smile with: the dark girl, now gazing directly at them, looked grave and blank.

As they went into the corridor and Pippa carefully closed the door behind them, she heard the red-haired girl say, "rolling on the floor, that's where they found her, never a word from him . . ."

When they returned to the compartment after dinner, the atmosphere had changed. There was a pleasant feeling of relaxation in the air and a strong smell of orange peel; there were cake crumbs on the floor; the crochet woman had laid aside her work and was folding sandwich papers neatly; an open thermos stood beside her on the seat. The young man had lit a cigarette and the dark girl, leaning against him, was daintily eating a banana, and gazing at a copy of the *London Illustrated News*, which he held on his knee. His almost inaudible comments on the pictures were making her laugh, and she would lean her head more closely against his shoulder, holding the banana carefully upright as though it were a candle.

"Excuse me," murmured Pippa, in the doorway, and the fat woman moved her knees to let them pass and smiled in a friendly way at Mary. The atmosphere had indeed mellowed: those less extravagant had also eaten and eaten, it seemed, well.

"Could we open the basket, now?" whispered Mary as they sat down.

Now or never, Pippa thought, and summoning up her courage, she addressed the dark girl direct. "Do you mind cats?"

There was a moment of startled silence, so prolonged that Pippa feared the dark girl had not heard. Then, suddenly, she spoke.

"No," she said quickly, looking in a bewildered way from Pippa to Mary, "no, not at all." Then her eyes slid away, embarrassed, and she flushed slowly — a deep, dark red.

But by that time Mary had opened the lid. Big Bicho sat crouched, his eyes staring, in a trance of fear; little Bicho lay quietly, fast asleep.

Tenderly Mary lifted out the beloved creature, he to whom she was "still loyal", and he lay on her lap without stirring. "Let me be still," he seemed to say, "let me be as dead."

"That's a lovely white cat," said the fat woman, feeling in her bag for her crochet. "Taking her to a cat show?"

Mary bridled with pleasure. "No, it's just an ordinary Cornish cat," she said. "We're taking him home to Oxford."

"A Cornish cat!" exclaimed the fat woman, impressed, as though this were a rare breed.

The young couple were leaving the compartment, on their way to the washroom. They went without a word, closing the door carefully behind them; neither had looked at the cat.

"Good boy," whispered Mary, stroking the soft white fur. "Brave boy."

"You don't object to his being out?" Pippa asked the fat woman.

"Me? Oh, no, it doesn't seem fair to keep 'em shut up all those hours."

"That's right," said the red-haired girl. "Animals — you've got to think of them."

Pippa lifted the kitten out of the basket; he stretched happily and yawned — the roof of his mouth a minute shell of pinkish mother-of-pearl.

"Well, I never," exclaimed the fat woman, "a kitten!" She seemed amazed. "Look at 'im, Doris. I'n't'ee lovely? White, too!" She seemed almost stupefied with delight. "Put him near his mother," she said to Mary.

"He's not his mother —" Mary began, when the door to the corridor reopened. "Excuse me," said the fair young man, blinking a little behind his glasses, "I think my wife left her bag —" He hesitated in the doorway, as though not liking to push past.

"Oh," said Pippa, "yes. Here it is." And she passed it.

But still he stood, half-smiling, looking in on them, the bag in his hand.

"She's stone-blind," he said after a moment.

"What?" Pippa exclaimed sharply, almost rudely.

"Stone-blind," he repeated. "Her mother was too."

"But you can't mean —"

"She can't see a thing," he said gently, and closing the door, bag in hand, he walked quickly towards the washroom.

There was a moment's silence in the compartment, then the women began to speak.

"Poor soul, who'd've thought it?"

"The way she was looking out of the window!" exclaimed the red-haired girl.

"That's right. And looking at the magazine, did you see?"

"Yes, looking at the paper!" The red-haired girl's voice rose to a wail of stupefied amazement. She turned to Pippa, "And when you spoke to her, you know, about the cats? She looked right at you —"

"She looked where the voice came from," said Mary, stroking Big Bicho's fur.

Both women turned and stared at her. "He nudged her," explained Mary; she looked up at Pippa: "you remember? At first, when she didn't answer?"

"Yes," admitted Pippa uncertainly.

"I saw him nudge her. I thought perhaps she was blind when they were looking at the paper."

"*You* thought, Mary —"

"Yes. She'd only stay quiet when he read her big pieces from under the pictures, but sometimes there was only a picture and hardly any writing, and you could see he wanted to look at it, but she'd laugh and turn over because he'd gone all quiet and didn't speak. Sometimes, he tried to turn back, just for a minute, to finish looking." Mary bent her head to the white cat. "Poor boy . . ." she whispered. "Good boy . . ."

"You saw all this, Mary?"

"Yes," said Mary.

"Well," said the fat woman, and they all became silent.

When the girl returned to the compartment, both women moved their legs and made fussy, adjusting movements to bags and parcels to give her free passage. Their consideration was lost upon her and she moved towards her seat with the gay, almost defiant, insouciance that previously had puzzled Pippa.

"Quarter past seven," she said to her husband, and Pippa noticed that her fingers were lying, careless and unobtrusive, on the face of her watch. "Three more hours and twenty minutes."

"Tired?" he asked her.

She shrugged, drooping a little, and then, with a sudden impetuous movement, she leaned towards the window, pushing her face into the moving air; the gesture was too sharp — and she struck her cheek a painful blow against the woodwork. Beyond an involuntary flinch, she made no sign, half-smiling to herself her secret smile.

She stared at the landscape with eager concentration, as though she searched for a familiar house or some well-known landmark. What if she knew, thought Pippa, that the mist is rising through the early dusk and the fields already have sunk to darkness?

Her husband had picked up the magazine and was glancing through the pictures; he, too, looked tired — but still tautly attuned to the girl at his side, marking time — so it seemed, until she wished to speak. But he should not have told us, Pippa thought. Out of the pride and gentleness of his heart, out of the longing to share his burden of compassion, he has betrayed her. Even to the porter.

Suddenly the girl sank back into her corner. Her husband turned quickly. "Piece of chocolate?" he asked gently.

She shook her head; her hands lay open on her lap, empty, suddenly listless.

"Like to see the pictures?" His eyes swivelled round to Pippa — and he smiled apologetically, as though to say: "We have to put it like that — we have to play her game."

Again she shook her head.

11

"Come and walk down the corridor a bit? Get some air?"

"No, I'm all right."

He hesitated, then he laid his hand into the cupped palms in her lap. She grasped his fingers, gently, sensitively, but almost avidly — as though they spoke to her. "Soon be home," he said comfortingly.

"Where have you been staying in Cornwall?" asked Pippa quickly.

His face lit up with gratitude: "Land's End, we had a lovely holiday."

"Lots of sun," said the blind girl.

"And Cornish cream, we had. You're not supposed to because of the butter ration. But she got round the man."

The girl laughed. "That cream!" she said gloatingly.

"Lovely walks," he said, "but those cliffs . . . they're terrible!"

"So high," said the girl, "but it was lovely — the sea, and everything."

"She picked flowers," he told Pippa proudly. "Great big bunches of wild flowers. Didn't you, Ivy? What were those flowers called?"

"Sea pinks. You could pull them off — in cushions — like. They're pink," she added after a moment, "a lovely pink . . ."

"Against the grey stones," said Pippa.

"Yes," she agreed eagerly, grateful, as though Pippa had made her a present of the thought, "against the grey stones."

They talked for a while, and the women in the far corner listened, nodding their heads from time to time and giving little laughs — of nervousness, perhaps, or pity — until the lights came on and all their faces became monochrome, sharp cut with weary shadow.

"Like your lipstick, dear?" She shook her head and then she rallied. "All right." He passed her bag — and, sensitively, she touched her mouth with colour and flicked her forehead with a swansdown puff. She stowed the cosmetics carefully, each in its compartment, and as though her hands took pleasure in such tasks. Then she sighed. "Soon be home," he told her again.

The blind girl leaned her head against the upholstery, composing herself for sleep — but the dark eyes remained open, focused, it seemed, on Pippa's lap.

"Give her the kitten," whispered Mary.

Pippa had thought of that, but how? She looked at the husband and down at the sleeping kitten. He leaned forward, smiling, and touched the small body with his finger. "How old?"

"A few weeks. He misses his mother." Pippa picked up the kitten and laid it in his hands. He held it awkwardly, a little wonderingly, as one not used to cats.

"Isn't that his mother?"

"No. His brother."

The kitten mewed weakly and began to climb the man's chest, seeking a warm corner in which to snuggle. He smiled awkwardly.

"Sweet little thing," he touched it gently. "Soft, isn't it?"

The blind girl's eyes had turned towards the kitten. She seemed to be holding herself taut.

"Here," he said, "like to take it?"

13

She looked startled. "A kitten?"

"It's ever so white," he said, pulling it off his chest.

"Yes," she said deliberately, "isn't it?"

"You take it," he suggested.

She did not put out her hands; she seemed uncertain of the direction from which the kitten would come; she seemed just to avoid trembling. Very gently, he laid it in her lap.

"Oh," she said and laughed, "oh, I say!" The kitten crept into her hands and her hands went round the kitten. The kitten began to purr. "Oh," she said again, delighted, "listen to it!"

"He likes you," the husband pointed out.

"Yes," she said.

Her hands followed the kitten as it began to climb about, guarding it, checking it, directing it. "No, you don't," she said to it, "you come back here. That's right." The kitten defied her and began to play biting her sleeve buttons. "Oh, you naughty!" she exclaimed. "I'll take a stick to you in a minute."

Later, when the kitten was asleep, lying against her neck below her chin, she spoke to her husband.

"What?" he said.

She blinked a little and stroked the kitten casually, laying her cheek against the soft fur. "Why couldn't we have one of these?"

He hesitated. "Well —" another helpless one to care for, his eyes seemed to say, another tie — "we could. But —"

"Mm . . ." she said, rubbing her cheek on the fur.

"You can't ever go away," he said, "if you have animals . . ." A myriad tiny lights flashed through the windows as the train rushed through the outskirts of London. "But we *could*," he said, "if you really —"

"No," she said, "it's all right."

He stood up. "We're nearly there. I'd better get the bags down the passage. You'll sit where you are, won't you, till I see about the car?"

Directly he had gone, Mary leaned across to the blind girl. "You have the kitten," she said.

The blind girl looked startled, "Oh, no —"

"Yes. Of course, Put it under your coat, then it won't run away."

The blind girl began to smile. "Under my coat?" she repeated slowly.

"Yes," said Mary, the practised deceiver, "then it won't run away."

The fat woman in the corner, reaching for her suitcase, paused and made a shocked sound with her tongue. "Well!" she said — but she seemed delighted.

"Oh," said the blind girl, "I couldn't —" but the smile had deepened.

"You do it," said the fat woman breathlessly, heaving down her suitcase. "Under your coat, like she said. No good thinking. That's what I always say. Never gets you anywhere."

They passed the compartment again later, Pippa and Mary, on their way back from the luggage van. They had to run a little to keep up with the porter who was wheeling their trunk. The blind girl sat in the stationary

15

train under the light, in the corner — as she had been told. Her eyes were downcast — and her face, leaning forward, was deep in shadow.

"She isn't alone," said Mary, reading Pippa's thought, "she has the kitten . . ."

"Yes," said Pippa, hurrying on, "it was kind of you . . . kind of you, Mary."

"Not really," said Mary, running to catch up, "because —" she added, a little breathless, "— now she knows we knew she was blind."

CHAPTER
TWO

The Blown-Glass Decanter

"This is the kind of house that frightens me," whispered Lucy as Julian rang the bell.

"Why?" asked Julian quickly. There was a trace of alarm in his voice.

Lucy heard it and it increased her nervousness. "It's something to do with the very white doorstep," she said. But it was more than that; it was the ferocious gleam of the eighteenth-century brass door knocker; the black-leaded shoescraper, glossy with brushing; the closely curtained square-paned windows. It was a wing-collar, dark-suit, silk-umbrella sort of house; reticent, self-respecting, a trifle suspicious, discreetly prosperous — the house, in other words, of Leopold Makepeace Donne.

"Late Georgian," whispered Julian, and added unconvincingly, "he's quite a nice old boy."

Lucy nodded. Julian, she knew, was on probation with the firm — if a publishing house as old and famous as Donne's could still be described as a firm — but, until this moment, the fact had not troubled her. Julian was respected in the office, a leisurely, civilized establishment, and she had almost forgotten the background existence of Leopold Makepeace, the last of the famous name. "But he's a power to the land, my darling," Julian had explained. "He still has the last word."

Nervously, Lucy twisted her leg and looked to see if the seam of her stocking was straight. "Is Mr Donne very old?" she asked.

"Yes," said Julian, "He is, rather. And don't you feel you have to talk to him about books. They don't really interest him very much."

Then what shall I talk to him about? Lucy wondered, and absentmindedly she pulled off her glove; she put it on again quickly; the sight of her hand reminded her that she had been drawing all afternoon and should have renewed her nail polish. But what does it matter? she asked herself with sudden impatience. It's Julian I'm going to marry, not Mr Donne.

All the same, she had begun to feel that this sort of thing might matter. An article in one of the women's papers had unnerved her — one of those tracts about the kind of wife who is an asset to her husband's career. It had been well-written — one degree from the truth, perhaps, but running parallel — and was insidiously convincing. Odd things were said about clothes, about entertaining, about the running and appearance of "the husband's home", about a wife's attitude and behaviour to the husband's "boss", and about not making too close friends of the people "your husband will pass on the way up".

All at once, the qualities that had made her a loved and respected member of a large, untidy family seemed inadequate; she felt uncertain, suddenly, about the rambling studio flat on the top floor of an old-fashioned London house. The house, she realized now, was not old-fashioned enough, and they would have to eat in their living room, the stairs were not quite right, and there were far too many of them, and although the house overlooked Battersea Park, it was on the wrong side of the river. "But the light's so good," she had cried, waltzing about on the bare boards, "and the space! I can draw in here all day, while you're at the office."

Even that, now, didn't seem to be quite the right kind of idea. But she knew they would be poor — it might be years, if ever, before Julian became a director — and she had hoped her illustrations would bring in a little money. Never mind, she comforted herself, I will make it so beautiful, so unusual and spacious and sort of luxurious, that people, when they come through the doorway, will forget the stairs and the trams and the dusty laurels in the front garden.

Now, when the door opened, she was still smiling. Julian introduced her to the fresh-faced woman who let them in. "Mrs Thring," he said. "This —" he drew her forward "— is Lucy."

A little old man puttered fussily out of the shadows. Yes, there was the wing collar, the dark suit, and, for good measure, a tie through a ring. At least, thought Lucy, to him I can be friendly; here is one Julian is not likely to "pass on the way up".

Mr Donne shook hands quickly, as though he disliked physical contact. "Glad to see you," he said, in a dry, staccato voice, and turned his back on them immediately, leading them out of the hall. "Good of you to come."

Lucy, as she slipped out of her coat and ran to catch up, remembered suddenly that old Leopold Donne, or so it was said, had proposed to Julian's mother before she had accepted that penniless young writer, Julian's father. Now the world had "discovered" Julian's father and Donne's had reprinted his books. Did they see in Julian something of his father's judgement? Or was it just for old association's sake they had given him this chance?

The morning room, like the hall, seemed too full of furniture. Mr Donne was swaying a little, in a lawyer-like way, on the balls of his feet. He glanced at her keenly as she came in. "Pour Miss Lambert some sherry, Julian," he said.

So they're in a standing-up mood, noted Lucy, and looked about her. "You have some lovely things," she murmured. In cold fact, the crowded furniture, under the bright overhead light, could have suggested a junk shop, but somehow did not; the polished surfaces were too meticulously cared for, and there was loving thought behind the cramped arrangements. On each door and above the valanced curtains was an out-of-date type of burglar bell.

"Yes," agreed Mr Donne, and drew in a long breath, "that thing you are touching now — gold filigree — is Marie Antoinette's own manicure case. No, don't put it down." He stood beside her. "Open it."

She heard the tremble of emotion in his dry voice, the quiver of loving pride. It was catching; her fingers became all thumbs.

"Let me," he said. This time he did not mind touching her hands. Delicately, he pressed the springs, the lid flew open, and Lucy saw the tiny instrument, strange to modern eyes.

She caught her breath and, as she did so, felt the sudden prick of tears behind her lids.

He glanced at her swiftly and slyly, as though to catch her expression. "Ah," he said, "you are crying?" and as she prepared to deny it, "I cry, too, sometimes, when I touch these things."

"Lucy cries for anything," put in Julian unkindly. "Have you seen this?" he went on, in a different tone, holding up the decanter. "Oh!" exclaimed Lucy and moved towards it.

It was two globes of blown Venetian glass, one large and one small, joined by four tender stems.

"Watch it pour," said Julian, and as he tilted it, Lucy saw the golden sherry flow into the hollow stems like living streams of amber; poised, it seemed, in air, they joined at last to fill the gleaming bubble below the neck.

"Oh," exclaimed Lucy again, "may I please pour it?"

The old man laughed. "It's amusing," he said, "not old — at least, I don't believe it is — but it is blown in the old tradition."

"I like this thing," Lucy said. Delicately, delightedly, she filled two glasses. "It's alchemical — a Borgia thing — a thing for potions — a kind of magic."

"No more," said Julian to Lucy. "Mr Donne doesn't take it."

"I shall suspect him," said Lucy, without looking up, "if he doesn't." She half-filled the third glass and carried it to him. "Drink first," she told him.

He took the glass awkwardly and raised it a little. "Your happiness!" he said, and she saw a glint of amusement in the shrewd eyes.

After that, things went easily. Lucy was shown Doctor Johnson's ink-well and the desk from his study; a cupboard iron-hard and black with age, from the Doge's palace; a pair of embroidered gloves belonging to Charles the First, and the actual key of his cell. Gradually she began to realize that almost every object or piece of furniture in the house had some specific association with a great name of the past. Each had been acquired for this reason alone, and not for its age or workmanship. Even the spoons and cruets, she learned at dinner, had belonged to Beau Brummell, and the china bore the crest of Napoleon the First.

Ever since he was a young man, her host explained, he had laid out his money in this way. He bought carefully and with steadily increasing knowledge. "I have spent on these things," he said, "what other men spend on horses, servants, food and motor cars. I am not what the world would consider a wealthy man."

After dinner, the white cloth was replaced by green baize, and Lucy was shown the watches. This, Julian explained later, was a great honour. Out of the safe, in a chipped black box, they came — exquisite examples of eighteenth-century workmanship, glittering with jewels and pale enamels. Mr Donne took out one watch at a time; eyes and fingers were allowed their brief tribute, before Mrs Thring, summoned from her sitting room, re-wrapped each sparkling object in chamois and consigned it again to darkness.

There was, to Lucy, a sadness about this procedure, and as the safe clanged shut upon the padlocked box, a sense of banishment and wasted beauty. Quite suddenly the old man looked tired — he is drained, Lucy thought, exhausted by his passion; he cares too much for these things — and at ten-thirty, he dismissed them. "You must go now," he said, with royal simplicity. "It's my bedtime. Thank you for coming."

On the way home she said to Julian, "He's stranger than you told me. But I enjoyed it. I liked him."

"He liked you," Julian said. "You were a great success."

"Was I?" asked Lucy anxiously, remembering the tired old face. "Was I really?"

"Terrific." He squeezed her arm. "Well that's over!"

And then she knew he had felt as she had — uncertain.

They did not get Mr Donne's present until after the wedding. It was there, in the large studio room, when they returned from France — a tall cardboard box. There was no need to be careful with shavings and paper; the room was knee-deep with straw and packing cases and dishes stood in corners, and a divan bed was upended against the wall.

"Julian," called Lucy, "do come. You'll never guess what he's sent us!"

Julian came in, wiping his hands on a towel. "A Regency watch, I hope."

"Don't be silly. Look, it's the blown-glass decanter!"

"By Jove!" said Julian. He walked slowly round it as it stood on the table. "It's got legs."

"It always had legs. They're to match these stem things. Julian, it is sweet of him."

"Well you made such a fuss about it the night we were there. You practically asked for it."

"Oh, Julian, I didn't make that much fuss. I was trying to make him happy."

They stared at it curiously. In these surroundings it really did look alchemical, like a complicated retort.

"It's certainly a funny-looking thing," said Julian.

"Yes," Lucy agreed. "Like some kind of new invention for making coffee. Perhaps," she suggested, "it looks better full. Do you think people will laugh when we give them sherry from it?"

"No," said Julian, then hesitated. "But they might expect a blood transfusion."

Lucy aimed a mock blow at him, and he caught her wrist. "Don't, Julian," she gasped, laughing. "You hurt!" The table shifted slightly, and there was a light, musical crash. Their eyes met in mutual fear, and they stood frozen. Slowly, Julian let go her wrist, and Lucy looked down. "Oh, Julian," she moaned and went down on her knees.

At first glance, the decanter, Lying among the shavings, looked whole but as soon as, tentatively with one finger, she touched it, the neck fell away from the stems. She picked up the broken pieces and held them tenderly.

"It wasn't my fault," Julian said, like a child.

Lucy looked up at him. Her face was white. "No," she said. "It was mine."

"Let me see." Julian took the glass and fitted the two pieces together. "We could get it mended," he said.

"I don't think so," Lucy told him. "It's blown glass."

"Can't they sort of melt it down and stick it together?"

"I don't think so," Lucy said again. "Otherwise it wouldn't matter if glass blowers made mistakes."

"All the same," went on Julian, "I think there's something they do now. Take it to Baddeley's in Regent Street."

"It'll cost the earth," said Lucy.

"Well, it can't be helped. We're a couple of clumsy idiots."

Lucy bent her head. She picked up a handful of straw and let it fall slowly through her fingers. "I was going to start saving for a carpet," she said.

Carefully, Julian placed the decanter on the table and sat beside her in the straw. "My darling," he said, "you know we couldn't have afforded a carpet, anyway — not for a bit."

"I was just going to start saving," said Lucy, running her fingers through the straw. "Secretly," she added.

"Your mother's going to lend us rugs," Julian reminded her.

"Yes, but only three." Impatiently, Lucy pushed the straw aside, revealing the boards. "Look at this floor. All nails and cracks and shapes and sizes."

"You see," began Julian, "the trouble with this decanter —"

"I know, I know!" exclaimed Lucy. "If only Uncle Henry had given it to us — or someone who lives abroad. But we're so caught up with Mr Donne; he's part of our lives. And he cares so terribly about things."

Julian was silent. Gently he took her hand in his and brushed the listless fingers free from straw. "One thing," he said after a moment. "He hardly ever goes out."

"But we can't bank on it," Lucy cried. "You know how things happen — never as you expect them to. Oh I know he can't sack you for breaking his decanter, but people's reactions can be so unreasonable. Even when they know they are being unreasonable, it doesn't change what they feel inside."

"You know, darling, I hate to say it, but it was your fault that we got the decanter at all."

"How do you mean?" Lucy asked him, stupefied.

"Well, he was going to give us a cheque. I went into the office one afternoon before he met you, and he said something about not knowing what to give people when they got married, and did I feel a cheque would seem too much like a bonus."

"But nothing could seem too like a bonus," Lucy exclaimed. "Oh, Julian, it would have gone towards the carpet."

"Yes, or even bought it. He gave Cole fifty pounds when he got married." Julian dropped her hand. "But it's beastly to talk like this."

"Yes," Lucy said. "But why did you say it was my fault?"

"For being so jolly charming."

"But I thought wives had to be charming to their husband's bosses. I was trying especially. I was —" The words faltered into silence and Lucy's eyes filled with tears.

"My precious darling!" Julian pulled her to him, through the straw and kissed her. "If you had been a boring lump, he'd have stuck to the cheque idea. The decanter, you silly creature, was his personal gesture to you." She looked thoughtful, and he touched her cheek with his finger. "See?" he asked.

She caught his finger and held it tight. "Yes," she murmured and, after a moment suddenly began to laugh.

Lucy took the decanter to Baddeley's. They were sorry, but they could do nothing. Then Lucy pleaded to see Mr Baddeley himself. She knew he was a crony of her mother's. Her mother had many such cronies in London shops. "Mr Baddeley," she told him when he came at last, in his neat morning suit and stooping a little under the weight of his considerations and kindness, "you must save me." And she told him the story of the decanter.

Mr Baddeley was human, and Lucy, pink with desperation looked more than usually pretty. "Well," he said, "I'll see what I can do. Leave it with me. I'll ask one of our buyers if he will be kind enough to take it round the factories. But," he shook his head and pursed his lips "I'm not very hopeful."

On the way home, Lucy stopped at the wine merchant's. Someone had told her about a simple way of saving money. "You take", she had been told, "an empty whisky bottle and put all your odd sixpences in it," and if it was the squarish, dimpled kind, when it was full it held forty pounds. This, Lucy knew, was about what it would cost to carpet the studio.

"You see," she said to Julian at supper, "there's no harm in trying to save."

Julian, only half-convinced, put in five sixpences; Lucy's mother contributed some quantity unknown, and Lucy herself started it off with twenty.

Lucy then set to work painting and decorating the flat and was swept away on a wave of creative frenzy. Friends and family were made to keep their distance. Comment tormented her before a certain stage. "Wait," she'd cry to Julian. "Please wait until I've done the overmantel. Then you'll see."

Occasionally Julian would suggest bringing someone home for dinner, but Lucy was adamant. "Not yet. Please, Julian! It will be such fun. It will look so lovely — these moonlight bluish walls with dark plum colour."

Now and again, there were gatecrashers, intrepid relatives whom Lucy allowed to make coffee and bring her a cup to the foot of the ladder. Julian suspected them of adding sixpences to the bottle. And he himself became more generous than was really prudent.

There came a day when the ladders were cleared away and the furniture was put in place. Mrs Kithatton from downstairs was got in to scrub and polish the floors. That evening Julian was made to walk about the room in a trance-like manner.

"Look up and round," Lucy exhorted. "Don't look down. You must imagine the floor."

Julian was impressed. "It's amazing," he kept saying. He was immensely proud of her. The lighting, the way she had arranged the flowers, the judgement with which she had placed their few good pieces of furniture. "Darling," he began, "couldn't we ask —"

"No," said Lucy, "we couldn't. The men are coming tomorrow to measure the floor. There's no harm," she went on, pulling off her pinafore, "in getting some idea of an estimate."

The estimate was thirty-three pounds, fifteen shillings, and Lucy had thirty-five pounds and sixpence in the bottle. When Julian unexpectedly came home for lunch, he found her simmering with excitement. He helped her lay the table by the window; they put out the Breton plates and the yellow, wedding-present napkins. The room had suddenly become fun to live in. Outside, the trees moved swiftly in the spring air, and they could see a glimpse of the river.

Lucy made a tortilla, a large one, and a great dish of salad. "You know," she said as they drew up their chairs, "those sixpences in the bottle — they're a kind of magic. We haven't missed a single one."

Not yet, thought Julian. Aloud he said, trying to sound casual, "Talking of bottles —" and stopped. After a moment he tried again. "Old Mr Donne came into the office this morning," he began conversationally, and he saw Lucy lay down her knife and fork. "He asked after you and sent you his kind regards. He wondered if — well, if you still found the decanter amusing."

"Oh," exclaimed Lucy. "What did you say?"

"I said — well I said, yes, you did. Have you heard again from Baddeley's?"

"No, not since their buyer went to Italy."

"To Italy?" echoed Julian.

"Well it couldn't be mended, it seems. I told you darling. But Mr Baddeley said he'd send the pieces with the buyer when he went to Italy and possibly he could get it mended."

"You mean reblown?"

"Yes, I suppose so."

"How long ago was this?"

"About three weeks."

Julian looked worried. "I rather think that decanter's a special kind of job. I don't think any Tom, Dick or Harry could blow it. The man may be dead or something."

"Well, then, that'll be that. We can't do more."

Julian ate the rest of his tortilla in silence. After a while, he wiped his mouth nervously on the yellow napkin and pushed aside his plate. "Darling," he said, "I rather think you ought to ring up Baddeley's. Suppose Mr Donne suddenly called, or we asked him to dinner, or something."

Lucy laughed. "But he wouldn't. You know quite well he wouldn't. He never goes out. He'd loathe to be asked to dinner." Suddenly she became silent, her eyes on Julian's face.

"I'm not so sure," Julian said. "He liked you, and perhaps because of my mother —"

"Shall I ring up Baddeley's now?" Lucy asked.

Julian's face brightened. "Would you?"

"Yes, of course." She got up from the table, napkin in hand, and walked deliberately into the hall. In a few minutes she was back, "They've got it," she said in a stunned voice. "It's there in the shop. It arrived yesterday. They say they've just written."

Julian sprang up, his face almost anguished with relief. "I'll go there now. I'll go and collect it." He hesitated. "How much is it?"

Lucy looked at him steadily. "Forty guineas," she said.

There was silence. Julian's eyes flew to the bottle on the bookcase and back again to Lucy's. "What did you say to them?" he asked.

"Nothing yet. The man's holding on."

Julian jerked his shoulders. "What can we say?" he asked her. "We've got to have it."

Lucy's voice began to tremble. "We could tell them the truth — that we can't possibly afford it. We could ask them to put it into stock."

Julian sat down at the table. "Darling," he said, "I was going to tell you. He's going to the opening of the Chelsea Flower Show on Thursday. This morning he asked, as we're just around the corner, if he could come along here afterwards, about six o'clock, for — these were his exact words — a glass of sherry."

"He doesn't drink sherry," Lucy said.

"I know," agreed Julian. He really means he'll call between tea and dinner. He's being considerate. Don't you understand that, darling?"

As she did not speak, he went on. "You see, he asked to come. He couldn't very well propose himself for a meal or anything that entailed trouble for you."

"Yes," she said, in a light, constrained voice, "of course I see."

He got up and went towards her. "My poor darling."

She backed away from him. At the concern in his voice, her lower lip had begun to tremble. "No," she said, putting out her hands to ward him off. "I must go to the telephone. I must go and tell the man." He let go her hands, and she ran to the door. On the threshold she turned. "You better take the bottle to the bank," she said, the tears running down her cheeks. "We don't want to pay in sixpences."

While Julian and Mr Donne were talking, Lucy, pale and quiet, sat curled in an armchair. She felt peaceful and a little chastened, like a justly punished child. "Mustn't snatch," Fate had said, rapping her lightly over the knuckles. "All in good time you will get your furnishings — as you earn them and your man gets on." Fate, in the form of a blown-glass decanter.

It sat there smugly on the round table. It seemed taller and narrower than the old one, and there were two slight flaws in the glass, but she could look at it now without resentment. And the room looks pretty enough, she decided, in spite of the floor. The pinkish sky had turned the blue walls to opal, and in the early-spring dusk, she had lighted one lamp — a converted crystal vase. She was aware gradually of silence, a silence curiously prolonged. Julian, suddenly standing up, was pouring himself more sherry; his face stiffened, and he was smiling oddly.

Lucy uncurled her legs and sat up. She searched wildly on the surface of her memory for some echo of the last spoken words. Mr Donne's voice, it had been. Something like: "I may be speaking out of turn. I thought Beckman had told you."

"No, sir," Julian said, as Lucy stared, bewildered, at his face, "no one has told me."

"Yes, Friedman Cole retires in June," said Mr Donne. "But better forget it for the moment. I seldom go to the office and I never interfere."

Julian raised his head. "I'll try to forget it," he said, and Lucy saw his hand on the glass tremble.

There was a short silence, and the old man turned to Lucy, and she saw the shrewd eyes glitter between the reddened lids. "So you like my decanter, do you?" he asked abruptly. He stretched out an arm and laid his knotted fingers on the smooth glass; he stroked it gently with his short-nailed thumb.

Lucy, distraught, kept her eyes on his face. Don't change the subject, she longed to cry. Tell me — tell me at once — what you just said to Julian.

Mr Donne lifted the decanter and held it awkwardly between his eyes and the light. "Strange-looking thing, he remarked, smiling. "As you so aptly describe it — alchemical."

Lucy, gazing at his face, did not see the globe slide round in his fingers or the golden liquid rush up into the transparent stems; she saw only, with a slight start, his free hand come up convulsively in a vain attempt to save it as it slipped between his knees to the floor.

In the second of shocked silence following the crash, Lucy understood suddenly. They were taking Julian into the firm — now, soon, in June. That's what he meant when he spoke of Friedman Cole. She hardly heard Mr Donne's distressed apologies, his offers to replace the decanter, or, if they would allow him, to find some other little thing to take its place. But she heard him say to Julian that it wasn't old, had no associations. "Perhaps," she heard him say, "there is something you'd prefer, some little thing you need, something you'd like to choose yourselves."

Lucy turned suddenly. "Please, please don't worry," she begged him and laughed shakily; almost she took his hand. "These things just happen. We know how they happen." And as Julian appeared with a bowl and cloth, she went down gratefully to her knees. "I'll just clear away the worst. It won't take a minute. It's easily done. It isn't", she heard herself say, " as though we have a carpet."

CHAPTER
THREE

Talking of Television

It is unfortunate that the telephone should ring, as it so often does, while you are in your bath.

"Yes?" you say, in a get-it-over-quickly voice.

"Miss Smith? This is the BBC, television casting, would you be able to manage a transmission on February the fifteenth or seventeenth, rehearsals from the first?"

Magically, your scowl dissolves. "The fifteenth or seventeenth? Yes, I think so . . ."

"The fee is twenty-five guineas. Would that be all right?"

Yes, marvellous — it is on the tip of your tongue to reply but you remember, just in time, to hesitate — so often has it been drummed into you that you must not sound too eager.

"Twenty-five?" you say uncertainly. Then you hold your breath: please, please, don't snatch it away . . . I should love to do some television . . . this is the first opportunity . . . I wonder what made them think of me . . . of course, twentyfive guineas is all right . . . even fifteen . . . possibly ten . . .

"Well," says the voice from the BBC as the drips plop softly on the polished floor, "we could go, I think, to

35

twenty-eight," it sounds gentle, reasonable, not in the least put out, "but not as much as thirty, I'm afraid, on this particular play."

Kind, kind BBC, of course you can't! Why should you? Trustingly, on some half-guessed recommendation, you are hiring an unknown quantity — a pig in a poke.

A few days later, the script arrives — very heavy, in a long brown envelope. You take it away to a quiet corner but, after a hasty perusal of the first few pages, your heart sinks. It is a dialect play, written in broad Devonshire, full of "thees" and "doan'ts", "surelies" and "midears". At the head of the title page in pencil, you see your name — Jane Smith: Miss Nellie Masters.

"Oh dear, oh dear . . ." you murmur to yourself as you turn over the pages. Dialects never were your strong point. But gradually, as you read on, you become aware that, after all, Heaven may be on your side. It seems that Miss Nellie Masters is a twin and, not only a twin, but an echo. It falls to her lot to repeat word for word, intonation for intonation, the end part of every sentence spoken by Miss Minnie Masters. Provided the actress playing the part of Miss Minnie Masters can speak Devonshire, all will be well. Anxiously, you turn back the cast list and find, to your joy, that Miss Minnie Masters is to be played by a dear friend and one to whom you are said to bear a superficial resemblance. Hence, of course, your engagement. Hastily, you dial her number.

"Darling, can you speak Devonshire?"

"No," she wails.

"What shall we do?"

"We'll have to hope the rest of the cast can and we must pick it up quickly by ear."

"This is my first television."

"I know. You'll hate it. It's like acting in a vacuum. Shall I pick you up for the first reading? It's at 20 Dash Street, mews entrance . . ."

Your taxi driver does not really believe in the address you give him but, at last, you persuade him to set you down in a most unlikely-looking cul-de-sac, lined with disused coach houses. When he has driven off, you do not believe in it much yourselves. But, after a painful scramble over drains and cobbles, you see the dusty back of what seems like a warehouse and the welcome but not particularly conspicuous letters: "BBC".

Inside you are confronted with a bleak stone staircase and double doors, half-glassed and lined with chicken wire, on which are displayed with shattering finality the words "NO ENTRY".

You are aware that the BBC has many curious hide-outs in the remoter parts of London but none, you feel, more discouraging than this.

You climb the staircase, to be met with a replica of the double doors and the prohibition. Up again to another floor — still, no luck. On the top floor of all, there is an unused garbage can and a single door marked "PRIVATE".

You climb down again and peer unhappily through the half — glassed doors on the ground floor. The minutes are ticking by. You are already late for your first reading. Inside, the place looks even more like a warehouse — stacked folios on silent shelves. No sign of human life. Tentatively, you push the door marked "NO ENTRY". It opens easily and you walk into the morgue-like shadows of things dim and stored. Your two pairs of heels strike a hollow flight of echoes from off the ringing stone. But you are approaching civilization. There in the distance is a glow of artificial light and, as you approach, a man in shirt sleeves.

"Oh, no," he says, when he has heard your lament. "They must have said "*not* the mews entrance". This is the BBC music library. Now, it's a bit complicated . . ."

It is. You walk up flights of stairs, you cross glassed-in bridges, you pass through swing doors, you soar in elevators, but at last you are in the familiar atmosphere of polished wood, warmth, light and uniformed attendants. A famous film-star in slacks passes you; you meet a fellow actor you have not seen for several years; and there at last is room 51 with the rest of the cast — hatless and coatless, chatting and smoking, not only very much at home but as if they had been there for a considerable time.

"Ah, at last!" says the producer, coming forward to greet you. Then his expression becomes quizzical: "Odd how two people so alike can look so different."

With dismay you realize that as prospective twins you and your companion leave much to be desired. One of you is tall, the other is short; one has a round face, the other pointed; one is plump and one is slight.

"Well," says the producer, "it can't be helped now. Anyway," he adds, as if to comfort himself, "you're both equally crazy. Better see what Mrs Thompson can do about clothes . . ."

When this is over, you draw chairs into a circle and begin to read the play. Several of the cast know you slightly; others know you by repute; some are strangers. Surreptitiously, you try to suit names to characters on the cast list. There is nothing outstanding or particularly theatrical about anyone. The women, for the most part, wear coats and skirts; the men tweeds or sports jackets.

As the reading progresses, you become aware that — with two possible exceptions — none of the cast is Devon-born. There are inflections of Lancashire, Yorkshire, Irish and Scottish — slightly modified, but none the less recognizable. You turn the page and see that your scene is about to come. You feel not nervousness, but a sudden tautened awareness. Miss Minnie Masters is speaking (ah, Welsh inflections, or your ears deceive you) and you echo her last words with suitable inanity. The cast laughs. You feel immensely cheered. Confidence flows back until your character, speaking independently for once, surprises you with an intonation which might be described as Czechoslovakian.

"Well, well!" says the producer mildly. The cast laughs again and you, rather ruefully, with them.

"I suppose," says the producer mournfully, at the end of the reading, "it'll be all right on 'the night'. Rehearsal on Tuesday, 10.30, at St Martha's Convent, please."

St Martha's Convent has been a girls' school — gloomy, rambling, Victorian-Gothic and utterly inaccessible. You rehearse in what was once a classroom. There is a blackboard fixed to the wall and a chalky feeling about the floor. You find your twin has been given a day off for filming and her place is taken by the producer's assistant, a charming, fair young man who is delectable in the role of prim spinster. But your prop, your stay, your inflections have gone!

The two authentic sons of Devon succeed in imposing their accent on the rest of the cast and the play begins to take shape. As usual, you are overwhelmed by the prowess of the other actors and aware of something like a thin sheet of glass between the performance you yourself are giving and the performance you could give were the invisible barrier not there.

"Very good," said the producer, at the end of the morning, "with one exception." On this happy note, you find yourself dismissed.

After that, each day is like another. The play emerges and has charm and humour but repetition dims the charm and familiarity the fun. You work blindly on the inspiration of those first few days when impressions were fresh and still untarnished. You seek opportunities, as if the classroom were still in a school, to play hooky and slip away for weak cups of canteen coffee. Your fellow actors have become friends, almost your family. Their backgrounds and home lives take shape for you, your dreams and ambitions mingle in the buzz and clatter of the lunchtime canteen — where a cabinet minister must queue beside a typist, poets are interspersed with producers, and where, unwittingly, you once sent a famous conductor to fetch you another slice of cake. No longer are you "Miss Smith" but "Jane darling," "Jane, my pet" or "Dear, dear Jane . . . not like that!"

There are clothes fittings and wig matchings and then, at last, comes The Day — "the worst day of your life" your twin tells you cheerfully.

You meet at Broadcasting House, hatted and coated, and carrying little bags with extra stockings, sandwiches, cold cream, tissues and fal-lals. Alexandra Palace is your destination.

Soon the bus is there, so roomy that you each have a window seat and more to spare. There is amongst you the carefree exuberance of children on an outing, laced with the grim foreboding of a tumbrel full of victims bound for the guillotine. So much can go wrong in television. No script to read from as before the microphone, no prompting as in a theatre, no retakes as in a film: once on the air, you are out on a tightrope, perilously balanced. There can be no mistakes, no hesitations, no turning back: for if you should falter, the illusion will be broken and the play spoilt, not only for your vast invisible audience, but also for your fellow actors, who rely on your support. (We will not — this being on the whole a cheerful article — even mention the probable effect on the producer.)

So you rattle along through the London streets in your private bus. You try to comfort yourself with the reflection that, whatever happens tonight, it will make no odds in a hundred years' time. But this is your first television and you want to do well. You are not at all certain of yourself in this role. You are still aware of an invisible barrier between the performance you have been giving at rehearsal and the sharp, clean authenticity of the part as it should be played.

The bus stops suddenly in a side street and several minutes elapse. "What are we waiting for?" "They're fetching the parrot." The parrot; of course. You had forgotten the parrot; or you thought he might be stuffed. But here he is, at last, a little surprised but very much alive, freshly fed and sanded. You make room for his cage and address him in his stage character of "Ko-ko". He meets all overtures with a wary, misanthropic eye and shows no vivacity.

The bus has reached the suburbs and, as the road twists, begins to climb. The air feels cleaner, fresher, and there — glinting above you in the sunshine — are the glass roofs and windows of the Alexandra Palace; a Victorian pleasure dome perched above London's grey-green panorama, now the home of British television.

No longer, as in the eighties, are the gardens sweet with flowers and gay with music. The grass looks ragged and there are weeds among the gravel. The glinting windows have known total war and are still patched and cracked; the doors need paint, and the whole place wears a misanthropic air as long-suffering as that of the parrot. Both are being put to uses of which neither had ever dreamed.

Through the swing doors are uniformed attendants, a smiling lift-girl and, as you glimpse the studios, you are aware for the first time of an underlying atmosphere of efficiency, of essentials without frills, an aura of work well done for its own sake. What matters here is the actual forward leap of television, not paint on doors and window frames.

And now, at last, you are in your dressing room. A row of these line the passages which flank your particular studio, as bathing cabins flank a swimming pool; except, in this case, the "swimming pool" is enclosed in soundproof walls and thus hidden from view. The dressing room, which you share with your twin, looks clean and bright but has no ceiling. The four walls converge at great height into the glass roof. There is a nightmarish sensation of being an ant at the bottom of a square drainpipe.

There are your clothes on hangers, pressed and altered in accordance with many ankle-aching fittings. You begin to unpack your cold cream, your sandwiches, your soap, but "Come and have a peep at the sets!" says your twin and drags you into the passage and through the soundproof door, which swings back heavily behind you with a sad, hydraulic sigh.

The studio is a blaze of light and sound. It seems immense. Round the walls are built realistic sets, scenes from your play: a village street, a cottage interior, a sea wall, a piece of beach with nets and boats. Compared with the films, each set is miniature in circumference and has the charm of most small things. Part of the difficulty of television technique is the limited space in which the actors have to work: a wide gesture, a sudden turn, may waft you off the screen.

The main part of the studio floor is a terrifying jumble of machinery on wheels — all the complicated paraphernalia of cameras, sound and lighting. Pipes and tubes, linked to mechanical nerve centres, sprawl and writhe with the undulatory intelligence of pythons. There is a sinister hum and an almost jungle heat. Strangely at home in this inferno, is a rare species of man: keen-eyed and jersey-clad; authoritative but young; swift but unhurried; calm but vital; sometimes vituperative but never bewildered. Here is none of the easy leisure of the film studio. These people seem to be working against time as indeed, poor wretches, they are. Their show must be on air at 8.15 tonight, photographed straight through, alive on the quivering ether.

"Come on," says your twin. "Dress rehearsal at 2.30. We'd better hurry if you want to have some lunch . . ."

There is a good deal of knocking at doors up and down the dressing-room passage: "Oh, so here you are! My basin leaks . . . oh you've got a bath! . . . Are your clothes all right? They haven't sent my feather boa . . ."

With the help of the dresser, you and your twin set about to achieve a mythical identicalness. Very high heels for her; heel-less monstrosities for you (feet do not appear in a television play); hems turned up for her, let down for you; identical scarves; hair screwed back; dowdy little boaters and suddenly, in the mirror, you are faced with two passably similar little maiden ladies. You whip off the hats, shake down your hair and join the rush for a canteen lunch. In the canteen, you meet your colleagues, several of whom have become unrecognizable.

You are only half made up when your call comes for the dress rehearsal. With your twin you are seated before the mirror and gentle-calm, pastel-coloured young women have been at work on your faces, modifying and enhancing until potential resemblance is fast becoming incontrovertible fact.

You seize your hats, you rush through the swing doors and take your places, panting slightly, in the cramped wings of the set. A few seconds still to go. You straighten each other's lockets and ribbons, pin up stray pieces of hair and then on, when your cue comes — into the blaze of light, the false and dreamlike travesty of a cottage interior.

The infernal machines have lined up into a fourth wall. You are hemmed in by electricians, photographers, mechanics, cameras, lights and microphones. The machines press in upon you with their glare, their heat and their throbbing, thought-destroying hum. Beyond this hum, no voice is heard besides the voice of the actor, no sound but that made by the characters on the set. Your funniest lines are sucked up with grim, mechanical imperturbability to be spewed out again, you feel, upon the ether devitalized and flat.

Did this really seem a charming play? Why, it is terrible . . . it is inane . . . Vaguely it seems to you, in those first moments of blind panic, that nobody is giving a performance except the parrot. That gloomy entity appears now as a transformed being, climbing about his cage in this welcome, unhoped-for glow of tropic heat, interspersing the dialogue with irrelevant remarks of his own — helping out, when pressed for matter, with jungle cries of painful intensity and shrillness. Never, you think, critically, have you seen a more pitiful example of overacting.

A voice booms out, seemingly from heaven, and calls a halt. The parrot must be taken off; he must make one swift appearance and an even swifter exit.

"Foiled!" you murmur below your breath as, frustrated, he is carried past you.

Once again the heavenly voice rings out — disembodied, quite unearthly . . .

"Where is he?" you whisper to your twin.

"Floating on a cloud," she replies matter-of-factly.

"That's where you'll be, any minute," booms the voice, in Jove-like accents, "if —" and adds a phrase which sounds less Jove-like but rather more to the point.

"What did he say?" you ask your twin, sotto voce.

"He? Oh, you mustn't take any notice of him."

The electricians laugh. Your twin straightens her scarf, looking primly down her nose.

The play goes on.

An imaginary cake is passed round (the real one is still at the baker's). The twins, who have spread clean handkerchiefs, napkin-wise, upon their knees, find this easy to manage — the dialogue allowing no time for the eating of cake, imaginary or otherwise. The long neck of the microphone sways from speaker to speaker, twisting and dangling above heads, almost trembling in its insatiable, mechanical curiosity; making its fluttered rushes from one to another in a panic of semithwarted eavesdropping.

"Do NOT — I beg you, I implore you — turn away from the mike! Now, we'll take that bit again . . ."

The rehearsal seems interminable. Now you are on the actual set, there are countless unforeseen considerations and pitfalls. Scenes are played and replayed. You are most unsuitably dressed for the heat and, as hours pass, begin to feel slightly faint. Oh, for a brief respite away from the lights and heat! Just ten minutes, you feel, in the cool silence of the corridor would be sufficient to set you up. But this is the last chance before transmission, the final grooming. If the pitfalls are not circumvented now, they never will be.

At last, however, you are free — to toss off your hats, pull out heavy pins securing false hair, throw off your coats, kick off your shoes and relax for five minutes on the hard chair before your dressing-room table.

There is a knock at the door. It is the producer. "Very nice, darlings. Could be a lot worse . . ."

Dinner in the canteen is less of a scramble. Tables have been booked and a special meal ordered. You long for a cocktail but dare not drink.

This time, your make-up is more leisurely and carried through to completion. Clothes seem to go on with greater ease. In fact, you are dressed with alarming suddenness and much too early. You try to read the evening paper.

Your colleagues look in, bright-eyed, overfriendly: "Good luck, darling . . . all the best . . . the same to you . . . soon be over . . ."

The callboy announces five minutes. There is a faint flurry which dies, in passage and dressing room, to a tense calm. Transmission is on.

You are not on until halfway through the first act. You skulk for a while in your dressing room. For the hundredth time you cast your eye over the props laid out for your quick change. You powder your face. You wash your hands. You light a cigarette. You tiptoe out into the quiet corridor where red lights are burning warningly outside the studio doors. You walk up and down, lightly, nervously. You see your fellow actors crossing and recrossing the passage for their exits and entrances. You do not worry them with conversation.

After a while, you find courage to slip silently through the swing doors. The play is well into its first stride. You cannot see much of the set above the solid blockade of cameras, electricians, mechanics and workmen. A grey-haired carpenter is leaning against a post, making giraffes of cotton wool and wire. His job is over for the night. You envy his calm.

You slip round behind the set, where there is a small television screen. Two secretaries sit before it, making notes. With morbid fascination, you watch the play unfold as it is actually going on the air, purged of colour but alive as no film is alive. You sneak quietly back to your dressing room whose nightmarish properties, you find, have become intensified. Far above you, through the glassed mouth of your deep cavern, you see stars in a night sky. A living sky, you know it to be, pulsating with poetry, music and captured vision poured into its vastness by just such other ants as you.

"Miss Smith, please," shouts the callboy suddenly, close beside your door.

You are on.

Memory of transmission dissolves into a kaleidoscopic blur. Attention is too concentrated for conscious thought. You are aware that the parrot is rushed on and off and allowed no time for ad-libbing; you are aware that so-and-so seems nervous and that what-you-may-call-him is giving a very good performance; you are aware that the cake is no longer imaginary and is extremely concrete and sticky and that, having no time to eat it, there is absolutely no place to put it; you are aware that an electrician stifles a laugh at one of your best lines and, in a rush of gratitude for this tribute, you are suddenly and gloriously aware that your glass wall has splintered and your character has come to life.

The rest is anticlimax — the scramble to catch the bus in time; the hurried sorting of props; a brotherly kiss from the producer; a last-minute look round . . . The rattling drive back in the only available conveyance, a cross between a station wagon and a tradesman's van, into which you are locked, since the handle is insecure. Each of you carries a spotted giraffe and, deep in each pocket-book, a comforting cheque (twenty-eight guineas is, after all, as near to thirty pounds as makes no matter). Laughing, affection born of imminent parting, congratulations, recommendations . . . goodbyes . . .

And then at last, your key in your own front door; the smiling faces of your family; the unbiased comments which, added up and sorted out, appear on the whole to be favourable.

You find a steaming bowl of soup and the day's letters placed beside your plate — a dentist's bill, a letter from a friend in Cyprus, the water rate, the electricity account, a letter from your son at school asking for a new blazer, the invoice for repainting the front of the house . . . You push them aside, then struck with a sudden thought, you take out a pencil. With your pay cheque in mind, you make a rapid calculation . . . thirty-seven pounds, two shillings and eight-pence.

Sighing a little, you turn back to the soup.

CHAPTER
FOUR

Once upon a Time
(Some Random Thoughts on
Story-Writing for Children)

Have you ever listened to children telling stories to each other? Tired perhaps, having cooked them a meal, you ask them to wash the dishes — when they have finished, you think, we'll play a round game. In the meantime, you pick up the paper.

But the washing-up goes on and on. There is a half-hearted clink of china, the sound of aimless footsteps and a voice — one voice, raised and interminable — holding forth.

You open the kitchen door. One child is at the sink, mop in hand. Another is wiping a plate — round and round, round and round, as if in a dream. The third is sitting stooped and hunched upon a stool. The stack of crockery looks as big as it ever was. There are drips on the kitchen floor and the tap is running slowly into a flooded bowl which overflows with throaty gurgles down the drain. The plate-wiper is telling a story.

"And then," she says, "this man — not the first man but the man who had the dog. That was before the dog ran away. No, it was after but they didn't know it then. Except the first man. He knew because of the soda-water syphon. Well, when the girl went to see this man's mother, the first man's mother — oh, I forgot to say this was all before the man was standing under the wall, the other one — the one with the moustache. And they said they hadn't seen the dog. So this man, the one whose uncle was President of the Bank . . ."

And so it went on. And on. And on. It was the story of a play or a film. The movement of the mop in the cloudy water was barely perceptible as the dish-washer listened. The stoolsitter made no movement at all but gazed forth from under a tangled fringe, chin in hand. Not one of those three substantial entities was even in the kitchen. Another world had caught them up and would hold them rapt and elevated until, with a sharp reminder, you broke the spell.

What was the plate-wiper's secret? With what magic did she hold them still? Her facts were hazy, the sequence of her incidents was muddled, her enunciation was none too clear and the story itself left much to be desired.

Was it because the teller herself was interested? Because she was living the story as she told it? The loss of the dog was her loss; she shared the apprehension of the man who stood beneath the wall and sensed the mystic aura of a "Bank President". Such impressions sincerely felt can convey themselves automatically to the hearer. Eyes, voice and gesture weave the spell and lame words speak.

Perhaps. All the same, I cannot get rid of a sneaking suspicion that this is not the whole secret. Or rather that what secret there is lies in a very simple fact: the child's love of a story — almost any story. An indifferent, bad or even a boring story is better than no story at all.

This is a terrifying thought. It turns the field of story-telling for children from an enclosed and sheltered pasture into a vast, horizonless prairie. "Quick," we gasp. "Quick! Make rules! Put up fences! We can't have this! This will never do!"

So theories come into being and policies are formed. These are communicated to authors by quiet-voiced women across (juvenile) editorial desks: "Charming. But we find our children like stories about real happenings and real people. Couldn't you? . . ." "Yes, very nice, but some of the words are rather *long*, if you understand. We find our children prefer stories which use words within their own vocabularies . . ." "Well, we *really* wanted something for the eight-to-ten year olds . . ." "Fantasy? Well, that's always a bit problematical . . ." and so on. Behind the gentle words are the iron rules, barely indicated but quite inflexible.

Sighing, the author picks up his MS and in a few months' time your son can buy a book called *Armies of Other Lands* and your daughter, perhaps, a charmingly illustrated pamphlet entitled *Katinka, a Day in the Life of a Ukrainian Village*. "On Sundays —" she will read (and read it she will in case by the time she gets to page 19 something will begin to happen), "we wore our high-headed dresses and sometimes as many as ten petticoats . . ." "Ten petticoats!" she is supposed to exclaim. "Mother, on Sundays in the Ukraine the little girls wear ten petticoats!" and Mother, looking up from her darning, reflects smugly on this painless acquisition of general knowledge by the young — sugar-coated culture for consumption out of school.

But let us examine some of the editorial shibboleths more closely. (Oddly enough, these are less apparent here in England than in America. Matter-of-fact as we are supposed to be, a submerged vein of poetry and individualism runs like a streak of silver through our solid Island clay. Mist and magic are indigenous with us — even in publishers' offices — whereas in the USA, fantasy is still slightly suspect until proved sound and saleable — and an English child will treasure many a tale which his transatlantic counterpart might look upon as "sissy".) It is indeed true that stories about Real Children From Other Lands (or Other Climes or Other Periods) will always find a market. They call for sound knowledge rather than inventive facility on the part of the author and attractively illustrated are a safe buy for nieces and nephews at Christmas time. How "real" they are depends entirely on the skill and imagination with which they were written.

Strange pieces of general knowledge do come your way as you watch little Yosh build his Eskimo hut, share with little Masha her Christmas on a farm in Czechoslovakia, hear how little Abdul tends his camels in El Cantara or pursue Little Ivan across the Russian steppes. Such books combine a double function and are seldom the true narrative which children love. They resemble in some subtle way the London greengrocer who will only sell you oranges if you buy cabbages as well — "half a pound of what we've got for a quarter pound of what you want; besides," he might add, "green stuff is good for you."

"Yes, yes," says the editor kindly. "But some of the words are rather *long*, don't you know . . ." She waves her pencil over the MS which lies upon her desk. You look at it too although you are much too short-sighted to see what is written there. "Oh," you say rather lamely, "do you think so?"

"Yes," she replies with an even kinder smile. "Children apart, I think anything we have to say is better said in quite simple words, don't you?"

"Well," you think wildly of some way of stopping her before she says it but she is there already.

"Look at the Bible," she says. "Now, I'd like you to take this home and rewrite it in language intelligible to eight-to-ten year olds. You see, we must . . ."

Must we? Must we really? With all the richness of the English language to choose from must we only use the words which are completely intelligible to a specified age? Do not stories compounded entirely of such words resemble those light, digestible dishes, the invalid diet of childhood, which are too quickly assimilated and which leave one's hunger vaguely unsatisfied? Richness and variety of impression cannot be achieved on a paucity of material. Could we not give the child, within sensible limits, the right word in the right place? How else can we lead him towards his heritage?

Words have colour and feeling as well as sense. The child's imagination can catch the former without perhaps his conscious understanding of the latter. And yet more often than we think the meaning too is conveyed to him by the context. He might not be able to define this meaning in words but it is acceptable to his understanding and is assimilated within the story.

In the language sense, are we not apt to spoonfeed our children too long? The unknown word creates an effort to understand and the consequent, almost imperceptible, discipline of increased attention. Few recreations are enjoyed in complete passivity, even should active co-operation confine itself to a wider exercise of the understanding. A story which demands nothing of the reader cannot help but be insipid.

If we review in our minds the great classics of childhood, we find very few of them if any are written in artificially simple language: *Uncle Tom's Cabin*, *Robinson Crusoe*, the fairy tales of the Grimm Brothers and of Hans Andersen, *Alice in Wonderland*, the *Just So Stories* . . . When one re-reads these one is struck at once by the richness of vocabulary and maturity of thought as compared with children's books of today.

In the *Just So Stories*, Kipling went out of his way to find fascinating, barely intelligible words with which to spice his tales: "Said the Ethiopian to the Baviaan, 'Can you tell me the present habitat of the aboriginal fauna?'" and we can none of us forget, so often are we told, that the Shipwrecked Mariner was a man "of infinite resource and sagacity". Lewis Carroll, who would have us believe he wrote simply, well knew the value of a "slithy tove" or a "borogrove". (Much of *Uncle Remus* is completely unintelligible to English readers (and I suspect to some Americans). My mother read and loved

Uncle Tom's Cabin at the age of eight but I doubt very much if my small daughter of ten would tackle it. Listen to the description of Mrs Shelby:

> To that natural magnanimity of mind which one often marks as characteristic of the women of Kentucky, she added high moral and religious sensibility and principle, carried out with great energy and ability into practical results.

As for *Robinson Crusoe*, he too must speak for himself. Although not primarily written for children, it was the younger generation of its own free will who adopted this story for their own. Here, he speaks of his father's counsel:

> He bade me ... observe I should always find that the calamities of life were shared among the upper and lower part of mankind; but that the middle station had the fewest disasters and was not exposed to so many vicissitudes as the higher or lower part of mankind, nay, they were not subjected to so many distempers and uneasiness either of body or mind as those who, by vicious living, luxury and extravagances on one hand or by hard labour, want of necessaries, and mean or insufficient diet on the one hand, bring distempers upon themselves by that natural consequence of their way of living ... that temperance, moderation, quietness, health, society, all agreeable diversions and all desirable pleasures were the blessings attending the middle station of life.

Is it that children of earlier generations were more intelligent than those of today? I very much doubt it. I think they, as the children of today, passionately loved "a story" and would hunt through no matter how deep a welter of words to find it. Even the least intelligible of these would be taken in their stride as they rode hell for leather on the scent of the plot. As the chapters slipped by, repetition and context would give such words their meaning, the child a vocabulary and the book its true perspective.

We do not give children this chance nowadays; when all is said and done, deny it as we may, we write down to them. The bookshops are filled with "easy" books for children. When the children of the eighteenth century had passed the "cat and mat" stage, the English language was handed to them *en bloc*. Today, we dole it out to them. In order to enjoy his reading, the child of the past had to learn new words and a great many of them. We have short circuited this process. We give a child his story almost before he has earned the right to it. It is we who must tie ourselves in knots in order that he may understand it. We meet him more than halfway. In the early stages, this is an incentive; but if he continues to read easy stuff for too long, he will jib at anything harder. The habit of reading only those things which are assimilated without effort will remain with him all his life.

"Maybe," says the juvenile editor politely. Then suddenly she frowns, tapping the MS sharply with her pencil. "I don't like this bit where the little dog gets run over."

"Oh . . . you don't?"

"No."

"Dogs do get run over —"

"Children's books shouldn't be sad."

"But the rest of the book is quite gay."

"I think books for children should be gay all through, don't you?"

"Yes, I mean — no. Did you ever read a book called *Froggie's Little Brother Bennie*?"

"No, I can't say I did." (Has the kind smile become slightly derisive?)

"Well, it was a terribly sad book. About two London waifs. They were hungry and cold and often homeless. I adored it as a child and wept quarts over it."

"Oh?" Her gaze seems more puzzled than critical. "But life is sad enough, don't you think? Children should be happy while they are children."

"Perhaps you are right."

All the same, it comforted me as a child to read that other children had troubles too — graver ones, so often, than my own. Books about children who had nothing but fun were oddly irritating and faintly boring: so I alone in the world had troubles! Obviously I was peculiar — sadness, however fleeting, being absolutely alien to normal childhood.

Is there perhaps too much of a conspiracy among modern writers to construct our tales entirely of sweetness and light? We swerve away, when writing for children, from anything which approaches grim reality. We set out to convince them (eventual disillusion being none of our affair) that all is for the best in the best of possible worlds. There is much to be said for preserving as long as possible the El Dorado of childhood but, in our anxiety to achieve this, we are sometimes apt to err on the side of timidity and, as a consequence, to the quick sensibility of a child, our work will lack conviction. Never completely deceived by the persistently idealized picture we so doggedly glimpse of honest human frailty.

Children will not be denied knowledge of life as it is (or as they fear it may be) and if the better class literature of their day lacks virility where do they seek it?

In comics.

We bowdlerize Grimm because "some of it, my dear, is too ghastly" but, in closing a window, inadvertently we open a door — a trap door, and one which creaks with blood and fear.

I would far rather my children read in Grimm of the maiden who had no hands or of "The Man who Could Not Shiver" than of the Ape Man, the Green Monsters and the Blind Killers of the American penny-dreadfuls — products of minds, uneducated and opportunist, swift to exploit a childish love of savagery.

When in the old books grimness appears, it is skilfully woven into the fabric of the tale by the hand of a master, and fantasy, soaring to whatever dizzy height, flies on wings of poetry. We cannot say as much of comics. Our Canadian nieces and nephews read with equanimity of shapely young women, with Veronica Lake hair-dos, sitting gagged and bound and entirely at the mercy of a race of pale green, subhuman monsters, the very sight of which should make their blood run cold. Starved of the miraculous, these are their fairy tales; this is their folk lore.

All very well to push forward *A Day in the Life of Little Baku of Malay*. The children will make short shrift of that too, and back once more to comics.

This literature, besides being of the stuff of which nightmares are made, has many other curious properties; one of these is the ability to reproduce itself. In America and Canada it positively breeds in any house where there are children. However often one makes a clean sweep, other copies — just as brightly coloured, quite as tattered — mysteriously appear under pillows, in toy cupboards, under beds. Forbidden the house, they lurk in the woodshed. They have penetrated my house in London. Three thousand miles some of them have had to come — but they made it, sure of a welcome, tenacious as homing pigeons, straight to their roosts under the chair cushions in the nursery. When read, tenderly the torn pages are gathered together, the loose parts fitted into the right order, the copies solemnly counted and then, with many injunctions, the whole clutch is passed on to the children next door (strictly on a lend-lease basis) and another unsuspecting household is injected with the virus.

Yes, it takes more than Little Baku to counteract comics. Only vigorous and arresting literature can do it. Stories which break through the shibboleths on their own momentum, stories such as *Bambi*, *The Wind in the Willows*, *National Velvet*, *Smoky*, *Dr Dolittle*, the Arthur Ransome books, *The Wizard of Oz* and many others.

There is no infallible recipe for a good story — either for children or adults — just as there is no infallible recipe for a great painting or a fine piece of music. We can put into our tales for children all the skill and inspiration of which we are capable and then, if still we lag far behind the great storytellers of the past (or fail even to get abreast of comics), it will not be because we consider writing for children easier than writing for grown-ups but simply that we lack the spark which turns the simplest, homespun story into magic or makes the wildest flight of fantasy seem real.

CHAPTER
FIVE

Take of Wormwood
Seven Scruples

*This book can teach you everything —
except the fortitude to follow implicitly
its extraordinary suggestions*

I suppose most of us, however confident a front we show to the world, have felt at times, some inner sense of personal inadequacy. Now, happily, for me all that is changed, and I find myself, almost overnight, a useful, not to say indispensable, member of the community — all due to a little book called *A Shilling's Worth of Practical Receipts*, Houlston and Stoneham, Paternoster Row, in London, published in the early years of the nineteenth century. Thanks to this modestly priced volume, I have suddenly become the fortunate possessor of many new and startling accomplishments: I can dye kid gloves purple, manufacture Daffy's Elixir and Sympathetic Ink, undertake the French Method of Embalming, prevent cold feet at bedtime, cure cholera, and ventilate a ship.

True, I have not yet found myself called upon, suddenly and without warning, to ventilate a ship; but it is a comfort to me to know, should a distraught captain approach me on this point, that I would be able to whip from under my coat the piece of metal tubing (which is all that is required and which it has now become second nature to carry) and explain to him how "the rarefaction produced by the fire causes a current of air," which arrives at "the extremity of the pipe", located in the "place which it is designed to purify".

I have learned, too, to make Artificial Stone; but for those who have really suffered through a lack of this commodity and who contemplate sending me an order, I must explain that this takes a trifle longer than ventilating a ship — a matter of eight days or so for the drying, and a good forty-eight hours for the polishing. There is also a recipe for Artificial Sea-Water.

Moreover, I can whip you up all kinds of beverages: Clary Wine, Mead, Noyeau, Persico, Perfetto Amore, and Usquebaugh. You *must* try my Usquebaugh, which, after I have filtered it through paper to remove the traces of liquorice, cloves, mace, coriander seeds, nutmeg, cinnamon, rock alum, aniseed, peppermint, stoned dates, apricot kernels and caraway, I may "colour to my liking". I can toss you off Brown Caudle, Rich Caudle, or Cold Caudle; and I do take a few orders, under special circumstances, for Common Caudle, which I dispatch in a "plain bottle" and which, to the uninitiated, you can pass off really quite simply as Caudle.

I have decided against making English Sherry for export, as I find that, under the present rationing system, my grocer and wine merchant tend to be uncooperative as far as even the simplest ingredients are concerned. So I am only too glad to pass on the following recipes.

No. 227. English Sherry
Loaf sugar, twenty pounds; sugar candy, twenty pounds; pale ale wort (good), ten gallons or more; raisins, eight pounds; yeast, eight ounces. Ferment, then add brandy, one gallon, or less; bitter almonds, three to six drachms; orris powder, three to six drachms. Bung down.

I explained to the wine merchant that, as far as brandy was concerned, the recipe called for only one gallon or less. He replied, rather acidly, that it would have to be a good deal less. So I reluctantly abandoned the project, because I had never considered — and told him so — his pale ale wort to be particularly "good". As I turned away and left the premises, he seemed to repeat, with unnecessary emphasis, the last two words of the recipe.

There is, of course, the second method: "English malmsey, fifty gallons; Cape Madeira, forty gallons; cassia (bruised), half an ounce; cloves, half an ounce; bitter almonds (bruised), three ounces; spirit, five gallons. Bung —" No, in this case, it says, "Macerate, rack and rummage". There I draw the line; surely this is something no right-minded person should be asked to do. The recipe for "cyder" doesn't require such violence. "To make it work kindly," the book says, "heat a little honey, three whites of eggs, and a little flour, together: put them into a fine rag, and let them hang down by a string to the middle of the cyder cask." We may not think it proper; but the key word here is "kindly", so we could do just this, and call it a day.

Common Syllabub is familiar to us all. But my book, not content with evolving a Solid Syllabub, has hit on a method of making what it calls Everlasting Syllabub. Now, this is very useful. We all know those households where there is never enough syllabub. But in my home, thanks to this useful little book, that situation no longer obtains. I make just one small breakfast cup of Everlasting Syllabub, which goes the rounds of the family in strict rotation, and the problem is solved.

A useful hint: "With the thin part left at the bottom, mix strong calf's foot jelly, and sweeten it to taste; give it a boil." This will turn your syllabub into "a fine flummery".

There is, of course, a certain amount of leeway in the making of hartshorn jelly, whose ingredients, according to my recipe, "must be regulated by fancy". It suggests that "when finely curdled, and of a pure white, have ready a swan-skin jelly bag over a china basin, pour in your jelly and pour it back again, till clear as rock-water."

Talking of hartshorn reminds me (for some reason) of horehound, which, my book tells me, is delicious candied. Personally, I find this one of my least successful experiments, and I should be glad if any reader who has specialized in candied horehound would be kind enough to enlighten me on several points. My recipe says, "Boil some horehound till the juice is extracted. Boil up some sugar to a feather; add your juice to the sugar, and let it boil till it is again the same height."

Now I am unsuccessful in boiling up sugar to a feather. The book tells me that, in order to test the sugar, one should "dip in the skimmer and shake off what sugar you can into the pan. Then blow with the mouth through the holes, and if bladders or bubbles blow through, you may be certain of its having acquired the second degree." So far, so good. However, although I have managed an occasional bubble, there has been little manifestation of what might honestly be described as a bladder. But let us accept the hypothesis that I have reached the "second degree". It is the next bit I find difficult: "Shake it over the pan, then give it a sudden flirt behind you; if done, the sugar will fly off like feathers." To where?

The "sudden flirt behind you" worries me. Why "behind you"? In a life dedicated, one might say, to the art of cooking, it has never once been suggested that I do anything "behind" me. Anyway, I should be most grateful for any suggestions from readers who have mastered the art of candied horehound — or have mastered the art, as well it may be, of a sudden flirt.

There is almost no situation or emergency appertaining to human life that this ambitious but pocket-size volume does not cover. Its modest dimensions enable it to be taken anywhere, and I, for one, dare no longer be caught without it.

I realize now, for instance, that white veiling, after washing, should be clapped with the hands until dry; that shoe polish, besides the more usual inclusion of lampblack should contain white wine, treacle, loaf sugar, powdered galls, and copperas; and that two quarts of good beer poured on Herba Angali Ruber, or red chickweed, are a cure for hydrophobia. If, in our day, this simple remedy has been abandoned, it is due, no doubt, to the interchangeable nature of modern kitchen utensils. My book is explicitly against this interchanging: "Boil it in a new earthen pot," it says, which "must be kept very clean and used for no other purpose."

Happily, the "receipts" are arranged in no particular order, which makes for pleasant reading devoid of monotony. They provoke, in fact, a stimulating succession of mental shocks, as will be seen from the following headings:

336 Elder shoots to eat like Bamboo.
337 Factitious Emeralds.
338 Elastic or Waterproof Paint for Boots and
     Shoes.
339 Transparent Soup.
340 Egyptian Marble for Leather Book Covers.
341 To Dye Grey or Red Hair Black.
342 Hasty Pudding.
343 Appearance of Sudden Death.
344 Spanish Ladies' Rouge.
345 Leech Bites, to Stop.
346 Odiferous Esprit.
347 Mineral Metallic Cement for Filling Decayed
     Teeth.
348 Horse-radish, to have in keeping.

349 Liquid Laudanum.

350 To Destroy Insects in Vines.

351 Pearl Water for the Complexion.

352 Sir H. Davy's Corn Solvent.

353 Eau Divine.

354 Leeches, to Fix.

355 Asiatic Dentifrice.

356 Restoring Drowned Persons.

This lighthearted flouting of traditional laws of classification has drawbacks; the juxtaposition of, say, Nos 342 and 343 could be more happily conceived; and it is sometimes necessary to thumb the book through several times in order to find the requisite antidote to the particular emergency. But it was a leisurely age of leisurely accidents: it took even longer to drown. According to No 356, "the greatest exertion should be used to take the body out of the water before the lapse of one hour". One hour, I feel, would give reasonable time, not only to find the place in the book, but also to read and digest (despite the ignorant shouts of the drownee) the series of really excellent hints on this subject: Do not, insists the author, "roll the victim on casks". Frankly, it would not immediately occur to me to do so. For me, casks are out; also any "other rough usage" such as holding the victim up by the heels. This I seldom attempt; somehow, especially with a grown man, it is not always easy to get the right swing. Instead, we should carry the victim "with the head raised, to the nearest convenient house".

"For young children," the author continues, lay them "between two persons in a warm bed". For older persons, this treatment is not considered suitable, and one can see why: in the case of an elderly lady, for example, any unexpected return to consciousness might constitute a secondary shock. Evidently our author prefers not to risk such a contingency and, for those of riper years, has other treatments. "Introduce", he says, "the pipe of a pair of bellows (when no proper apparatus is available) into one nostril; close the mouth and other nostril, then inflate the lungs, till the breast be a little raised." Any cinders thus introduced into the bronchial tubes can, I suppose, be removed later by a surgeon. One or two leeches, he suggests, might not come amiss, and tobacco smoke, too, has its mysterious uses if you have a "proper instrument".

On the patient's return to consciousness, a few drops of Eau de Cologne no doubt would refresh him and "counteract the stench of Thames Water". You will understand with what joyful alacrity I rush to perform this small service when I tell you that I have made, according to the directions in my book, seventy gallons of the Eau de Cologne stuff.

True, one certainly uses a dab on the handkerchief every Sunday, before morning church; but I am beginning to realize that I have overestimated further sources of consumption. Thus it is with a slight lifting of heart that I see poor wretches dragged from the river and rush to sprinkle them; but never, as my friends so unkindly suggest, do I push them in. In cold fact, my book actually allows for no smaller quantity: Take, it says, "spirit, seventy gallons", so I took it.

Later, when I found the courage, I added sage, thyme, balm mint, spearmint, *calamus aromaticus*, angelica root, orange flowers, wormwood, rose petals, lavender flowers, nutmeg, cloves, cassia, two sliced lemons and a couple of sliced oranges. "Macerate", the book then told me, "for twenty-four hours, then draw over fifty gallons". I ignored this direction. Even without such phrases as "rack and rummage", twentyfour hours of maceration sounded too much.

Next day I added, as the book directed: seeds of anthos, essence of bergamot, essence of jasmine, essence of cedrat, essence of balm mint, essence of Portugal, essence of rosemary, lesser cardamoms, neroli and *eau de melisse des carmes*. I have for this last a separate recipe, which contains hyssop, thyme, marjoram, angelica and aniseed. Then came my Waterloo: "Agitate for twelve days." We will draw a veil over this period. I can never be grateful enough to kind friends who stood by me throughout the ordeal, feeding me sandwiches and answering the telephone. Some of them alone agitated it.

But, somehow, it was done. And the evening of the twelfth day, I could set down the cask and turn once again, with the courage born of exhaustion, to the book. Allow it to rest, the book said, for a week. Allow *it* to rest! I have allowed it to rest ever since.

CHAPTER
SIX

Pauline and Bertha

The two women sat opposite each other beside the open window. Pauline sat in the Regency chair and, as she talked, her eyes slewed backwards and forwards beneath their carven lids. How beautiful she is, thought Bertha (sunk a little humbly on the sofa beside the tea-table), so beautiful that, to watch her face, makes me feel beautiful, too . . . Below them, beyond the grimy London balcony, a buddleia bloomed — its purple, powdered blossoms alive with butterflies.

"And there you have it, darling," Pauline was saying, hurriedly, "the same old pattern, over and over again. Ad nauseam." And, suddenly, she laughed.

"How do you mean?" asked Bertha.

"The way things always go . . . the way I come to you, with the same old story: first it was Malcolm; then John; then that dreadful time —" wildly, the eyes slid now, "with Julius. Then there was that thing with Freddie; that wasn't so bad, of course . . . but it was pretty bad — his wife going to see my mother and the sleeping pill incident, do you remember? And now," the eyes challenged Bertha's, "Edward."

"So you see the pattern?" said Bertha, after a moment.

"Yes, I see it. Of course I see it. But I can't do anything about it."

There was silence. Bertha, finding a drain of tea left in her cup, swilled it gently round, catching a transparent ring of sunlight within the china's green and gold; the buddleia wafted its breath towards them — bland it smelled, and spiced, like perfumed custard.

"If only," Pauline's anxious voice went on, "he'd say — 'I don't love you. It's finished.' If only he'd say that. I could take it. It would hurt — of *course* it would hurt — but I'd know where I stood: I'd know 'the form'."

He won't say it, thought Bertha unhappily, watching the sliding reflections within her cup, and you couldn't take it.

"These things," said Pauline, "aren't just physical. There's something . . . something else . . ." Pauline hesitated, "Or what do you think, Bertha? Tell me. I can bear it."

"No," said Bertha, "they're not just physical. It would be better," she added vaguely, "if they were." She hesitated a moment, "Would you like some more tea?"

"Bertha," cried Pauline suddenly, leaning forward (her face looked stretched and curiously dry like a lovely death-mask), "tell me. Is it over? Have I lost him?"

Bertha looked back at her, her hand on the teapot. Yes, she might have said, it's over and you've lost him; by the time you come to me, you have always lost him. Instead, she stammered unhappily, "My darling, how can I know?"

"You do know," Pauline accused her.

"Yes," said Bertha and glanced down at the teapot: her hand on the handle looked suddenly smug and hostess-like; ashamed, she drew it away.

"But how do you know?" went on Pauline, "What right have you to know? I mean — you're so immutable — tucked away here, with Charles and the children . . ."

"Immutable?" said Bertha, staring uncertainly.

Pauline stared back. "But have *you* ever had anything — anything like this thing I've had with Edward?"

"Oh," said Bertha, "is that what you meant? No, I haven't really."

"But why not, Bertha? You must have been terribly pretty."

"Yes, I was rather."

"I mean, you're pretty now. Edward thinks you're adorable. He thinks you're rather cagey, Bertha — too good to be true; he believes you have a past . . ."

Bertha laughed and reached for Pauline's tea-cup. "Does he?" she said and flushed a little, as she made room for the cup on the tray. "I never quite know what that means — a 'past'. I haven't, you know. Unless —"

"Unless what?"

"Unless," slowly Bertha raised her face, "well, once," she said, "I held a man's hand," she hesitated, smiling a little, "but that wouldn't be quite what Edward means?"

Pauline laughed. "Not quite —" she began and stopped, surprised by the sudden tears in Bertha's eyes.

"Because," said Bertha and the tears spilled over, "that's about all it was — my past," she fumbled in her pocket for a handkerchief.

"Bertha! Darling —"

"It's all right," gasped Bertha, dabbing her eyes, "I'm quite all right. I don't know why I . . ." she blew her nose, "I'm sorry." Suddenly, she was smiling again and pushing her handkerchief away, deep in her pocket, push upon push, "Let's have some sherry."

"I'll get it," cried Pauline, whisking away the tea-tray. "Sit still. Let me . . ."

"After your things," said Bertha apologetically as Pauline came back with the glasses, "it sounded so jolly silly . . ."

"My things are 'jolly silly', too," said Pauline. "Sorry," she added, pouring too hastily.

"And yet," said Bertha thoughtfully, "it wasn't silly." She stared a moment at the spilled drops on the table. "It was everything," she said, at last. She took out her handkerchief again and wiped the drops away.

"How long ago?"

"About three years. No, four. The winter Charles was abroad."

"Since you knew me?" said Pauline, surprised.

"Yes."

"But where did you meet him? Here, in this house?"

"No, at Woolencote. I was staying with Phillipa. You know Phillipa, Charles's sister?"

"Yes, I've met her. Once, I think. A little hearty, isn't she? Like Charles?"

Bertha hesitated. "She was very good to me," she said, at last.

"Well, tell me what happened!"

"Not now — not when you're so worried. And it's quarter to seven. I must go and cook in a minute. And there's nothing to tell, really. Nothing happened. No sleeping pills, or anything."

"Bertha!" cried Pauline, hurt.

"No, no," Bertha reassured her. "I just mean that if I say to you, 'tell me what happened', there are things you can tell: they are actual events. But," nervously, she sipped her sherry, "with me —"

Pauline moved across and came to sit beside her on the sofa. "Tell me," she said, "all the same." As Bertha hesitated, she went on, "It would help me, Bertha. Somehow, now . . . at this moment . . ."

"How would it help you?" asked Bertha.

"Because of what you are now. Don't you see? — Whatever it was, you've absorbed it into your life, and digested it; you've grown on it; it's — it's just made you 'more Bertha'."

Bertha laughed. "Is that a good thing," she asked, "to be 'more Bertha'?"

"Yes," said Pauline, "it is a good thing. A very good thing indeed." She picked up her glass and stared into it. "What was he like — this man?"

Bertha threw her a startled look. "He was a Greek," she said.

"And you met him at Phillipa's?"

"Yes. At Woolencote. He was spending Christmas there."

"And you fell in love at first sight?"

"Yes," said Bertha, "at first sight." Her hands, Pauline noticed, were tightly pressed together in her lap.

"What was he? By profession, I mean."

"He was a doctor — a surgeon. But he'd written a book on Greek history. A very good book. He'd come to England when Greece was occupied —"

"What did he look like? Was he good-looking?"

"Yes. No. He wasn't very tall. He was dark, of course. He had a gay, alive sort of face. But, sometimes, something would close down in it and it could become like a mask."

"Really," said Pauline.

"Yes," said Bertha; she hesitated and, glancing down, she noticed her clasped hands; she relaxed them and picked up her glass. "Have you ever stayed at Woolencote?" she asked.

"No," said Pauline, leaning forward, "I haven't."

"It's rather a lovely house to stay in — especially for children. Or it used to be — something seems to have gone out of it now. Or out of me, perhaps." absent-mindedly, she drank up the rest of her sherry and set down the glass, smiling a little. "That Christmas, Phillipa was in bed when we arrived, recovering from a sprained ankle, and we were summoned to her room before dinner. I shall never forget the look of the house that evening . . ." Bertha laid her head back against the cushions of the sofa and half-closed her eyes; her cheeks, Pauline noticed, had become a little flushed. "It had a dramatic look," Bertha went on hesitatingly, "like a stage set; there was something mysterious and magical about the perspective of the passages — do you know that look? And about the holly, crooked on the pictures; half-open doors; and the glimmer of the firelight in curtained rooms, — and —" she added, almost in a whisper, "the frost outside: dark lawns still and stiff with frost . . . no wind." She was silent a moment. "And there was the sudden sight of the long, familiar bedroom, the tray of cocktails on the dressing-table and a wad of shadow beyond the high, carved bed. On a sofa beside the fire, I remember, there were things like string and tissue paper, half-opened boxes of crackers, and piles of football socks. There were voices . . . introductions . . .; someone was writing names on slips of paper; everybody seemed to be laughing and talking — except one person, who stood in the shadow beyond the bed; someone, I realized suddenly, who was standing particularly still. It was Andreas.

"I could not even see his face — he stood silhouetted against the lamp, almost stocky, he looked — but I remember feeling something fateful about him; a curious shock of inward recognition — as though he were the core of all that strangeness I had sensed about the house. As I turned away to talk to Phillipa, I felt his watchfulness; and when she addressed him directly, he started slightly and came quickly, almost apologetically, to stand beside her. 'Bertha is my Number One in-law' Phillipa told him as she introduced us, and he looked at me again. 'What a curious label,' he said, after a moment, and I heard his gentle laugh.

"Standing there, at the foot of Phillipa's bed, I had a moment of panic — a paralysing attack of shyness — in which I thought, I cannot go down to dinner, without Phillipa, and perhaps sit opposite this man . . .

"But it passed and we did go down to dinner and I did as it happened, sit opposite to him. There was a white-ish soup, I remember, and, in the candlelight, for the first time I saw his face.

"It was a charming face, as I think I've told you. But he turned it away from me; he talked, bending his head and laughing a little, to those on either side of him. I saw the way his hair was brushed, back and sideways from his parting; and to see it hurt me, Pauline, with a kind of familiar pain. If ever he glanced in my direction, it was with his mask-face, a fleeing white-jawed look; and once, for a flickering second, our eyes met.

"After dinner, we went upstairs again to fill the stockings and I caught a glimpse of my own face in the looking glass on the landing — wildly beautiful, it looked, almost incandescent with beauty. For a startled second, I did not recognize myself and then I thought it must be something to do with the lighting of the passage; but I saw it again in Phillipa's room; it frightened me: my kind of prettiness, I thought, was never meant to look like that.

"All through that evening, he did not speak to me. We filled the stockings with cheap, funny toys; with hair clips for the women and tie-clips for the men; with powder-puffs and coloured handkerchiefs; and dates and figs and oranges and bright-barred sticks of candy. There were whisperings and secrets and sudden gales of laughter and late at night, there was a so-called wassail-bowl beside the library fire and Phillipa in her dressing gown. It was then, for the first time, that he spoke my name: 'Berta,' he said, avoiding the 'th' and raised his glass in a smiling, deliberate toast.

"There was a woman there, pale and wispy, but with fine eyes: she wore, I remember, a magnificent diamond brooch. Her name was Hester Friburg. I noticed her because he was so gentle with her — and teasing, as though she were a child. He had helped her fill the baby's stocking, scolding her a little, and had accompanied her down the dark passage to where the child was sleeping.

"Next day, there was Christmas dinner — at mid-day, because of the children — and the tree, after tea, in the early dusk. There were presents for everyone from everyone else. I gave Andreas a calendar, one I had bought for an absent aunt; and he gave me a little red diary, purse size, and bound in leather; in it he had written, on January the fourth, 'Quaglino's, 1.30. Lunch with Andreas.' I did not mention this. I pretended I had not opened the diary. But afterwards, for some reason, I found it easier to talk to him. And not only to talk to him but to laugh with him and counter his subtle teasing: he guessed, I think, that I must have seen his message.

"On his last night, we walked across the fields to church to hear the carols, in borrowed coats from the pegs in the hall; there was Andreas and myself and Hester Friburg and two others. On the way back, I lost my glove and, scolding me a little, he took my cold hand and placed it in his pocket. Until that moment, he had been laughing and talking but then, suddenly, he became silent. There was frost on the snowy grass, which rustled, and a clear full moon. I could not speak either and I could not withdraw my hand. The silence between us swelled out and out and became, each second, more fragile, more perilously balanced, until at last we reached the house and I managed to break it: I made some laughing remark and thanked him. He did not reply and, as we hung our coats in the shadowed hall, he turned and looked at me.

"The others had gone on, along the passage towards the library. He stood, blocking my way and I leaned back, afraid, among the hanging coats. He took my hand and turned it, palm-upwards, and stared at it. I stared at it too, in the dim light — hearing my heart beat. 'We must wait, Bertha,' he said hurriedly; he spoke as though I had been arguing with him; as though our silent walk had been one long argument. Then Phillipa called him and he left me — standing there, with upraised hand, among the coats.

"He went next morning, soon after breakfast. We said goodbye across the toast and marmalade: there was a car at the door and his bags were in the hall. Others called out to him about meeting in London but I sat tongue-tied beside the empty chair: he had not mentioned the diary nor asked me where I lived.

"When I got home, I tried not to think of him. I did try; as much for my own sake as with any thought of Charles. I missed Charles: I wished he would hurry back; I needed his sanity, his breeziness; I needed (I hoped that might cure me) to be called "old girl". But there was no Charles; and Andreas, of course, did telephone — he must have got my number from Phillipa: he telephoned at seven-thirty in the morning of January 4th. He awoke me from sleep and, as I stretched out my arm to pick up the receiver, it was as though I had been dreaming of him — and here, at my bedside, was his voice. I had forgotten how familiar he would seem; how real; how close; how threadbare excuses could sound and how easily and sharply they could be dismissed. He laughed and made me laugh at myself; he spoke a good deal and very quickly; there was a hint of anxiety in the speed with which he spoke. When I hung up the receiver, I felt dazed and there, in the wardrobe when I opened it, hung my beautiful French blouse — why, yesterday, had I pressed it so carefully? And the room looked different: it suddenly had meaning; the whole house felt different . . ."

"Oh, I know," cried Pauline, "I know."

"And do you know that moment," said Bertha, "when one first walks into the restaurant . . . their half-rising from behind the table and that look they have? One sees it only in the first half-second — an incredulous look, of relief." She hesitated, "Or something?"

"Yes," said Pauline, "I do."

"It was like that," said Bertha, and was silent a moment. "But only at first. All through the rest of luncheon, he talked about himself; not egotistically — he had never spoken about himself before — but with some kind of purpose. He spoke of his parents, his boyhood, his university, his war experiences; he touched, very lightly, on his attitude to women: and I, sitting there — watching his face and disturbed by his presence — did not understand. He spoke so lightly and this, perhaps, was what puzzled me: I wondered why he was telling me these things. I took them for a series of anecdotes; I thought he was being a 'good host'. Why am I here, I wondered, why did he invite me? It was only afterwards, a long time afterwards, I realized that he was trying to establish some kind of picture which I would remember if, from now on, the shape of his life should change.

"When luncheon was over the waiter ran forward to pull out the table for me to pass; I felt bewildered. What now, I wondered, as I walked ahead of him, between the tables towards the door. I pushed through the swing doors without turning because, at that second, there were tears in my eyes. He knew this, I think, for he took my arm and held it firmly against his side. 'I must get back —' I remember saying, pulling away from him slightly as I saw him call a taxi. 'Of course,' he said laughing and opening the car door, 'Jump in. I'll take you. But not yet,' he added slyly, as the car moved off. 'First, we shall call on a friend.' I believe I made some kind of protest but he laughed again, I remember, still gripping my arm as though I might, even then, open the door and jump out.

"He took me to Hester Friburg's flat. I did not realize it was her flat and was surprised to see her when she arose from where she had been sitting — rather disconsolately, it seemed — in the corner of the drawing-room sofa. And she to see me. But she was pleased. She pulled an armchair towards the fire and Andreas took my coat. She chattered eagerly — her spindly little legs and her small, smart shoes placed neatly together, as she leaned towards me from the edge of the sofa.

"It was a typical furnished flat of the more luxurious type — that kind of luxury which, so soon, can become sordid; there was a good deal of beige satin about, I remember, and mother-of-pearl trees with sea-shell blossoms. Andreas went into the kitchen to make coffee while Hester took me in to see her baby; the room he was in was not a nursery but a bedroom, in which toys and napkins seemed out of place; he sat in his play-pen, glum and stolid, beside his German nurse. The German nurse was a dour-looking woman and there was a limp sadness about the whole flat.

"Back in the living room, as we drank our coffee, Hester plied me with questions; her curiosity was disarming; like that of a child, one could not resent it; there was something wan and empty about her, needing to be filled. She volunteered odd pieces of information about herself and I realized that she belonged to that cosmopolitan set whose ways seem foreign to me: that she had, or had once had, a husband who 'brought off deals'; yachts floated into the picture — and out again (perhaps when the deals were less successful); country houses were glimpsed; and Mediterranean villas; these reared up, had their day, and subsided once again, a little mysteriously, into the landscape. Strange people flashed in and out, some notorious; she saw these matter-of-factly and accepted them, with naive comment, but without criticism. Andreas, alert and watchful, seemed to efface himself. He sat back in his chair, his head against the light — like a producer, invisible in the stalls, watching a 'run-through'. Hester occasionally threw out a request: 'Draw the curtains, will you, Andreas . . . More coffee, please . . . Bertha needs a light . . .' and he would perform these tasks with alacrity — a kind of loving willingness as though, it seemed, he could not do too much for her or — was it? — for us.

"At four o'clock, the door-bell rang. It was Phillipa, up for the day, with goose-eggs for Hester. I realized, watching their friendly, perfunctory kiss and knowing how little they had in common, that there was a special reason, hidden still from me, for being 'kind' to Hester.

"Phillipa, protesting that she could not stay a second, was persuaded to stay for tea. Hester went off to make arrangements; and Andreas, I think, to buy a cake.

"'What is all this about Hester?' I asked Phillipa, directly we were alone.

"She looked at me a little oddly: she was surprised, I think, to find me in this flat, 'Darling, don't you know? She was married to Otho Friburg —'

"'Who is Otho Friburg?'

"'A company promoter or whatever they're called. You must have heard of him. He started it all on Hester's money and he loathes her for it. Andreas says he beats her.'

"'Andreas —?'

"'Andreas was staying with them when they had one of their worst rows — surely they've told you? It was Andreas who persuaded her to leave him; he arranged everything and found her this flat; it was Andreas who asked me to have her for Christmas. Friburg doesn't know where she is; and Hester's terrified of him; she won't set a foot in the street unless someone's with her.'

"'But what will happen?' I asked, after a moment.

"'Well, they leave for Greece on Saturday. Now things are settled there, Andreas can go back.'

"'Will he marry her?'

"'I suppose so,' said Phillipa, 'eventually. I suppose he must.'

"'She doesn't love him,' I said.

"'Well, it isn't a question of love, quite. Andreas has engineered all this and he's responsible for her. Hester's very helpless. He's all she's got.' Phillipa hesitated, 'Hester's his child,' she said.

"'Yes,' I managed to say, 'I felt that.'

"Suddenly Phillipa stared at me: she looked absolutely stunned. 'Bertha,' she exclaimed, 'you're not in love with Andreas?' And I remember staring at her face as she moved towards me — a little ludicrous, it looked, with shock: she seemed about to say a good deal more but Hester came in then with the tea-tray and Phillipa sat down, rather suddenly, in one of the deep armchairs and stared fixedly at her shoes.

"Hester was begging us both to stay to supper; if we would stay, she said, we could all go in Phillipa's car, to the French film at the Academy. Phillipa excused herself — rather abruptly, I thought: she had promised to dine with her sister. Andreas arrived with the chocolate cake but his expression changed, I noticed, as he came into the room; he glanced quickly from me to Phillipa. 'Then Bertha will stay' Hester was saying, 'Please, Bertha, you must —' I could not reply and Phillipa did not help me; she sat there, silent, staring at her shoes.

"The half-smile faded from Andreas's face; he became suddenly grave: 'You will stay, Bertha,' he said. I tried to laugh then and stammered something about the house, the children . . . 'You can telephone your house,' Andreas said, 'I'll get the number.'

"He stood beside me in the hall while I telephoned. As I put down the receiver, my hand was trembling and it missed the rests. He straightened the receiver and turned to look at me. 'Bertha —' he began but I ran past him down the passage to the bathroom. I ran past Phillipa, too, and saw her turn. As I closed the bathroom door, someone knocked; it was Phillipa; after a moment, I opened the door. 'Bertha,' she urged — as I sat on the edge of the bath, the tears pouring down my face — 'it's hopeless. You must know it. You must pull yourself together.'

"'He said — Wait,' I managed to gasp, 'Once he said, Wait —'

"'Yes, but what for? And for how long? And he's not well-off, darling. With Hester he would have a good marriage —'

"'He doesn't care for her money —'

"'I know that,' she exclaimed impatiently, 'I know Andreas. But what could you offer him? He's in a bad enough jam as it is. What could you bring him but further complications?' I was crying so much that she passed me the bath-towel and I buried my face in it. 'And what about your family?' Phillipa went on, 'What about Charles? You must face up to things, darling —'

"'Please go, now,' I managed at last, 'Please go back and talk to them. Don't let them miss me,' and I turned away to the wash-basin and began to run the taps.

"'Come *with* me,' begged Phillipa, 'I can drop you at home on the way to my sister's. A clean break. Now. This minute. It's the only way —'

"'Please go,' I asked her again, standing — my back towards her — running the taps, 'Please go and talk to them. We can't both be here, like this —'

"'Then you'll come?' she said.

"'Yes, I'll come. But not now. Not yet. I'll stay to supper —' I turned and faced her, 'You can come back for me. Please, Phillipa —'

"'All right,' she said, slowly, after a moment, 'I'll leave my parcels here . . .'

"We did go to see the film and I sat beside him in the darkness. I held my head very straight and still, I remember, and there were strange tears which ran, quite gently, down my cheeks — unchecked and unwiped so they should be unnoticed. I did not feel unhappy — these tears, I think, were left-overs. Luckily, it was a sad film and Hester cried too.

"On the way back, Andreas stopped the taxi at a wine merchant's. 'We shall be very gay,' he announced, when he rejoined us. He held the bulky package on his knees and took the small seat opposite and, as the street lights flickered their white shadows across his face, I saw he spoke to me.

"We *were* very gay at supper. I don't know why. Nothing we said or did seemed to matter very much; there were no longer any problems. Hester, repeating gossip, became very funny. After supper, she turned on the radio and Andreas pulled the sofa towards the fire; he told Hester to stop talking: 'Pablo Casals,' he said, 'we will sit quiet and hear . . .'

"He switched off several lights and the room (with one lamp and all its near-good-taste condemned to shadow) seemed, as slowly it filled with the music of the 'cello, to change its character: it became a timeless place. Hester sat curled in the corner of the sofa and I, on the floor, towards the other end; Andreas, after a while, came to sit between us: he dropped behind me on the sofa and stretched his legs towards the fire; and he let his hand fall — seemingly by accident — upon my shoulder, just beside my neck. I reached up, after a while, and unseen by Hester, I took his hand.

"This is one of those things impossible to describe — the depths and stillness of the living present: all that we could have been, all that we were to each other, was in that moment — acknowledged and mutual. That is all I can tell you. That is all I know. Soon after that," Bertha went on lightly, "Phillipa called for me and drove me home."

There was a long silence until, at last, Bertha stood up. And Pauline, lithe and long-limbed, swung round on the sofa towards her: "but didn't he write or anything?"

"No," said Bertha, moving towards the door.

"Then that was the last you saw of him?"

"Not quite," said Bertha, "I met him at a cocktail party not so long ago."

"And what happened?"

"Nothing happened. It was just after Nigel was born. I was rather fat and my hat didn't suit me."

"Oh, Bertha!" cried Pauline, in an anguish of pity.

"It didn't matter," said Bertha.

"But it must have mastered," cried Pauline, "Oh, Bertha!"

"It didn't matter," Bertha repeated; she spoke a little wildly. "It did not matter. Can't you understand?"

"No, I can't. You mean — you had that moment?"

Bertha looked down at her hand on the door-knob, "I can't explain," she said, at last.

"Yes, you can," urged Pauline, "I half-understand. You mean — experience isn't gauged by numbers, isn't that it? Or something like that? Oh, do come back and sit down!"

"I can't —" said Bertha, opening the door.

"Why not? What have you got to do? Please, Bertha —"

"I must put the potatoes on," cried Bertha irritably and, as Pauline stared at her — surprised, Bertha hesitated and half-smiled; her expression softened, "for Charles's dinner," she added lamely.

CHAPTER
SEVEN

Mr Sequeria

Mr Sequeria was slightly diabolical-looking. He lived next door in a long, white house from which the plaster was flaking. He would sit all day at the open window in a black overcoat and a shabby, homburg hat. His hands and face were long and white and he would sit very still.

I was startled the first time I saw Mr Sequeria. It was the day after we had moved in — in early summer. The village — if about twelve houses could be called a village — was hung upon the mountain side, surrounded by woods and grouped around the church. The houses were perched at odd angles on rocky promontories and we each had some unorthodox view into another's property. Mr Sequeria's house and mine stood cheek by jowl so, although I could see across his large, cascading garden straight into the back windows of Mr O'Malley's house which stood at right angles, I only had a complete view of Mr Sequeria's house when I approached my own across the square.

Coming back from a first walk, that early summer, I had glanced absentmindedly at the long house beside my own. And then, shocked, had looked away again — so quiet, so pale, so baleful, had seemed that brooding presence.

"Who lives next door?" I asked Ludavina as we unpacked the china.

"Next door? Why — *Senhor* Sequeria."

"He looks very ill."

"Yes, he has a bad illness. Sometimes he is not himself."

"Does he live alone?"

"Oh, no *minha Senhora*. There is Donna Maria his wife, and his daughter and his son."

Within two days, I had discovered the son, a wizened child of eight named Luiz, who was subject to violent outbursts of hysterical rage. He played in the square outside my window and one or other of the village children was always bruised or bleeding from encounters with Luiz. But they played with him all the same and he often talked to me through my window. There was something likeable and unusually intelligent about the child if one could prevent his becoming excited. He wore very short, tight trousers and his head was shaven against lice.

Of Donna Maria I had only an occasional glimpse. She was a florid woman with a peasant's mania for shaking things in the back garden — rag mats, mattresses, blankets, bolsters cases, — everything incredibly patched and worn.

In spite of Donna Maria's obsession, the house, when one passed the front door, smelled of smoke, stale wine and earth. And there were fish bones, melon seed and broken crocks beside the threshold. Rumour had it that she had been his cook in the days when Mr Sequeria had been rich.

For rich he had been. He had owned almost the entire village of Santa Marta. The O'Malleys' house had been his home — and the O'Malleys' house was pretty grand, with its Moorish arches, mosaic tiling, french windows and stained glass. Mr Sequeria had been a great painter — the greatest painter (it was said in Portugal) of his day. He had lived ostentatiously, surrounded by property and objets d'art. I never saw any of his work.

The daughter was a pretty girl, shy and gentle. She taught sewing in the local convent and was away for the greater part of the day.

Gradually Mr Sequeria and I became upon bowing terms. Returning from my walks, I would smile up at his window and he would incline his head. Only when he spoke, would he remove his hat and that came a long time later.

One afternoon, returning from a rock climb, I found our back door locked.

"Who is there?" called Ludavina, fearfully.

"It is I — the *Senhora*."

With much creaking of bolts and many tuggings, the door was opened.

"What is it, Ludavina?"

"Oh, come in, *minha Senhora*. Come in quickly. *Aie* — Mother of Jesus, this door! The *Senhora* must have it seen to. The wood is warped. Like this, it is dangerous."

"Why is it dangerous?"

"Because one cannot shut it. Come in. Come in, *minha Senhora*."

"But what is the matter?"

Ludavina gave me a look. "It is *Senhor* Sequeria," she said. "He has had one of his attacks. He has tried to kill his daughter."

"To kill his daughter!"

"Yes, they've taken her away now. They're keeping her at the convent."

"And Mr Sequeria —?"

"They've locked him in the upstairs room." Ludavina clasped her hands. "Oh, *minha Senhora*, that you must sleep alone in the house this night!" Ludavina slept in the village.

When I went up to my room, I found Ludavina had closed the heavy shutters. I opened them and the windows too, as I did not think Mr Sequeria would climb to the first floor. The side of Mr Sequeria's house was white with moonlight and everything was peaceful. The air was heavy with the scent of pittosporum and the acrid smell of eucalyptus. Across the riot of Mr Sequeria's garden, the lights glowed in Mr O'Malley's house. There was a sound of music. Mr O'Malley was entertaining friends.

Perhaps Mr Sequeria, too, was sitting — still and pale in the moonlight — staring across the untidy valley of his garden at the house which had been his.

Some days later, Mrs O'Malley asked me to tea. She was a sharp little Belgian woman and the house seemed prosperous. It was a tea-napkin-best-silver affair. The children came in to say "*bonjour*" and were hustled out again. They were crisp, short-skirted, well-nourished children, safely insulated from human contact by a formal insecurity of manner. Later, in the garden, I heard them scream like maniacs.

A young French poet passed the scones and cakes. He was a left-over, I learned, from a greater French poet — a real man of letters — who had been staying with the O'Malleys. The young poet's name was Alfred and he had remained behind as "*au pair*" to teach the children.

Later Mr O'Malley came in. He was pink and dapper. He had pleasant, easy manners and seemed, in spite of speaking only French and Portuguese, a man of the world. The O'Malleys, he told me, descendants of Irish kings, had been domiciled in Portugal for over five hundred years.

The young French poet walked home with me. When I spoke politely of the O'Malleys, he replied evasively and I guessed he was not happy with them. As we passed the white house, I noticed Mr Sequeria sitting, once again, at his window. I smiled at him and he bowed.

"*Méphisto lui-même!*" whispered Alfred, as we went down the steps into my garden. He left me at my door but asked if sometimes he might call on me.

"*Senhor* Sequeria's daughter is coming home again," remarked Ludavina as she gave me my supper, "to prepare for her wedding."

"I didn't know she was engaged."

"Yes, yes. It was that which excited *Senhor* Sequeria. She is marrying a clerk in the Water Board. They will live in Campolide."

I sent Mr Sequeria's daughter a piece of old lace for a wedding present. She wrote me a formal letter of thanks, beautifully spaced out and in copperplate handwriting. I felt rather snubbed by it, until, meeting her in the square, she smiled at me warmly and told me she was happy.

"Your parents will miss you," I said.

"Ah," she told me, "after the wedding they are going to move. My mother has persuaded my father to sell this house. She has found a new one, down in the lower village, very small but all modern with an indoor lavatory."

"Oh," I said.

"Yes," she went on. "It's better they move. Luiz can go to school. It's sad up here in the winter when the mists come on the mountain."

"Will your father — does your father —?"

"Oh, he likes this house, of course. He likes the garden. There isn't a garden at the new house but there are more people and we'll have the trams."

Alfred began to call in the evenings after supper. I found he was only seventeen; but his knowledge of French literature would have shamed a scholar twice his age. He bitterly resented his youth — a ludicrous facade, he felt, for his disillusioned and erudite maturity. Alfred would have signed thirty years of his life away for a shock of greying hair and a place in the Academie.

He had an indulgent compassion for my ignorance and began to educate me. He would come at dusk when the windows were open on to the square and we would light one lamp. "*Ainsi,*" he would say, "*nous créons une petite féerie.*"

We could not see Mr Sequeria but, if he sat at his open window, he could not fail to hear Alfred's vibrant voice, upraised and lyrical, as he recited long passages from Racine or Corneille. And Moliere — Mr Sequeria would have been startled no doubt by the bitter peals of stagey laughter with which Alfred did Cyrano.

One morning, Ludavina came up to my room in a flutter.

"*Minha Senhora*," she said, "*Senhor* Sequeria is downstairs."

"Downstairs? Where?"

"At the kitchen door, *minha Senhora*. He wants to see you. He has some things to sell," she added.

I was filled with dismay. We were all poor in Santa Marta — even Mr O'Malley whose prosperous-seeming establishment was, they told me, run on credit. "What sort of things?"

"One or two little things. I suppose," said Ludavina, "it's because of his daughter's wedding."

"Will you ask him to come up?"

"Up to the salon?" asked Ludavina, surprised.

"Yes, of course."

The stairs creaked under Mr Sequeria and he breathed heavily. Ludavina threw open the door for him and he stood on the threshold, panting slightly.

He seemed enormous, like a great black crow, his overcoat hanging in dead folds from his gaunt shoulders. His face was ashen. Ludavina held his hat.

"*Minha Senhora*,"he said and bowed.

I went towards him. "*Senhor* Sequeria. This is a pleasure —" As he kissed my hand, I noticed the blackness of his hair. "Won't you sit down?"

"You are too kind," he said.

There was a leaden slowness about his movements and, at such close quarters, he smelled cold and earthy like his house. It was a strange, reptilian smell. His hands were large and very long, with stained fingers, but he used them with simplicity and grandeur. He smiled at me and there was a haggard kindliness about his eyes. They were dark and luminous and they seemed to see too much.

"I know the *Senhora* likes beautiful things," he said.

"Yes," I told him, "I do."

"I have brought the *Senhora* one or two little things which might please her. She can buy them or not as she wishes . . ." He felt into his pockets. "As they are to be sold, I wished to show them first to *Senhora* my Neighbour in case one or other of them might take her fancy. She will, I hope, forgive my presumption . . ."

I bought the things Mr Sequeria showed me (a snuff box, a piece of Chinese embroidery, an ivory fan) for the price he asked for them — two hundred escudos. I bought them with the money I was saving for a coat and skirt. It was but a fraction of their real worth.

"The *Senhora* is sure she would like these things? They can be sold elsewhere should their possession be superfluous or in any way incommode the *Senhora* . . . ?"

"No. I am glad of the opportunity. *Senhor* Sequeria is kind to have thought of me."

Ludavina brought sherry and biscuits. Mr Sequeria, as he raised his glass, remarked lightly on my drinking a Spanish wine in Portugal: "Jerez . . . a goodish, light aperitif but no better than many we make here." In the mock gravity of this gentle disparagement, I caught an echo of malice — the pale, fleeting ghost of past audacity.

We talked of Portugal, of wines, of pictures and of painting. We did not speak of his daughter's wedding nor did I refer to his leaving his house and I felt, as I said goodbye to Mr Sequeria at the front door, that never again would I feel afraid of him. It was from that day that he began to raise his hat to me from his place at the window.

Mr Sequeria's daughter had about twenty yards to walk from the door of her house to the door of the church in the square. She wore the lace I had given her as a wedding veil. Mr Sequeria did not join in the little procession to the church. He watched it, no doubt, from his upper window as I did from mine.

After the wedding, came the move.

I did not look much as Mr Sequeria's possessions were carried piecemeal down the hill. It took several days. Donna Maria seemed very red and panting and the pile of rubbish by her front door reached alarming proportions. I wondered who would come to take it away; it could not be burned there, so close to the house.

Luiz ran in and out to me in a state of wild excitement. And then one night, he came to say goodbye. I did not say goodbye to Mr Sequeria nor did I see him go.

So the house next door became empty. I asked Ludavina who had bought it and she said: "No one yet." The pile of rubbish remained by the front door and the flies buzzed about it. Loose pieces of paper blew into the square.

Mr Sequeria's deserted garden lay dreaming in the sunshine, with the melons rotting and the grapes ripening. Scum formed on the dark water of the stone irrigation tanks and golden nasturtiums ramped over everything.

Then, suddenly, like a grey back-drop, fell the first autumn rains. The lanes and cobbled alley ways of Santa Maria became rattling cataracts. After the rain came the mist. Our huddled village was wrapped in cloud. Grey mould appeared on tiled floors; marquetry tables fell apart and doors and windows warped still further.

Sometimes a gentle wind from the sea would blow the cloud away. It would go unwillingly, clinging in shreds to the curved roofs and tree tops. And then, generous and autumnal, the sun would pour down — on the jade needles of new grass and the sudden crocus. This was St Martin's time — the time of sucking pig and roast chestnuts. Mr Sequeria had been gone a month.

I would wonder sometimes, as I walked down to the lower village to pay my bills, which of the several new houses was his. There were about six of them, stuck together by the tram line, and built by the man who had built the cinema. They looked moulded with their stucco trimmings, as if he had baked them in an oven and then iced them. Each had a fancy bird bath by the front porch but, as yet, there was no water laid on.

"Oh, *minha Senhora*," said Ludavina one morning, when she had returned from shopping, "the worst has happened. *Senhor* Sequeria is back!"

"Back?"

Ludavina set down the heavy basket on the kitchen table. There were beads of sweat on her upper lip and she looked very solemn. "*Minha Senhora*," she said, almost as if it were my fault, "he nearly strangled Luiz. But for the Grace of the Blessed Virgin and the banisters breaking, that little innocent soul would now be with the Saints. And he broke all the windows in the house and two lamps and a wash-basin. They say he put an iron bedstead right through the ceiling —"

"Through the ceiling?"

"Yes, *minha Senhora*, through the ceiling. He is very strong."

"But, Ludavina, he should be shut away —"

Ludavina shrugged her shoulders. "They tell that to Donna Maria but she takes no notice. It's the new house which has excited him."

"Are they all back?"

"No, *minha Senhora*, only *Senhor* Sequeria."

Mr Sequeria was back indeed. He was locked in the empty house with a man to guard him.

From the outside nothing seemed different. The windows had always looked blank and staring; the garden had always been untidy. The man who looked after Mr Sequeria wore a stocking cap with a tassel. His tight wrinkled trousers and heavy boots made his legs looked gnarled. He had a whiskery, wine-sodden face and spent the greater part of the day leaning across the lintel of the door. He rolled his own cigarettes and used so little tobacco that they would bend limply in the middle. I wondered how much he was paid.

Donna Maria would come panting up the hill with food on covered plates. She never greeted me and I sensed her dislike and fear of me.

Mr Sequeria came often to his window. But now, when he saw me, he would melt away, slinking backwards into the shadows of the room. There was something infinitely sad about this movement as if he were ashamed.

My English friends became alarmed. It was not right, they said, to go on like this — with a homicidal maniac locked in an empty house next door. I, too, felt something should be done. I knew little about Portuguese asylums; perhaps, like the prisons, they would be surprisingly enlightened and modern. But I didn't know. I sent for a man to make my doors shut. He said it would be difficult and would need new wood.

I got used, after a while, to having Mr Sequeria there, haunting his own house. Sometimes when friends were with me and there was music, I would suddenly remember and think of him sitting quietly there in his overcoat, sunk in the greyness of the chilly dusk. I knew he could hear the music, and that the careless sound would break inanely against the empty silence of his walls. But it was better, on the whole, not to think of him; to take him for granted — like the rain which fell or the shutter which banged in the night. Gradually this came about; and so completely that, when Alfred clattered into my house one pouring wet morning, I did not, at first, connect his excitement with Mr Sequeria.

Alfred's cheeks were pink and his eyes shining. His

wet hair was plastered flat against his forehead. Gone was the disillusioned poet, the sophisticated man of letters, the blue-ribboned Academician; he dripped and stuttered on the threshold like an incoherent child.

"Madame, I pray of you — could one take the liberty of using your telephone?"

"Yes, yes. Of course. Whatever has happened?"

"Monsieur Sequeria is breaking into Monsieur O'Malley's house with a hatchet!" He could not disguise his pleasure at being the bearer of such news. "He's broken through the glass doors of the vestibule and he's working on the main door now."

"Oh, Alfred —"

"The maids have all run out of the back, into the garden. He could get in quite easily through the kitchen door or the french windows of the salon —"

"But Mr O'Malley —"

"He's in Lisbon. Madame O'Malley and the children are all up in the attic."

I picked up the telephone and asked for the Republican Guard. As I waited for the connection, I asked Alfred how he got away.

"Oh, I ran out of the kitchen and across the garden. I knew you were the only person who had a telephone."

"But how did he get out?"

"Monsieur Sequeria? The man must have gone for tobacco. The rest was easy —"

"But he may be killing them now —"

Alfred seemed quite pleased with this idea. Or perhaps it was the general drama of the situation which intrigued him. "No, I don't think so," he said, upon reflection, "I threw the attic ladder out of the window."

"Well, he'll put it up again."

"Oh, he won't have got the door down yet."

The Republican Guard seemed a little sceptical about my story. They felt sure I was exaggerating. They would come up, they said, as soon as it stopped raining.

"You must come up now," I told them.

"*Minha Senhora*," said the man patiently, as if I were being unreasonable, "I would not send a dog out in this weather. If we came up now it would have to be in a taxi —"

"Then come in a taxi!"

"Who will pay for it?" asked the Guard.

"*Senhor* O'Malley will pay for it. Gladly," I added.

"The one who summons the police should pay for the taxi."

"Then I will pay for it. Only come."

As I put down the receiver, there was a distant crash and the musical tinkling of glass. Mr O'Malley's maids, taking refuge in Mr Sequeria's garden, let out a chorus of shrieks.

"I'd better go," said Alfred. He was radiant with excitement. "A thousand thanks, Madame. A thousand apologies. *A bientôt*." He was off into the rain.

I ran to the window which overlooked Mr Sequeria's garden. Trails of mist and rain were blowing across the prostrate vines. Mr O'Malley's house was hidden. I could hear, but not see, the maids at their crying.

When the Republican Guard arrived, about twenty minutes later, all was calm. They came to my house to get the money for the taxi.

It seemed that when Alfred arrived back, he found Mr Sequeria being led away quietly by the peasant who was paid to guard him. He had the axe in his hand and he looked very tired. Mr O'Malley's ground floor was a shambles. Mr Sequeria had broken all the doors as he came to them, whether or not they were locked. He had not got as far as the attic.

The Republican Guard stood about the square. A few people had collected near Mr Sequeria's house — not too near. They stood at a respectful distance.

Later, when Mr Sequeria was led away, the sun came out. The whole square was lit with a glistening, watery radiance. There was no need to go to the window. I could see from where I stood in the middle of the room.

Mr Sequeria passed my house with his shoulders bowed and his face shielded by his arms. He walked with quick, shuffling steps — quicker than the Guards, who hurried to keep up with him.

Donna Maria came afterwards, panting a little, and carrying his overcoat, which was soaking wet.

CHAPTER
EIGHT

Supper in the Kitchen

Fran was so quiet later that Charles asked if "anything was up". She sat amongst the unwashed dishes, a little beyond the lamplight.

"I'm tired," she told him, "after London" and she stared at him as beside the hearth he cleaned his gun. In a moment she would have to pile the dishes on to the dented black tray, light a candle and set it amongst them, and carry the tray down the stone-flagged passages to the scullery. She would have to use a primus to heat the washing-up water: Charles, out in the fields all day, had forgotten the boiler fire.

"Did you shut up the geese?" she asked suddenly.

"Yes."

"Sarah go to bed all right?"

"Except for a bath."

"Did she wash?"

"She was a long time in the bathroom."

"Oh."

She wished he would look up. "Your husband is so good-looking," people said — a banality applied to flesh and bone, but not to that inner grace which made these rare; she wanted to reassure herself about that face, that it was what she knew it would be and would seem so to others. "Charles!"

He looked up, surprised (yes, it was all there, touchingly unconscious of its own distinction).

"It's all right," she said, smiling.

He smiled too, rather slowly, meeting her eyes, and she looked away, humbled by the message of his glance: "London was dreadful," she said quickly, "it rained rather . . . I met Marilena."

Charles picked up his polishing rag. "Marilena? Who's she?"

"We were at drama school together. I've told you, darling —"

"Oh," he exclaimed, with ponderous enlightenment, "Marilena . . ."

"We hadn't met for twelve years. That's a long time . . ."

She glanced down at her hands and then, instinctively, she closed them, hiding the roughened nails. Marilena's hands had been almost spidery in their delicacy — no, not spidery, but the bones had looked like birds' bones, fragile and flexible, and her hands as she talked had flickered. "She's married. I went to her house. I think she's rather rich."

"Oh," said Charles absently, "good for her."

"Yes, and she's lovely, Charles."

"Is she, by Jove?" exclaimed Charles, with feigned heartiness.

"Really lovely. We met on the step of a bus. I was getting on and she was getting off."

That elegant creature, how to describe her to Charles? — The little hat that was barely a hat, a wisp of sequined net following the curve of swathed dark hair; so enhancing the line of throat and brow that each turn of the small head created its own perfection; the shoes; the soft, soft gloves . . . And the vision had cried "Fran!" and Fran, startled, dull, had stared into the bone-smooth face without recognition, almost with fear. "Don't you know me, darling?" That catch in the voice, a little break as though a syllable cracked? Those startlingly, pale eyes with staring lashes: kitten's eyes? "Marilena!" Fran had gasped.

"Yes, yes. Where can we talk?"

In Marilena's house, of course. And on the way there, Fran had caught a glimpse of her own face in the taxi mirror: above the clutched parcels it had looked, not sunburned as she hoped, but shiny and sallow, with roughened, uncombed hair.

"Oh, Charles, I wanted her to have a lovely house! Really lovely. Unusual. I should have been disappointed if she *hadn't* had a lovely house, but —" Fran paused, "I wanted it to be the kind of house I didn't like . . ." her voice trailed off, ashamed.

Charles, aware of the silence, looked up vaguely. "Go on, I'm listening." He set his gun up on his knee, at arm's length, and smiled at it lovingly: "Seventy-five years old . . . you wouldn't think it?"

"No," said Fran gently.

"Well, go on about thingmebob's house," he stopped again for his rag, "— you hoped it would be the kind you liked?" As Fran continued silent, he looked up with a smile, pleased to have hit on proof of his attention, "And was it?"

"Yes," said Fran, smiling too, "yes, it was." She drew a long breath: "Do you know the kind of house that is all oyster and alabaster and pale curves and sudden urns of dark red roses — where the beds have sculptured hangings and are raised up like gay tombs; and all kinds of diffused lighting in unexpected alcoves; alcoves with just one thing, a strange shape — a thing they talk about carelessly after dinner: 'Oh, yes . . . fun, isn't it? A ha-ha shell from the Galapagos —'"

"What is a ha-ha shell?" asked Charles, interested.

"I don't know. I made it up."

"Oh, and was it like that, the house?"

"No," said Fran, "it was lovely." She turned to him, suddenly animated. "Oh, Charles, it was really lovely. A dream house. I could hardly bear it," she added, remembering the anguish of her sudden envy. "It was Regency — no, perhaps a little earlier — and it wasn't the mixture as before: satin stripes and spotty empire mirrors — anyone can do that; it was the house itself and the way it stood. And it was the way the front door opened; the width of the hall; the way the staircase curved up, so shallowly that, standing in the hall, you could see into the rooms on the landing above and out again through the long windows. I could see us in that house. Sarah coming down the little curving stairway which leads from the nurseries; and the park at the door; and there'd be so much for her so near; the open-air theatre — she's never seen any Shakespeare — the picture galleries; the zoo, concerts — you know, Charles, we ought to do something about her music — and —"

"Has whats-her-name any children?"

"Marilena? No, she can't." Fran paused, thinking this over, "I wonder if she minds. Shall I tell you about the drawing room?"

"Yes, do."

"Because the drawing room was the loveliest of all — and it was hushed and timeless, as though the past was there as well as the present; and such lovely combinations of light and shade that one could have furnished it with boxes."

"Oh, come . . ." murmured Charles, polishing.

"But I mean it," insisted Fran, "a house like Marilena's is so full of ghosts of lovely things that the merest suggestion is enough . . ."

"And what does Marilena use?" He breathed on his polishing, stared, and rubbed again. "Suggestions? Or boxes?"

"Oh, Marilena has everything. And it's all right — nothing leaps to the eye." Fran hesitated. "She's terribly charming, Charles. I had forgotten. We were so young. She lived in digs, with a gas-ring, somewhere behind Victoria. My mother used to worry about her and ask her to meals and things. But when Marilena came to tea and looked, with those clear eyes, round my mother's drawing room, I never dared to guess at what she might be thinking —"

"But it was a charming room."

"Yes, yes, I know. I know now that Marilena loved that room. She looked like that because she loved it. Charles, I've found out that Marilena was shy."

"Really?" said Charles.

"But it's a funny thing to have discovered suddenly, today, after twelve years —"

"Yes . . . I suppose so."

"Darling, I'm a bore . . ." Fran pushed back her hair and stared, bent brow on hand, at the worn table. "She said she liked my 'rough curls' . . . she said I looked young . . ."

Fran picked up a fork and drew it idly along the sunken grain. "Do I, Charles? I wish I'd worn my best black . . ."

A clock ticked (the cheap alarm which ruled their days) and away down the scullery passage a tap dripped. Charles's breathing deepened as, with passionate absorption, he began to assemble his gun.

"Her husband owns the Comedy-Empire," went on Fran suddenly.

"Oh," Charles straightened his back, stock in one hand barrel in the other, "does whats-her-name act?"

"Marilena. It's quite an easy name, Charles. No, she doesn't. She lost her nerve."

She fell silent, twisting the fork. She had talked so much and told so little: nothing of the conversation in that timeless room, Marilena sitting so beautifully with lovely collected lines, as people sit on a stage; her arms loose on the arms of her chair and her hands — those helpless hands whose fingers seemed to curl with their own fragility — alive with flickering gesture. Fran had thought (shrunk a little into the depths of the sofa) that it was only a woman secure in the achievement of sartorial perfection who dares sit as Marilena sat — carelessly royal, inviting scrutiny.

Carelessly, too, Marilena had spoken of her life — in that odd voice with its musical break; but amusedly, happy in Fran's perception of mocking understatement and connivance in the small, deliberate flights of imagination. Marilena (it had seemed to Fran) had been everywhere, had done everything. When she spoke of the famous, she reduced them to life-size, and drew them with light, indifferent generosity into a circle, accessible to Fran; and when she spoke of the past, she spoke with a disarming frankness: "I was madly inhibited," Marilena had confessed and had added, with what seemed deliberate inconsequence, "it's stupid to be poor."

Stupid? Marilena had used the word gently, almost reflectively, but the impact of it had shaken Fran. She, too, had suspected (and dismissed the thought) that it was stupid to be poor. Stupid, just that. There were things one could do; other values . . .

A manservant had brought tea, very quietly and with little paraphernalia. Once or twice the telephone rang and was answered promptly on some floor below.

"But tell me more about you," Marilena had said, "the farm and everything."

And Fran had told her. But the charm of country life had seemed curiously elusive: she had tried to be amusing about buckets and oil lamps; a little poetic, even, about hayfields and moonlight and the scent of honeysuckle; she had played up the flagged floors and the oak beams; she had attempted to dazzle Marilena with the prospect of unrationed butter, fresh cream and occasional home-cured ham, but somehow —

"How did you learn it all, darling?" Marilena had asked, a little incredulous.

"From Charles mostly, and we have a man; and a girl who comes in . . ."

"How did Charles learn?"

"From the men," Fran had said, smiling in spite of herself.

"Oh, Fran!"

"No, Charles has always known about land. You see, his father —" Fran had hesitated: one could not, like that, trade on the past; it was only local die-hards to whom Charles, estate-less, seemed still the squire. "But," she went on, "he does 'learn from the man'; we all do —"

"Do you scrub the floors and all that?"

"Sometimes. When there's time. We mostly live in the kitchen."

"Are there any people — anyone interesting?"

Anyone interesting? Fran · had reviewed her neighbours from this strange angle. The Rector? But one so seldom saw him except in church: all his non-duty hours seemed to be spent in a loft over the stables carving his altar screen; Colonel and Mrs Stoddard? She, perhaps, was interesting — riding to hounds with a broken neck. The Trevellyans? When they were there; but they lived mostly in the South of France, and their woods, Charles said, were a disgrace (but to Fran enchantment, with their overgrown drives and rotting tree-stumps). Miss Pill and Miss Plunket? Fran loved Miss Pill and Miss Plunket, who ran a market garden; she loved their teaparties, the manless comfort of their tiny house and their deliciously circumspect preoccupation with the occult — but could they, by London standards, be called "interesting"? Who else were there? That red-haired woman who wore slacks and sunbathed rather too opulently for one whose bungalow overlooked the main road? Miss Whale, that was her name but Fran, on the unavoidable country encounters had never dared use it: it seemed too apt. And the dreadful, affluent brother who drove a Rolls Bentley and came for an occasional night, the "male whale", as Charles called him? Might these, on closer acquaintanceship, prove "interesting"? Not, Fran thought, as she sat there, silent, by Marilena's standards: once when he came by train, Fran, cornered, had given the brother a lift from the station and he had laid a familiar arm along the back of her seat (she had sat poised like a ram-rod, not daring to brake) and, when he had got out, he had laid a deliberate hand on her knee; and she had stared, shrinking and speechless, at an uncut emerald worn as a signet ring . . . "Thank you, my dear," he had said, too slowly and with a lingering glance.

"Darling Fran," Marilena had exclaimed, watching her face, "are they as bad as that?"

"No, no," Fran had said, a little ruefully, ashamed of her silence; but how could she explain to Marilena that country neighbours, pleasant and unpleasant, were just there — to be accepted as one accepted the leaning oak which threatened the barn or the hidden spring which bogged the pasture; attacking the oak would damage the barn and deflecting the spring would dry up the cow pond. "We have a duchess," she proffered, tentatively.

114

"The real thing?"

"Yes, Bramhampton. But even she —"

"Even she?"

"Well," said Fran, "I don't think you'd call her interesting." (Not interesting, but kind, kind . . . that dear crumpled old face when Sarah lay ill . . . the tremble of the lip, 'My dear, if there is anything, anything . . .')

Marilena sighed. "Look," she said. "It's beginning to rain."

And both had stared, suddenly silent, at the grey mist beyond the long windows. "It's odd —" Marilena had said, after a while.

"What is?"

"Well," Marilena looked down momentarily at her exquisite hands and drew in her breath with her laugh, "— that I've never met people of that kind."

"Of what kind?"

Marilena hesitated. Then, "Oh, country people," she had said, escaping nimbly into vagueness.

Fran was silent a moment, puzzled by the light detachment of a tone which, in another, might suggest regret. What Marilena meant, of course, was that she had been spared the tedium. "It used not to be like this," Fran pointed out, "it's just that everybody's short-handed. There's so much one can't leave and on a little farm it's the same for everybody. Except for —" Fran hesitated.

"Except for what?"

Fran laughed. "I was going to say except for people like Miss Whale."

"Miss Whale?" Marilena had exclaimed sharply.

"Oh, she's just a woman who lives in a bungalow off the main road and does nothing but drink gin and play the gramophone —"

It was then that Marilena had said slowly, "My name's Whale."

Fran, thinking back, remembered with what reptilian quiet the shadowed room had slid from dream to nightmare: the chill of shocked compassionate foreboding as her note of laughter and disdain, unabsorbed and unmistakable, rang on the echo of its own finality. But they had managed well. Their eyes wide and their faces blank; too blank. A few words had established the connection and Marilena without a tremor had claimed her sister-in-law: "Florence . . . a good soul really. She's led a rackety life but Sydney's fond of her . . ." And then, mercifully, the telephone had rung — this time in the room itself — and Marilena had picked up the receiver.

Sydney — so that was his name! Fran felt again the meaning weight of the hot hand on her knee; she saw the green signet ring; she could even recall the face, heavy, and darkly aquiline with slightly protruding eyes and almost eastern curve of lip and nostril; there might have been (Fran realized suddenly), at one time and for some woman, a dreadful kind of charm about this man, born of his arrogance and masculinity — but for what type?

"Does it matter?" Marilena was saying and Fran, startled, had looked up, suddenly aware that for the last few seconds Marilena had been speaking over-quietly and in guarded monosyllables: "Yes, I know . . . Yes, I will . . . Why? . . . Of course . . . I said 'of course' . . . Goodbye . . ." and, as she laid down the receiver, she had stared at the instrument curiously, then calmly and deliberately, she had raised her eyes and it had been Fran who faltered, guilty in her recognition of those anger-thickened consonants: her own eyes had slid away, hunted and unhappy, towards the clock.

"Quarter to seven! Is that the time?"

"You said you had a picture of Charles," Marilena reminded her.

Fran gripped her handbag as though the shabby leather case might fly out of its own will. "Darling, not now. I must go . . . my train . . ."

"It won't take a moment —" insisted Marilena.

But paralysed with pity, Fran had sat quite still. She had stared at Marilena's outstretched hand as if its owner, bent on self-destruction, reached out for a sword.

"Darling!" protested Marilena, surprised, and Fran, crimson-cheeked, had opened her bag and proffered wordlessly the dog-eared slip of worn morocco leather.

Marilena had gazed in silence — "Is he really like this?" she had asked; the involuntary tribute was oddly hushed.

"Yes," Fran had whispered.

"What was he — Major?"

"Lieutenant Colonel."

"At that age!"

"He was twenty-eight."

"A gunner . . ."

"Yes . . ." and then, in spite of herself, Fran had added — just above her breath, "DSO and Bar."

Marilena had looked a little longer and then she had closed the case. "Thank you," she had said lightly, as she gave it back, "he is charming."

And Fran, as she turned away and began fumblingly to collect her parcels, had seen that the light, wide kitten's eyes were bright and blank.

"I'll wash the dishes," announced Charles.

Fran stared at him, a little dazed. "No —" she began.

"Yes," said Charles firmly as, with tender care, he laid the shining weapon in its case. "You go to bed."

Fran stood up; deliberately she crossed to Charles and wound her arms about his waist and laid her head, with its weight of tiredness, against his chest.

"What's this?" he asked.

"Nothing. Me." Her voice was muffled.

He stroked her hair. "I was just thinking —" he said, after a moment.

She waited. "Well?"

"I was just thinking that if the weather holds until we've cut the wheat, it'll mean a pretty penny."

"Yes," said Fran.

"It's rattling good land. Another eighteen months and no one'll know this place —" He pulled, with gentle malice, a lock of her hair. "No need then to envy whatsername."

Fran flung back her head. "Envy whatsername?" she repeated stupidly.

"Marilena Thingmebob," said Charles.

Fran's eyes slid past his face, past the lamp, across the shadowed kitchen and fixed themselves with wide clairvoyant terror upon the outer door; she saw through it, beyond it, across the darkening countryside towards the town: envy Marilena?

"Well, didn't you?" asked Charles, smiling.

"Yes, of course I envied her: her house, her clothes, her leisure . . ." She turned quickly, looking up into his face. "That's what it's for, that's what she lives on. I — I paid my tribute. Don't you see Charles? I can afford to envy Marilena." Sharply she bent her head and there, on her arm, lay his hand, steel-fine and work-hardened.

"Then why are you crying?"

Fran was silent.

"Why Fran?" asked Charles gently, "If you were glad to envy her —"

Fran raised her tear-wet face: "Envy her — yes, but not by a clumsy mischance, teach her to envy me."

CHAPTER
NINE

Pleasure Cruise

Fanny looked through the haze of cigarette smoke and wondered why she had come.

Lucien had had a headache. Lucien had said there was nothing to see in Lisbon. Colonel and Mrs Graft had packed into the cars for Cintra. The Waring girls had taken the train out to Estoril. The Miss ffaulkes had discovered, simultaneously, that it was Sunday and that there was an English church on the hill. And Fanny . . . here sat Fanny, completely at a loose end, in a café in the Rocio Square.

As far as she could see, she was the only woman in the café.

She had drunk a cup of strong black coffee; she had studied her neighbours with interest and circumspection; she had longed to light a cigarette.

But already her presence had made itself felt. They were polite but they had started a little: Latin faces — beautiful in youth, less so (much less so) in age; thus it seemed to Fanny as she gazed about her. Here were no frigid masks of shyness or reserve: generosity, greed, sensuality and kindliness blatantly displayed themselves. Sitting amongst them criticism melted into interest and interest into sympathy.

120

Two men especially attracted her attention; they were deep in argument and Fanny could watch them unobserved: one was old and paunchy, yellow as a Chinese idol; the other was young — it was difficult to tell his age — temple, cheekbone and jaw were lean and burnt dark by the sun; there were deep lines running from nostril to lip corner.

The old man talked slowly and emphatically, stressing his words with a single gesture — a chopping movement of his right hand, the fingers spread. The younger man listened, his eyes downcast, his face carven, non-committal. Suddenly, he looked up (at last, thought Fanny, I am seeing eyes that flash) and the words poured out, harshly staccato. The old man stared; his prominent eyeballs seemed about to start from his head; it seemed to Fanny that the two men must come to blows. But no; there was silence between them and deep thought. The old man began to nod completing, to Fanny's delight, his resemblance to a Chinese idol. The young man laughed, snapped open his case and took out a cigarette. He leaned back, smiling.

So that's that, thought Fanny, as the old man rose with difficulty to his feet, patted the young man affectionately on the shoulder and launched himself out into the sunlight.

The young man was still half-smiling, watching the tip of his cigarette, his chair slightly tilted. Fanny found herself trying to guess his occupation and background but in so foreign a country the odds were against her. "And how strange, how utterly foreign and strange my life and outlook would seem to him!" She thought suddenly of her Chelsea flat, the studio drawing room with its cool, summer smell — the curtains blowing, a glimpse of the river, Lucien's grand piano, the flowers on the console table; the Chelsea Flower show, Martha's white apron; Lucien lying down, Lucien bringing tea — arranged as no woman could arrange it; Lucien at the piano — "Charming couple, delightful couple . . ."

In less than a fortnight she would be back; in less than a fortnight she would be picking up bargain hats in the High Street, Kensington; in less than a fortnight she would be wrestling with account books, thinking about meals. She thought of washing up on Martha's day out (how lucky they were to have Martha — an old kitchenmaid-cum-cook of her mother's), the grease floating on the bowl, the flight of Lucien from the scullery — suddenly sickened; the nervous, delicate arpeggios in which he drowned the memory . . .

She smiled and, looking up, met the sudden bright stare. She looked down again quickly, almost shocked (so intent and shameless had been the scrutiny) and began to pull her light summer coat from the back of a neighbouring chair. Rather shyly, she signalled to the waiter.

"*Um escudo, madam,*" he said, his appreciative gaze on her cool, green-clad figure.

She opened her bag and gazed rather helplessly at the five pound note, two florins and a sixpence that lay within. What a fool! What an idiot! Why had she not changed some money? Now it was going to be embarrassing, just because she could not speak Portuguese. Looking up, she met once more an interested stare from the other table: he leaned forward, deferential, half-smiling: "You have no money?" he said in English.

"Yes, but no Portuguese money."

He stood up, taking out his notecase. "I will change it. How much would you like?"

"Very little," said Fanny, in a matter-of-fact voice as he came to her table. "I just want to pay for my coffee. I am going straight back to the ship."

"Yes, I see. You are off the ship?" Speaking English his voice was gentler, more uncertain. "You don't want to stop, to buy anything?"

"No, I don't think so. I can't speak a word. I thought I'd just wander a bit and go back to luncheon."

"I see." He hesitated. "In that case, will you not let me pay for your coffee? It is —" he picked up the bill, "roughly twopence-halfpenny in English money."

Fanny laughed. "Thank you very much," she said. "I'm so sorry. I don't know why — I didn't think. You see, we were going on that trip to Cintra. It's all inclusive — one didn't bother. We leave tonight at nine."

"Then, of course," he said, "if you don't want to shop it is not worth changing money."

There was a pause. He was standing with his hand on the back of the vacant chair. He seemed polite and a little uncertain as if he were waiting for her to make a move. Fanny picked up her gloves.

"You will see very little of my country," he said suddenly.

"I know." Fanny frowned. "It is disappointing. I meant to go with the others. I should at least have seen Cintra. But somehow —" She smiled suddenly. "Those trains of cars . . ."

He hesitated then he laughed. "You know," he said, "they are very terrible — those people who go in cars to Cintra." He paused. "Almost every day a ship comes in and those people — they always look the same — drive out in cars to Cintra."

Suddenly Fanny saw her fellow passengers through his eyes. Yes, some of them would indeed seem very terrible — with their peeling noses and scarlet chests; unruly, shapeless heads of hair dried up by sun and wind; goggle-eyed, toothy, eager . . . Even Colonel and Mrs Graft, gentle, precise, well-read and much travelled, with her flowing clothes and raffia bag for books and embroidery and her narrow shoes — good shoes, long, low, beautifully finished but very terrible, yes, very terrible below that strangely hanging dress of cream tussore. And Colonel Graft with his stringy neck and worried, gooseberry eyes, his cloth cap and slung camera . . . Before she could stop herself and with real anxiety in her voice she heard herself say:

"And I, too, I suppose . . ."

"No," he answered immediately, "you are dressed for a town. The others they are dressed — perhaps it is for the beach?"

"No," said Fanny, laughing, "they are dressed for 'abroad'."

He looked back at her seriously. "I see," he said. Then he looked at his watch, frowning a little.

Fanny coloured. "I'm sorry," she said, "I am keeping you. Thank you so much for my coffee."

But he followed her out into the sunlight. He was carrying his hat in his hand and, in that bright glare, she noticed that parts of his hair were an almost golden brown.

"You are not keeping me," he said as they paused on the pavement. "I was wondering what parts of this city I should have time to show you before lunch." He had very little accent but spoke with an almost painful care and hesitation.

"Please don't trouble," said Fanny hurriedly, "I shall just wander slowly down to the ship." Suddenly she felt a fool but, she defended herself, one had had such a drilling about "wops'; she glanced up at him but he seemed to have forgotten her: he was looking across the square, smiling at a friend on the other side of the street; he waved his hat, placed it upon his head, and turned again to Fanny.

"Well, I take you back to the ship, is that it, yes?"

He was examining her face; his own was puzzled. Fanny made a sudden decision. "Look, if you're sure you've nothing better to do, I should adore to see a little bit more of Lisbon."

"No," he said, "I am quite free until four o'clock."

"Four o'clock?" echoed Fanny. "But I must be back for lunch."

"No," he said, "you will lunch with me."

"But —" began Fanny.

"Your friends think you are in Cintra, is it not so?"

Fanny hesitated then admitted that it was so.

"You would not like then? Every Sunday before a fight I lunch always in some simple place."

Fanny was silent for a moment, feeling her way, "And where you are not recognized?"

He smiled, "Perhaps —"

"You mean, in the smart Lisbon restaurants you'd be mobbed?"

He laughed. "Not mobbed. They are very kind — but too much talk, it is trying."

"What about today?"

"What about today? Yes, I ask myself: what about today?"

"I too ask myself," said Fanny.

He looked thoughtful for a moment. "Every rule I suppose can have its exceptions: today is today."

Something in his voice decided Fanny; she said quickly, "Thank you. I should like it very much."

Without more ado he signalled a taxi. What am I doing, thought Fanny, as she sank back . . . poor Lucien, with his headache! If she told Lucien, he would not think it amusing; neither, she was forced to admit, would Mrs Graft: funny, perhaps, very funny, but not amusing.

"How grand!" she exclaimed aloud. "Are all the taxis like this?"

"More or less. In London, they are boxes."

"You know London?"

"A little."

"Do you like it?"

"Yes, I have friends there. And my mother loves it. Perhaps next winter I shall be in London."

"I hope then," said Fanny, "that I shall be able to return your kindness."

He laughed. "I thank you," he said, his amused eyes on her face. The effect on Fanny was disconcerting; she glanced out of the window. "Where are we going now?"

"A little way outside Lisbon to lunch first. You would like?"

"Yes, but we are early, aren't we?"

"Yes, but it is so hot. There we can be out of doors. Excuse me." He leaned across her and lowered the window.

Looking at his face, thus brought close to her own, Fanny said impulsively, "You know in the cafe I was amusing myself trying to guess your profession." How dreadful that sounds, she thought, how beastly and inquisitive!

He glanced at her, slightly raising his eyebrows.

"I am a bull-fighter," he said.

Surprise drained Fanny's face of expression. They were driving down the main avenue of Lisbon, a miniature and sub-tropical Champs Elysées. "A bull-fighter!"

"Yes. I — my name is Salvador Monteiro." He seemed to expect that she would recognize his name. She gave no sign and he added quickly, "You do not like bull-fights?"

"I — I have never seen one."

He smiled. "You are English. "Oh, the poor bulls . . . Oh, the poor horses"!" His voice altered. "Here in Portugal we do not kill the bulls or hurt the horses."

"Then how — Then why — ?"

"Oh, it is still a fight. You see," he laughed, "nobody has explained to the bulls. They still have their —" he paused seeking a word, "their old-fashioned ideas." He was watching her face, deeply amused. "You are beautiful," he said. "You have a beautiful skin."

But Fanny had become quite pale. "You are a toreador, then?" she asked.

"No, there is no word "toreador", except —" he paused, "in opera. I am what is called a *cavaleiro*. I fight bulls on horseback."

"*Cavaleiro*," Fanny repeated, "ca-va-lay-roo."

"It means a 'horseman'. We use the same word to mean 'a gentleman'. *Cavaleiro* . . ."

"You have a long sharp pole," began Fanny.

He laughed. "Not here. No weapons. We have what do you say — darts."

"Are they painful?"

"Not very — he has a tough skin — but they make him very angry and keen to fight."

"You want him angry?"

"Yes, of course. Otherwise there would be no fair fight —"

"Then you creep up behind him —"

He laughed so much that she began to laugh too, without knowing why.

"Forgive me," he said at last, his warm appreciative gaze on her face as if her last remark had, in some secret way, enhanced her charms, "there is no creeping: you see, it is all very fast."

"And you see," said Fanny, "that I know very little about bull-fights." Subdued, she gazed out of the window.

They were now driving through the suburbs of Lisbon. Tall, tiled houses and low, dark shops clung to the street and the tramlines. Beyond, through the gaps, she could see burnt fields with their cactus hedges and the untidy grandeur of the eucalyptus trees. "We should go further into the country," he said, "but there is not time. I must be in Lisbon before four o'clock."

"And I? You have not asked me when I must be back."

He gave her a direct and mischievous look. "You sail at nine," he said.

Fanny had a sudden mental picture of Colonel and Mrs Graft being whirled round Cintra in their high, open car — Mrs Graft with the scarf tied round her hat and knotted under her chin, her hair blowing in wisps . . . And I, thought Fanny, am about to lunch with a bull-fighter whom I picked up in a café!

The car stopped beside a narrow flight of steps, and they passed up the steps into a garden where weather-beaten, wooden tables were set under a trellis of vines.

How very lovely, thought Fanny, standing in the filtered sunlight. Beyond the shadow a trail of bougainvillea burned against the white-plastered wall. There were unkempt, drooping rose trees, heavy with bloom. White petals were scattered on the rough grass. There was a hot, sweet smell and the sound of bees.

"Where would you like to sit?"

Fanny pulled off her hat and shook back her heavy hair. It shone, dark red, in the green shadow. "Here in the shade," she said.

He moved back the bench. "*O Tiasinha*!" he called as he sat down beside her.

An old woman hobbled out of the white-washed house, a tablecloth on her arm. She was a forbidding old woman. She grumbled to herself as she spread the cloth, pushing his elbows from where purposely he had placed them. Her eyes, cold and dead as stone, stared into his laughing ones. "*Aïe, Menino!*" she said in a cracked, scolding voice.

As she leaned across him, he picked up a rose and pulled its stalk through the wool of her shawl. She gave him then a look of hatred, it seemed to Fanny — then she patted the rose with her wrinkled hand, her dead, staring eyes on his face. She began to speak and, with her hollow voice, the shadow of old age crept into the garden.

"What is she saying?" asked Fanny.

"Oh, that she had a house and a servant to work for her. That her husband, he loved her very much; that her children are dead; that she had been very happy and that now she is alone. She says this always. I have known her since a little boy." He picked up a twig of vine which had fallen on the cloth and crumbled it between his fingers.

The old woman drew a deep breath. "*Aïe . . . Aïe . . . Aïe . . .*" she sighed then, suddenly, she smiled — a strange contortion — and laid her twisted hand against his cheek. "Go on with you, you good-fornothing!" she seemed to say and then she hobbled off.

"It's hot," he remarked idly, "do you not feel hot?"

Fanny leaned back against the trellis. "I like this place," she said. "I like the heat, the silence. I feel —"

What did she feel? That in some half-remembered moment she had known it all before.

"It is an *adega*," he told her, "where wine is stored. After lunch I will show you. It is of a big vineyard but on Sundays the old woman sells lunch. She is a good cook."

"Poor old creature," smiled Fanny.

"Old fool!" he said shortly and, surprised, she glanced sideways. I wouldn't like, she thought, noting the arch of lip and nostril, to be a horse that played him up. "But she likes you," she pointed out.

His expression softened; he laughed but did not reply; he had forgotten the old woman — his eyes were on her face. "I have never loved an Englishwoman," he said reflectively.

After a surprised moment, Fanny laughed.

"You think that strange?" he asked, interested.

"Not strange," said Fanny. "Opportunity perhaps has not been kind." They looked at each other in silence for a moment.

"You are mocking me," he said — a disinterested statement — and turned away. *"O Tiasinha!"* He called so loudly that Fanny jumped.

"What does that mean?" she asked.

"It means 'aunt', 'little aunt'."

"Is she your aunt?"

It was his turn to look surprised. "No," he said.

"I'm sorry," said Fanny. "But this is all so strange. Nothing would surprise me."

The old woman returned with red wine, glasses, and a dish of prawns. They were giant, pink and succulent. As she pulled the first apart, Fanny said, "Tell me more about bull-fighting."

He frowned over the prawn that he was skinning and ate it in silence. Then he turned to her, placing his arm along the back of her seat. "If you want to see a bull-fight," he said, his bright gaze on her face, "there is one this afternoon. You would like?" Fanny looked back at him. "You would like?" he repeated.

"Yes," said Fanny, "if there is time."

"There is time. They start at five. Before eight o'clock all is over."

Fanny was struck by a sudden thought. "Are you," she asked with hesitation, "are you — fighting?"

"Yes," he replied still watching her face and smiling a little.

Everything became slightly unreal — the garden with its drooping roses, the old woman setting a dish of sheep's tongues on the table, the ridiculously blue sky. Her lip trembled. "I think I'd like to go," she said.

He was staring at her, half-smiling. She wondered what he was thinking.

"How old are you?" he asked.

"I am twenty-five," she said. During the pause which followed she had a feeling almost of panic.

"I am older," he said at last and dropped his eyes. His face suddenly looked tired; every line of it seemed familiar to Fanny.

"How old are you?" she asked gently. He looked up, smiling.

"I am twenty-five," he said.

There was silence, until at last Fanny broke it.

"Are there many *cavaleiros* in a bull-fight?"

"Sometimes only one. Sometimes there are two."

"You fight together?"

"Yes, but more often we take a bull in turn."

"Your horses, are they good horses?"

"They are beautiful horses," he said warmly. "Here in Portugal," he went on in his careful, hesitating voice, "it is a great wrong, a great disgrace for the bull to touch the horse. Our horses are agile like cats and clever — like men. They are brave."

"Like men," said Fanny, and smiled. He laughed, pleased.

"And the bulls?" she went on really interested.

"They too are brave and clever, so clever that they can come only once into the bull-ring."

"Why?" asked Fanny.

"Because they learn too much. The second time they are no good."

"Do you mean to tell me," asked Fanny, leaning forward, "that here in Portugal a bull only goes into the ring once in his life?"

He hesitated. "In theory, yes," he said and smiled, "sometimes in practice, no, but he is no good. You will eat this?" he asked, preparing to help her. "It is very Portuguese but it is good."

Fanny believed him. It looked delicious. "Tell me," she asked, as she held her plate, "if you are fighting today, how can you waste time with me out here? There must be many things you have to do."

"Not many. I like to be in Lisbon by four, to see my horses."

133

"What breed are they?"

"Local breed. These my father bred. I teach them."

"Have they Arab blood?"

"Some are three-quarter Arab. You like horses?"

"Yes, I love them."

"You hunt, in England? That is good sport. I should like it."

"No," she hesitated, "I'm not that sort of person."

"What sort of person are you?"

"I don't know." She clasped her hands. "I don't know. On my passport it says 'Housewife'."

"You are married?" he asked.

"Yes."

He looked at her wonderingly. "I should have said — a young girl." He smiled and then said gently, "So you are married?" He spoke as if this fact were curiously interesting and significant.

"Why are you surprised? I wear a ring."

He glanced at her hand as she laid it on the table but it was as though he did not see it; he then looked quickly up at her face. She drew back as though he were about to touch or kiss it, but he had moved no nearer. She could think of nothing to say to fill the pause. He looked down again at her hand. It lay on the white cloth, faintly brown, with curving fingers. Suddenly, he took it within his own. "So this is your marriage ring?"

"Yes," she replied evenly, forcing her hand to lie passive. "Don't you have wedding rings in Portugal?"

"Yes," he said, "we do." And he stared at her hand, without speaking.

134

After a while, gently, as though to straighten her hair, she drew her hand away. She laughed and the laugh sounded empty, a little foolish. "Do you —" she said, addressing a trail of bougainvillea on the wall opposite, "Don't you — feel terribly nervous before a fight?" He doesn't know what to make of me, she thought, and I cannot blame him; I haven't let myself open to anything. Life has run, so far, on such familiar tramlines; it's the first time, I suppose, that I've walked on foot up a side street . . .

He was answering her question; he was telling her that, once mounted on his horse, he felt no longer afraid. She asked him other questions about his life and, from his replies, learned of the low-lying, lonely land beyond the river, where the kites wheeled against the blue sky and the storks stood carven in the rushes; the great estates; the feudal feasts with oxen roasted whole; the herds of bulls — "*touros de morte*" — bulls of death; the local bull-fights, their colour and skill; the horse fairs — where every little urchin had a mount and priceless horses are ridden with a bridle of rope.

She saw it all: the sunshine, the dust, the sweaty hides, the wooden stirrups, the sheepskin saddles, the dark men with their scarlet cummerbunds and stocking caps . . . She realized, also, that this life of hardihood and danger was a luxury; that he was endowed with the careless riches of heredity, using his money, as his grandfathers before him, that the breed of bulls might be better and the level of sport kept high.

His arm, once again, lay along the back of her seat.

"And you have been married how long?"

"Seven years," she paused. "Why do you smile?"

He looked down, still smiling. "No reason. It's a long time."

"Not," she hesitated, "if you are happy."

"Oh no," he said reasonably, "not if you are happy."

"You don't believe — you don't think such a thing —"

"I? I have said nothing."

She sat silent, tilting her wine glass in the sun so the dark dregs turned to garnet. These Latins . . . how could one explain to them, how make them understand that — there were other levels, other values, other . . . but certain phrases slipped through her mind: "Charming couple, delightful couple . . . it was so nice to see nowadays . . ."

She turned quickly. "You see —" she began but, meeting his eyes, the words faltered and died: there was nothing she could tell him; he knew it all; she could not even look away.

He took her face in his hand, his fingers lay along her jaw. "You are a little child," he said, "a little, little child." There was silence.

Two tears rolled slowly down Fanny's cheeks. Amazed, ashamed, she tried to smile.

"This is done?" he asked, surprised and gently, "to cry?"

She could not reply and, very carefully, with the folded napkin, he wiped her cheeks. The rough linen was warm from the sun.

"And now?" he asked, smiling a little.

"No, it is not done," she said unsteadily. She smiled and her face, shaken out of its repose, was alive and tender.

"Drink your wine," he said and she saw her glass was full.

The old woman had brought them another dish. As he was about to help her, Fanny cried: "Please, no!" It was a pagoda of toast, steak, ham and a fried egg.

"But yes," he protested, "you have eaten nothing."

"But I can't," cried Fanny, "on a day like this . . ."

These amazing people — with a climate like theirs . . . She watched him, dazed, while he ate the steak, unhurriedly but with appetite. The heat crept round her, soaking into her brain.

"How can you fight on a day like this?"

He laughed. "You do not know what we say, that to enjoy a bull-fight it is necessary — a hot sun, a good lunch, sufficient wine, plenty of flies, dust and a little headache."

"I have a little headache," said Fanny.

How still it was! She pushed back the damp hair from her forehead. The feeling of unreality persisted. A dark, fresh stain of wine on the rough cloth matched so beautifully the heavy creeper on the white-washed wall. White and purple. Purple and white. There was coffee, fruit, *aguardente* — burning and golden in a little glass. She had eaten a peach, heavy and hard but full of flavour, chopped with sugar in red wine.

The sunlight lay across her eyes like white-hot lead.

"This will be a wonderful bull-fight," said Fanny, thinking of her headache.

He frowned. "Listen," he said, "I think you are very tired." He looked at his watch. "It is now three o'clock and a quarter. It takes nearly half an hour to get to

137

Lisbon and at four I must leave you. Perhaps it is better (do you not think?) that you remain here and rest a little. I will leave the taxi for you and, at half past four, he will take you to Campo Pequeno."

"Campo Pequeno?"

"It is the bull-ring. I will give him a card. He will take care of you. Do you think?"

"Can I rest here?" asked Fanny.

"Yes, yes. It is quite clean. I will arrange it."

"Thank you," said Fanny. "I think I should love that."

She leaned back against the trellis and, through half-closed eyes, watched him cross the grass and enter the dark doorway of the white-washed house. Why did I cry? she wondered. She felt limp as though she had passed through an emotional crisis. How silly I am, she thought, such a happy, even life as mine has been.

"Well?" she asked brightly when, at last, he rejoined her.

He picked up her hat and her light summer coat. "It is all right."

She followed him across the garden into the dark kitchen. He stood aside for her to pass up the narrow wooden stairway. On the threshold of a small white-washed bedroom, she collided with the old woman who was removing a dish of pears. The room smelt of pears and the sun poured through the open wooden shutters. She sat down on the edge of the narrow, iron bed with its rough white coverlet. The straw mattress rustled and, suddenly, she felt light with fear.

He laid her coat over the bed-rail. Her hat adorned the knob. She noticed there were pomegranates hanging from the ceiling in little raffia nets.

He crossed the room and partly closed the shutters, so that it became suddenly dark. The sunlight burned through the apertures, lighting the dusk. He came and stood beside her. They heard the old woman clumping slowly down the stairs.

"You will be all right here?" he asked, in a low voice as if there were already somebody asleep in the room.

"Yes," she replied but she did not move.

"It is all quite clean," he whispered. "Cover yourself up and you will sleep."

She did not speak. Suddenly she realized how far away was the ship, that no one in the world knew where she was; that she did not know herself. This, at last, was real.

"Take off your shoes," he whispered. As she did not move, he said: "You are very tired," and stooping down removed her shoes one by one and stood them together beside the bed.

"Now, lie down," he said, "and go to sleep."

She pulled her coat off the rail, spread it lightly over her knees, curled her feet under her and lay down. She looked like a child.

"I'm all right," she said. "Thank you."

He stood silent, smiling down at her. Then suddenly he stooped. She felt the weight of his arms, his cheek against her face. With all her strength, she pressed her hands against his shoulders. "Please," she cried, "please . . ."

He let her go, abruptly; he was kneeling beside the bed. After a moment, he said: "What is your name?" She heard the note of laughter in his voice.

She turned her head and looked at him. "Frances Vernon," she said and, in spite of herself, she smiled.

Very gently, with one finger, he smoothed back a strand of hair from her cheek. Suddenly grave, she turned her face away, towards the window. She was trembling. For about a minute there was silence and then he rose to his feet. At that she turned, looking up at him as he stood above her.

"They call me Fanny," she said.

"Fanny," he repeated and, immediately, was beside her, kneeling as before. She pushed a hand against his face. "I must think! I must think!" she cried.

There was silence, and no movement. Then he said gently, hurriedly, "I am coming to England in the winter. You know that? You remember? Oh, Fanny," he dropped his face into the hollow of her shoulder, "you are so beautiful, so beautiful. You have something the women here they have not. And you —"

She felt his sudden pause and waited, trembling; "And I?" she prompted.

"And you —" he said. "I know. I see. You have missed it all."

The silence was tense and rough, like words held back in the throat. Then Fanny said slowly, "I don't know you."

She heard him laugh. "Oh, Fanny *pateta* . . . how will you know me? In a salon? No woman knows a man . . . except like this. Don't you know that? Don't you know that, Fanny?"

"What did you call me?" she asked.

"*Pateta* — silly, foolish. You are that, are you not, Fanny?"

"Perhaps. Yes," she said, "I am."

"Look at me," he said. "Turn your head," but she held her face averted against the thin strength of his hand. "Please, Fanny . . ."

She turned suddenly, meeting his eyes. "Salvador," she said, speaking hurriedly, "that's your name, isn't it? I want you to go now. I am very English. I must think. It is all my fault. I —"

"You will kiss me," he said and took her face in his hand. "Like this."

She wrenched her head away; tears of vexation and excitement ran down her face. "Do what you like," she cried and heard her voice break angrily. "After today, I shall not see you."

In the silence that followed, she felt him draw away. "*Au revoir*, Fanny," he said. "After the bull-fight, you will wait in the box and I will come to you, yes?"

She did not reply and the smile left his voice and he said sharply: "You will wait, yes? You would not run away? You would not do that, Fanny?"

She shook her head. "No. I will wait."

"And then you will tell me where in London I shall find you, yes?"

"Yes."

"And you will think of me with — *tenoura*?"

"I don't know what that is?"

"*Tenoura*, it is —" He hesitated, "I think it is — tenderness."

Fanny blinked: something was hurting her throat. "Yes," she said.

The latch closed and she heard the descending echo of his feet on the wooden stairs.

Colonel Graft was at the gangway when Fanny came aboard at nearly nine o'clock, a rather fussed Colonel Graft, a Colonel Graft somewhat magnified by the dusk. "My dear young lady! We almost thought one of those young Dago film-star chaps had abducted you —"

"Where's Lucien?" asked Fanny; her voice dead.

"He was here a minute ago. The rest have gone down to dinner. There he is!" A few yards away, a dark blur was just distinguishable beside the rail. "Here's your wife, sir. Here she is, sir," called Colonel Graft, holding Fanny by the elbow.

The figure unmistakably was Lucien. "My dear Fanny, where in God's name —"

"I went to see a bull-fight," said Fanny quickly.

"Take her down, sir; she's cold; she's shivering."

Colonel Graft patted Fanny's arm and then turned his face towards the lighted harbour. "Goodbye, little Portugal. You've given us a pleasant day — a very pleasant day." He turned again to Fanny: "And you, my dear, what did you do with yourself? Oh, yes, you went to the bull-fight. By Jove —" his voice dropped, "then you saw . . . poor chap . . . the Purser was there . . . said he was one of their crack bull-fighters. By Jove! That's upset you. I saw something very similar once in the polo field. Pony fell and fellow caught his head, broke his neck . . . but this chap, they say the bull got him . . . poor devil . . . they say when the horse falls . . ."

"Colonel Graft!" cried Fanny. She was gripping the rail as if the ship was sinking and she with it. "Go down and order me a cocktail. No, a whisky and soda."

"Right. Just the thing."

"I'll go," said Lucien, slightly shocked by his wife's peremptoriness.

At the top of the companionway, Colonel Graft turned to Lucien. "She's upset," he whispered, "saw it in a minute . . ."

Fanny watched the darkening pile of the town, threaded street by street with light as the dusk deepened. In one of those houses, he was lying; there would be thick voices and eyes red with weeping; those who had known him all his life would be about him, those who had known him "since a little boy" — shadow people born of her imagination, pale ghosts of their breathing counterparts, among whom he that was dead seemed most alive.

Something moaned: it was the ship's siren; a raucous gasp which swelled and spread and burst at last into a bellowing flower of sound — remote and mindless — suspended above the harbour.

CHAPTER
TEN

The Lovely Evening

It wasn't lovely, really. But it could have been: all the ingredients were there, pressed down and overflowing.

". . . Like a stage set," Brigitte had said, looking about her: the dark lake, the shadowy mountains, the skeins of light below. Over the vines hung a single electric bulb; breeze-swayed shadows trailed across the stone. Little tables, ghost-white cloths, wine in carafes . . . And music (too loud for Sarah but not, it seemed, for the girls).

"Do you eat out here every night?" asked Miranda.

"Yes, if it doesn't rain."

"Oh, goodness . . ." Miranda breathed.

Sarah laughed: she had wanted "Italy" to be like this. It wasn't always. There had been windy nights when the tablecloths flew up and napkins slithered away into shadows: when the gay Campari umbrellas, threshing a little, swayed from their moorings and suddenly took wing; there had been nights of mist — the lake "perspiring": and nights of sudden thunder storms, which blew up without warning — crashing about between the peaks. On such occasions, one ate upstairs in a white-washed dining room, hung with last year's calendars. Then the place looked what it was — a village trattoria run by peasants, clean but second-rate. "Is it anything like you imagined?"

"Better," Miranda cried, "a thousand times better. Absolute heaven . . ."

How lovely their skins were, Sarah thought, marble-smooth with a patina of silvery shadows which slid quicksilver when they laughed or spoke. Miranda was Sarah's daughter; Brigitta — her daughter's friend.

"It isn't a smart place."

"Who wants a smart place? It's heaven!"

"You know," Brigitta went on, wrinkling her nose, "it's like a night club ought to be but isn't."

"Do you go to night clubs?" asked Sarah, surprised. Brigitta was just sixteen.

"No, I don't really," Brigitta admitted, laughing. "But you know what I mean — coffee bar places all done up with moonlight and imitation vine leaves. I mean," again she looked about her, "— this is the whole thing itself."

"It's very quiet up here," Sarah warned them, "you don't think you'll be bored?"

"Bored!" exclaimed Miranda, "darling Mummy, don't be *too* silly . . ." She laughed delightedly, catching her breath, "How long can we stay?"

"Three weeks."

"Sure you can afford it?"

"Yes, if we stay *here*."

"Tomorrow, may we swim in the lake?"

"Of course, if you don't mind the climb back."

"We've brought our painting things. At least, Brigitta has."

"Good," Sarah hesitated. "No young men, I'm afraid. At least, I don't know any . . ."

"Young men!" Brigitta gave a little snort: again she wrinkled her nose (really, thought Sarah, she's quite enchanting — that honey-gold skin, that honey-fair hair . . .).

"We've come for a holiday — we want a rest from all that."

All what? — wondered Sarah, amused.

The music stopped and, in the silence, a night-jar sounded its single calling note.

"What's that?"

"A bird."

"Yes," breathed Miranda, "It's a deep country: you almost forget." She lifted her eyes to the shadowy mountains and breathed in the mountain air. "Heaven . . ." she murmured again.

Brigitta turned her head and gazed across the courtyard at the lighted kitchen door: a young man came out and stood against the lintel. His white shirt gleamed in the dusk, a hint of gold light in the hair; and the pale face, caught sharply by the sideways gleam from the kitchen seemed curiously still.

"Who's that?" Brigitta asked.

Sarah narrowed her eyes: "Luigi, I think. The youngest son. I don't know him. He lives in Bolzano and has just come home for a rest . . ."

"Who else is there?"

"Candido. And a married daughter with a baby. And a boy called Nino. And Giuseppe . . ." Nice boys, all of them, she reflected, but a little shy of strangers.

"Do they —" asked Brigitta lightly, "ever come and sit out here or dance or anything?"

"Sometimes. Not often. They're rather serious . . ."

"Who does dance?" asked Miranda.

"The village boys. On Sunday nights."

Miranda inclined her head towards Luigi: "Isn't he a village boy?"

Sarah laughed, "No, he's a cut above."

"Tonight is Sunday," Brigitta pointed out.

The canned music, relayed from a loud speaker, blared out into the darkness above the lake: the softly moving air, neither hot nor cold, seemed to vibrate with it.

"Get up and dance yourselves," suggested Sarah suddenly.

"Who with?" — they looked appalled.

"With each other. The girls here often do."

"What," exclaimed Brigitta shocked, "me dance with Miranda ?"

"Why not?"

"Two girls dancing together?"

"Why not?"

"Good gracious," Miranda exclaimed, "We couldn't. I mean we'd have to practise first . . ." But her feet began tapping to the music.

"I will, if you will," said Brigitta, raising her voice (. . . little animated golden face, pony tail jumping on her shoulders).

"Oh, don't let's," exclaimed Miranda laughing. They both became silent, Brigitta swaying her shoulders, Miranda tapping her foot.

Luigi stirred suddenly and moved towards them across the courtyard. He walked purposefully with a swift, lithe step but he did not (as Sarah hoped) pause beside their table but went on past them to a chair beyond the light. He sank down into it — enfolded in darkness he sat, withdrawn and silent — too far to be with them, too near to be apart.

A party arrived, seven in all: village boys and three girls. The boys wore their best clothes — clean, white shirts and dark trousers: the girls wore blouses and skirts. They ordered white wine in a carafe and grouped themselves about a table.

"*Permesso?*" A tall young man stood at Sarah's side: he was asking to borrow a chair; as he spoke his glance slid quickly from one girl to another. "*Prego,*" murmured Sarah politely, trying not to smile: there were chairs and tables to spare at other tables.

"Please, do," cried Brigitta — a little too animated, a little too eager. He stared at her, chair in hand, without speaking, then, bowing, gravely turned, and walked away. It was almost a snub, not quite. Brigitta coloured and Miranda looked down at her plate.

Sarah leaned forward and began to talk (. . . conceited young ass, she thought); she spoke quickly, comfortingly describing places they must see, expeditions she had done and would do again with them; she told them about the play-suits one could buy beside the lake — and the funny, large straw hats: about the church processions in the village: about the alpine flowers.

They smiled brightly, sweetly, but they did not seem to be listening. They would laugh suddenly at the wrong places for no reason and Brigitta — one ear on the music — beat time with her fork.

The dancing began. Casually, correctly, the couples rose from the further table — one man left sitting alone. The girls' eyes, almost absently slid sideways: they knew good dancing when they saw it — the steady hips, the controlled, bored sway.

Then, out of the shadows, a voice spoke. Sarah, startled, turned quickly: she had forgotten about Luigi. "You do not like to dance?"

He was leaning forward in his chair, his hands lightly clasped above his parted knees, his drawn face lifted towards the light.

"I?" stammered Sarah, and gave a little laugh (was the "you" in this case, singular or plural?). "No thank you —" she glanced across at the girls, "but perhaps the *Signorine* . . ."

He rose immediately and came over to Miranda. She stood up, with a half smile, and glided off in his arms.

Little Brigitta dissolved into laughter: the ice was broken — now all would be well. "He asked *you* to dance," she whispered giggling, "do they always do that?"

Sarah hesitated: "Always do what?" she asked, after a moment.

Brigitta saw her mistake. "I mean —" she began and blushed.

"I know what you mean," exclaimed Sarah, laughing, "I'm not hurt really! Yes, they've got charming manners . . ."

"I didn't mean —"

"I know you didn't, I know you didn't!" she squeezed Brigitta's hand.

"Oh, *thank* you for having me," exclaimed Brigitta suddenly, and her blue eyes filled with tears.

Miranda danced shyly. Slender, dark-haired, golden-skinned — she seemed more Italianate than the fair boy who guided her. The couple moved softly, cut with trembling shadow; the arc lamp, slung on wires, glared down from above. "Like a scene from a play," said Brigitta again, "like something from opera. And I'm part of it," she added ecstatically on a note of surprise.

You are indeed, thought Sarah: the peasant skirt of white and scarlet, the little, short-sleeved blouse. Strange and charming quirk of fashion which made their clothes so right. Miranda, too, swam into the setting correctly dressed for the part.

The music stopped and, after a moment, the other two came back. Sarah leaned sideways in a gesture of welcome, and pulled up Luigi's chair. He sank into it, making one of the party.

"My feet hurt," he said.

The conversation, stilted but friendly, continued in Italian. How old was Miranda? How old was Brigitta? How old — "How old are you?" Sarah hastened to ask. Luigi was twenty-nine.

"*Permesso?*" Sarah looked up: the odd man out from the other table had emerged again from the shadows. He stood beside them, two paces distant, bowing towards Miranda. Miranda hesitated: it was Brigitta's turn. But Brigitta, beating soft time to the music, seemed lost in thought.

Nobody spoke. Nobody moved. And Miranda glided off. If only, Sarah worried, I could speak better Italian . . . She glanced at Luigi but Luigi did not look up; he had taken out his pocket-book and was thumbing through the leaves; smiling shyly, at last he produced a photograph. "You like to see?" he said.

Sarah stared at the picture without seeing it. Suddenly she looked. "Oh," she exclaimed and began to laugh. It was a picture of his motorbike, standing up alone.

Luigi looked anxious. "It is funny?"

"No, no. Not in the least." She said in Italian, "It's lovely. But . . ." she hesitated, searching for words, "I thought to see your fiancée —"

"I have no fiancée," he said.

"Or your wife, or your mother . . ."

He interrupted then, leaning across her, and began to describe the machine. He spoke quickly with a kind of modest pride. When he spoke of the gear box his voice deepened: there was a tenderness in it and something like awe. "You like?" he said, suddenly in English, staring into her face.

"Very much, yes."

"To ride with this on the mountain roads?"

"Well," began Sarah doubtfully just as the music stopped. Miranda returned, then, dropped by her partner, and the picture was passed to her. "You like?" Luigi repeated. Miranda liked very much. They talked awhile of motorbikes and Brigitta did her share. The music then struck up again but none of the party moved. Luigi aired his English, the girls politely helped.

Again the tall stranger approached and again he asked Miranda. "Oh dear," thought Sarah as the couple swept away; there was nothing she could do. Then at last Luigi stood up. Brigitta's lips parted, but he did not look her way. "I change my shoes," he announced and, bowing slightly, he left the table. They watched in silence as he crossed the courtyard.

"His feet hurt," said Sarah at last.

"Oh?" Brigitta said.

"Where's your sketch-book?" Sarah went on brightly (Brigitta's sketch-book, she thought suddenly, could lie on the table between them: Luigi would be impressed). But Brigitta merely shrugged. "In my room some-where," she muttered and went on tapping her fork.

The music stopped, Miranda came back to the table. Gaily, Brigitta looked up, "How was that one?" she asked.

"Not bad. Better than Luigi. Luigi's awful. He doesn't lead . . . Let's go and look at the lake."

They went out of the gate and into the shadowed lane. They stood against the parapet, looking down. It was still warm from the sun. Luigi joined them as the moon rose above the water. They talked of this and that . . . of dancing at home, of jazz and jive. "Jive? Show me," Luigi said. And, laughing, they showed him. Dancing together in the dust, flicked here and there by light, wary as fencers, light as flower-petals — it was charming.

Sarah moved away. She crossed the lane, into the courtyard. She went back to the table to fetch her bag. It was not there. Stooping, she felt on the chairs.

"You lose something?"

It was Luigi again. Sarah felt suddenly irritated: why had he left the girls?

"My bag. It's all right, it's here . . ."

She looked around; Miranda was dancing again. Where was Brigitta? Then she saw her, coming towards them. Forlorn and slightly embarrassed — threading her way through the dancers. "Get her, Luigi" urged Sarah. He went forward quickly and brought Brigitta to the table. Politely, he pulled out a chair.

They sat down together — Brigitta and Sarah. Luigi went off to fetch wine.

"Tired, Brigitta?"

"No, not at all."

Miranda came back. Down she flopped, panting a little and looking rather pink. "Gosh —" she exclaimed.

"How was that one?" asked Brigitta.

"Awful. He smelt of something. Not garlic exactly, more like chives . . ." and she fanned her face with her hand. Comforting Brigitta . . .

"Oh," said Brigitta. "Poor Miranda . . ."

"Yes, it was ghastly."

"Ghastly!" Brigitta repeated. They both became silent. Brigitta powdered her nose.

When Luigi came back with the wine he drew up a chair and leaned forward. "I go tomorrow," he said.

"Where?" they asked in chorus.

"Back to Bolzano. My work. A very fine city," he told them, "with mountains around and palms." He took out a diary, "I send you a postcard. Please will you write here the name?" (Who was he addressing? Brigitta or

Miranda?) Brigitta turned away; she stooped right down, below the level of the table as though to fasten a shoe.

"Here, Brigitta" said Sarah, pushing the notebook across, "he wants you to write your name."

"My name?" exclaimed Brigitta, as though she had not heard.

"Yes," said Sarah, "to send you a postcard."

"Me?"

"*And* Miranda. A picture of his town."

"Oh," said Brigitta, blushing. "There," she exclaimed, as she laid down the pen. She seemed happy again, at ease . . .

"Brigeet-ta . . ." repeated Luigi.

"What time do you go?"

"Early. Tomorrow early. Before you will be awake."

Miranda wrote her name and Sarah, too, wrote hers.

Luigi studied the page. His face seemed drawn again, a little tired. "*Grazie*," he said and put away the book.

"You are glad to be back?" asked Sarah.

He shrugged. "Here . . . there, it is the same." He stared at her, suddenly brooding. "You believe in a future life?"

"In a what?" said Sarah, startled.

He repeated the phrase in Italian.

Sarah floundered. "Yes, of course. I mean, I think so. It depends . . ."

"What does he say?" asked Brigitta. Sarah translated.

"Oh," gasped Brigitta delightedly. She leaned forward across the table, grasping her elbows: "You mean life after death?" she said. It was easy to say in Italian: she looked pleased that it rolled off her tongue. "Or," she added to Sarah, in English, "does he mean ghosts?"

"Ghosts?" repeated Luigi.

Out came the pocket vocabulary. They were off: pages turning furiously, fingers pointing, snatchings, arguments, laughter . . . Miranda joined in and they ran the gamut: premonitions, astral bodies, fortune-telling, astrology and yoga. I could leave them now, Sarah thought — I really could — and slide away to bed. She had done her best — expounded her philosophy and told her one true ghost story; translated Luigi to the girls, and the girls to Luigi. Things, she thought, would run on from here; and without her presence, Luigi might act as host.

She stood up. Luigi stood up, too. He looked a little startled. It's all right, Sarah wanted to say, the girls won't eat you . . . She put out her hand: "Goodnight, I'm very tired. And goodbye, too. Are you really going tomorrow?" He looked rather white, his face shrunken . . . She wondered if he had been ill. "Perhaps we shall meet again?"

"Perhaps," he said.

"Need we come?" asked Miranda.

"Of course not. Stay and dance." Sarah looked at Luigi. "You'll look after them?" And find a partner for Brigitta? But she did not say it, instead she took his hand: "Goodbye, again. One day, we'll come to Bolzano."

She walked away across the courtyard, threading her way among the dancers. She climbed the stone steps which led to the first floor. From the balcony she looked down. It was a romantic scene — no film studio could have done better — the shadows of the vine leaves, artificial light and moonlight. Brigitta, Miranda and Luigi splashed about the table. The dancing couples, the air alive with music . . .

In she went, and upstairs to her room: tin basin, toothpaste, peeling shutters . . . her nightdress laid out. She undressed, worried. Miranda was all right. Miranda was two years older — Italian village boys meant little to her.

But Brigitta — that was different: Brigitta was trying her wings . . .

One more look, before she went asleep. Across the passage to the girls' room, opposite, the creaking door, the ghostly beds — beds used as tables, covered with half-seen objects: paint-boxes, books, sewing materials . . . At the window, standing in the darkness, she pulled the lace curtain aside. The same scene — moonlight, lamplight and shadow, revolving couples — but, at the further table, under the arbour, Brigitta sat alone — still, sprawled, silent, the dress like a crumpled rose. Miranda, she saw, was dancing. Not with Luigi. Luigi, she realized had gone. And now what? Nothing she could do.

As she watched Brigitta rose and ran across the courtyard to the house, threading her way through the dancers. "Oh, don't do that," Sarah wanted to cry, "stay a little longer . . ." But Brigitta now had reached the courtyard steps — up she came, two stairs at a time. Sarah drew back from the window, and quickly ran out of the room. Across the passage she flashed, and shut her bedroom door.

Footsteps, up the stairs, along the passage. Running footsteps. A kind of gasp. A door creaked open. A door slammed shut. And there she would be, thought Sarah, lying across the bed . . .

Knock on the door and go in? No, she couldn't do that. She must not have seen; she must not have noticed. Sarah began to undress.

More footsteps. Sarah listened. Here now, was Miranda. Running, running — leaving her partners, leaving the dance. How kind they are to each other, Sarah thought. Miranda will make it right. The creak of the door. The slam of the door. Voices, voices. Sarah climbed into bed. They will talk, she thought, into the small hours.

Next day, Brigitta went sketching. She wanted to be alone. At lunch, she was quiet. At dinner, quieter still. They spoiled her, they paid her compliments, they tried to make her laugh. "It's no good, Mother," explained Miranda when they found themselves alone. "It isn't that. She knows she's pretty. She said last night "It isn't that I'm not pretty; if I were ugly, I'd understand. What's wrong with me?" she said."

"But there's nothing wrong with her!" Sarah exclaimed hotly. "She's adorable. Just because one stupid boy —"

"Luigi isn't a boy. And he didn't want to dance. His feet really hurt him . . ."

"Then why," cried Sarah, "did he ask me?"

"Out of politeness, I suppose, I don't know. I mean, he didn't know then that his feet would hurt."

"Nonsense," cried Sarah, "then why did he dance with you?"

"Out of politeness again. You practically asked him to."

"But why you and not Brigitta?"

"Because I was your daughter, I suppose. I tell you, Mother, he didn't really want to dance. He was awfully dull. Perhaps he thought that to dance with me was enough."

"But the others?"

"I think they thought that she just wasn't dancing. I mean, there she was sitting and there was Luigi at the table —"

"I know," said Sarah glumly, "it was all Luigi's fault."

"Luigi liked her. He called her *"bella bambina"*. But he thought her rather young."

"Well, she is young," said Sarah, "what's wrong with that?" "He thought me young, too," Miranda said, "but not as young."

"Brilliant," remarked Sarah, "considering he'd just asked both your ages."

"He said you looked thirty-five."

"That was kind of him. Look here, Miranda, if he sends you a postcard, don't —"

"Of course, I won't. I'm not so silly. I wouldn't show her. I'd tear it up."

"Perhaps," mused Sarah, "he'll send her one, too."

"He will, I think. He liked her. He liked her just as much as he liked me."

"Yes," cried Sarah, "that's it. That's what she's got to know. Explain to her, too, this thing about the others."

"I did. I have. And she saw the point. And now if we *both* get a postcard —"

"You think it'll be all right?"

"Yes, quite. I know it. As long as it isn't *just* me —"

"But did she *like* Luigi?" asked Sarah, after a pause.

"Not much. No."

"Did you?"

"No. Not much." At Sarah's expression, Miranda began to laugh. "That isn't the point, at all!"

But neither of the girls got a postcard. Sarah got it: an aerial view of Bolzano, set about with mountains, studded with palm trees. Tactful Luigi, this was a masterstroke. She set about to read it.

"Do show us," complained Miranda laughing. Both of the girls seemed amused.

"Be quiet. It's in Italian —"

"Oh, go on. What does he say?"

"Leave me alone. You're both jealous."

"Go on. Read it aloud."

Sarah frowned: "'*Per ricordo tenero*'," she said, "Really, the writing's awful . . . '*di una conversazione* —'" she paused, "Oh, I don't know . . ." she threw down the card, "It does look rather lovely. Look at the palm trees . . ."

"You're blushing," said Miranda. Idly with two fingers she picked up the postcard. "'*all una conversazione interotta*'," she read aloud. "What does it mean?"

"In memory of a pleasant conversation — something like that." Sarah began to pour out the coffee. "Two lumps, Brigitta?"

"'*Interotta*' doesn't mean pleasant," announced Miranda, squinting sideways at the card.

"Doesn't it?"

"You know it doesn't. It means 'broken' or 'interrupted' or something. What's 'tenero'?" she asked.

"'*Tenero*'?" repeated Sarah vaguely, "Here, darling, take your cup and pass the rolls to Brigitta . . ."

"'*Tenero*' . . ." repeated Miranda dreamily. "I know — Maria said it last night — about the veal. She said the veal was, '*molto tenero*' — very tender."

"Oh," said Sarah. She glanced across at Brigitta's face — parted lips, wide, mystified eyes.

"The correct translation of this sentence," announced Miranda deliberately, "is — 'in tender memory of an interrupted conversation.'" She looked sideways at her mother, her mouth lifted, "'From one who . . .' — really, Mummy." There was moment's silence. "So it was you after all!"

Brigitta began to laugh. Delightedly, happily, she gulped her coffee.

"Careful, Brigitta," said Sarah.

"Honestly," said Miranda. She looked genuinely indignant. "And you made me dance with him!"

Brigitta began to choke. Pink in the face, eyes brimming, she was coughing and laughing as well. They patted her on the back. "He asked you to dance," she gasped, when at last she could speak. "Don't you remember? He asked you to dance, first? It was her all the time," she exclaimed again to Miranda. "And neither of us . . ." she chanted. She leaned back in her chair, softly clicking her fingers: back and forth she tipped, swaying as though to music. "Neither of us . . . neither of us . . ."

CHAPTER ELEVEN

Lake Trout

"Rose darling," said Ella with a small exasperated laugh, "do eat up your fish; we can't spend all night over dinner: if we're going to pack."

"I know," said Rose. She gazed out across the lake to the mountains: peak upon peak they rose beside the setting sun — the profile of the range in one short week had become curiously beloved and familiar — "I wish we weren't."

"But you did want to take in Florence?"

"I did — yes."

"You used to love it. I mean, you *can't* go back to London without a glimpse of your beloved frescoes . . ."

"Why not?" asked Rose — delicately she pronounced the "why" with its hint of a phantom "H".

But Ella was used to this voice — the whole elocutionary miracle of Rose's art: "Darling," she said indulgently and laughed again, "you're not in one of your moods?"

"I think I am," said Rose lightly. Pensively she flicked off a sliver of fish, touched it with mayonnaise, and let it lie . . . salmon trout, pink as the pale vin-rosé in her glass, pink as that floating cloud above the mountain, pink as the sky-reflecting lake.

"We're not obliged to go tomorrow — not if you don't want to. I mean, would you rather stay on here? We've got until Friday. Just say, Rose."

"No," said Rose quickly, "I want to go." And suddenly she blushed: had Ella sensed that unspoken conditional — ". . . now you have come".

"Of course," Ella went on, glancing about her, "it's very picturesque . . ."

On the waterfront beyond their terrace, the fishermen were mending nets: gossamer-fine in pastel pinks and livid greens they hung, cobweb-like, among the jacaranda trees. Floss silk? Nylon? Of what could they be made? And the way the house stood over the water, the ochre-rose facade, the cypresses, the steep reflections . . .

"Charming," said Ella, looking about her; there was wonder in her voice —" clever of you to find it, darling. All by yourself!"

As though I were a child, thought Rose, or a moron — and so I am in some ways I suppose, compared with Ella. She glanced sideways at their reflections in the plate glass of the swing doors: two middle-aged women, neither particularly slim, neither particularly handsome. Ella had "style", of course: that arching nose and taut white hair. There was a continental "something" about Ella — the careless fling of cream lace, half scarf, half mantilla; the chunky lapis-lazuli earrings; the shrivelled, expressive hands with their one good ring. Of the two, it was Ella who would at once be taken for the celebrity.

"Why didn't you let Felix tell them who you were?" Ella was saying now.

Rose looked startled. "You mean here? At this hotel?"

"Of course. You'd have got better service. He'd have been interested."

"Who would?"

"The proprietor — Hercules, or whatever he's called. They have this album, not the hotel register — a kind of visitors' book. They'd have been thrilled."

Rose took a sip of wine; her eyelids quivered: she had still never quite accepted her fame — it seemed to her, at times, some kind of trick that she had played on the public and that one day they would find her out: the spinster teacher of elocution who, at thirty-five, had taken to the boards. She had married since, of course, and she could convey character — she knew that — but so could many others: it was her stardom which surprised her: this personal magic others found so touching and so delightfully amusing. "High comedy" they called it.

She had never been a pretty girl, never possessed what the moderns called "sex-appeal" and she must, she realized, have been about the most colourless, unpromising student who ever slid obliquely into drama school. Yet, here she was, twenty years later, at the top of her profession: "Couldn't you," tired managers would say to aspiring playwrights, "try to be a little more adventurous? Try something a bit more daring — with a good part, say, for Rose Emery . . ."

"They wouldn't have heard of me here," she said uncertainly.

"Darling," exclaimed Ella, "don't overdo it."

"Overdo what?"

"The modesty business. You might as well say that they never heard of Danny Kaye because he lived in Hollywood. What about 'The Stranger'? And 'Night's Lodging'? What about 'Swings and Roundabouts'? There is such a thing, you know, as universal distribution. You see what I mean? Just accept it."

"I do," said Rose, "but —"

"But what?"

"I couldn't have had better service."

"That ghastly room?"

"It looks out over the lake. I wanted it."

"And no bathroom —"

"There is a bathroom," murmured Rose.

"Nowhere to sit. They could at least have moved out that awful commode and given you an easy chair or something."

"I sit out on the terrace," said Rose, "or on the balcony. I've been happy here," she added obstinately.

("All right," Whittaker had conceded at last, "get right away from everything for a couple of weeks or so. Yes: find yourself a bit. Stand on your own feet. Cut loose from the leading strings. Even —" here he had jerked his head towards the waiting-room door to where, on that occasion, Ella had been banished, "even your friend Mrs Fleming. You'll be all right — you can work on the play back in London — you'll have plenty of time, if rehearsals don't start till the twenty-seventh . . .")

He was a good doctor but had he quite realized — Ella had asked herself — how unused Rose was nowadays to doing anything "on her own"? There had always been

George, her husband. And Ella herself, of course: Ella, her faithful stand-in for so many years. Or Florrie, her dresser: "You take it easy, lovey," Florrie would say, "nothing to worry about: you're lovely — everybody says you are and we'll soon get that grease-spot off your yellow . . ." And dear George, a little pompous, arranging a managers' evening: "a table for eight, please. Not too near the band. Oh yes, the usual: Chateau Guyonne '47. Cooled, if you please: last time it was a little . . . Thank you." Or there was kind Mrs Gimbell, spectacles on nose, answering the telephone, whipping through her mail: "Miss Emery asks me to tell you that she would be 'delighted'; that she would be 'unable'; that she was 'rehearsing'; that she was 'unwell'; that she was 'on tour'; that she would 'read your play over the weekend' . . ."

"You see, darling," Ella was saying breathily, "we were a bit worried, George and I." (George and I . . . Rose smiled.) "I mean Whittaker sending you off on your own like that. I can see it would work for some people and it's worked for you in a way. He's a good doctor, we thought, but —" Ella laughed again — that laugh which through the years Rose had grown to know so well — "but he doesn't *quite* know our Rose."

"What do you mean by 'he doesn't quite know' . . . ?"

"Well, darling. We were thinking of that time you ran off to Corsica by yourself. I mean . . . well, it was a bit of a muddle, wasn't it?"

"I had to get away . . ."

"I know, darling. But it was a bit hard on George — you'd only just been married."

165

"Yes," said Rose, "but I couldn't help it. I —" she hesitated. "It was hard for both of us."

"Well, never mind. That's all past and done with. You and George have settled down splendidly: he adores you, you know."

"Yes," said Rose, "I know."

But did he adore her? Would it not be more true to say that Rose, for George, had become a way of life? Contracts, billings, first nights — these, through the years, had become his raison d'être. To George, a retired soldier, the theatre world spelled glamour, and sustaining Rose's stardom had become his new career. But as a person, thought Rose, I rather irritate George: he has never quite seen what all the fuss was about. Nor have I, really, if it comes to that . . .

"He cares more for your success," Ella went on warmly, "than he ever did for all his own regimental business."

"What makes you say that?" asked Rose.

"He explained it all. One night when we were talking."

"Oh," said Rose, and sighed. People talked too much — especially to Ella. Ella had a social sense which carried her like a sail, whereas she, Rose — painfully shy — could just slide by on her name. Dear George: he was very kind, but if only when she was rehearsing he would forbear to interfere. Not with her acting. That never. But with extraneous, seemingly domestic problems; if only he would try to understand a little better the nervous tension with which, line by line, day by day, week by week, one drew out the secret of a part; erecting the invisible structure which, once secure, would earn for them all that heady sense of achievement. And earn it in sums which still, to George, seemed too substantial to be quite seemly: ". . . take a field marshal a couple of years to make this," he would grumble, poring over a contract. Now, poor George, he was worried . . .

"You see, darling," Ella was pointing out — more in sorrow than in anger, "you can't *go on* turning down plays —"

"I know," said Rose.

"People understand you've had a bit of a breakdown but you can't keep managers hanging about indefinitely. They aren't all like Felix, you know."

"I know," said Rose.

"George is scared stiff about the income tax. But it isn't only that: people are afraid that perhaps, well, afraid . . . that you may never —"

"I know, I know —" cried Rose, "I know . . ." the last words were nearly a wail.

"Have you written to Felix?"

"Not yet." Again Rose coloured slightly and touched the clasp of her handbag. "At least —"

Ella looked alarmed: her voice sharpened. "You are going to do the play?"

"Yes. Yes," cried Rose hurriedly, "of course." But her eyes slid away from Ella's questioning stare: it wasn't a lie — at least, not yet — that desperate letter to Felix still lay unposted in an outer fold of her handbag.

"But you look much better," Ella added. She seemed a little puzzled.

"I am better," said Rose.

"Has something happened?"

"What sort of thing?"

"A little romance or something?"

"Really, Ella —" exclaimed Rose, "with this face? — at fifty-six?"

Ella was silent for a moment. Then she said matter-of-factly, "Your face is all right: there is something about it. I don't know what it is. Nor does anybody else, for that matter. Not charm, exactly, more a kind of oddness, or perhaps it is charm, of a kind. I don't know . . ."

"People have always been kind to me here."

"But people are always kind to you."

"To me? Or to Rose Emery?" She spoke quickly for once, almost sharply.

Ella stared. "Yes, you have changed," she remarked thoughtfully. Rose was silent. "Is that", Ella went on, "why you have signed in as Mrs George Pullen?"

"It is my name," said Rose.

But after that journey, Mrs G.P. had not had the nerve to ask for anything: two wrongly advised changes and all that luggage! Dear Florrie, a wonderful packer but, after years of experience with theatre people, she had never even *contemplated* such a dangerous proceeding as "travelling light". At any rate, Rose had managed (with infinite tact) to evade the cabin trunk. That, at least, was something. All the same, she would not have liked Ella to know, nor George either, how rusty her Italian had become, and how useless at times her excellent French; how hesitatingly she had answered the customs (arousing instant suspicion) and how recklessly dealt with loose change: what to tip in francs — what to tip in

lire? *Who* to tip — and when? That porter at Domodossola:
she could see his face now, suffused and threatening; the
stream of invective had been happily unintelligible, but
she trembled still at the thought of that voice; it had been
so long, if ever, since a fellow human being had railed at
her in anger. It's no good, she had thought then, I can't
do it: I can no longer manage alone . . . No, on that first
night, she had not been in the mood to ask for anything:
the little room had been enough, with its starched shreds
of lace curtain and its healing view of the lake.

But Ella was right, she could have asked for
coat-hangers. A scene came to mind — unimportant but
revealing: Erculano, the proprietor, standing in the
doorway of her bedroom, a little anxious, ponderously
kind: "Anything you want you will ring? The bell is
there. Sometimes after dinner," here his voice had
become hesitant, almost timid; in the large, pale face,
she had seen a kind of uncertainty, "the water is not so
hot. But in the *morning* . . ." She had recognized
suddenly, as in herself, an anxious will to please: other
people, she realized had their "first nights"; she and this
nice top-heavy man had this much in common — for
either to live, the public must approve. She had smiled
and said quickly, "It doesn't matter. I don't need
anything. It's lovely here . . . goodnight."

But she had slept badly that first night: tossing and
turning, she had felt she was still in the train. She had
awoken tired, but Celestina, a little gruff-voiced maid,
had brought her rolls and coffee. Below her window, she
remembered, the lake had whispered and glistened;
shadows had danced on the ceiling. There had been

169

sunlight on the floor and sunlight on the mountains opposite: sitting up in bed, drinking her coffee, she had seen the tiny villages and the thread-like roads: she had seen blue chasms and soaring, misty slopes . . . She should cross the lake, she felt, faintly stirred by a first intimation of adventure; but how did one set about it? Tickets? Boats? She had thought then, nostalgically of Ella — Ella, her stand-in, who was always efficient and strangely gay, for one who sustained life on odd jobs, old friends and what she was amused to term her "gas-ring"; Ella, who so loved to travel and who could seldom afford to, nowadays, unless she travelled with Rose. If Ella were here, in twenty-four hours, she would know the inside story of every man, woman and child within a radius of miles, and Rose, in Ella's orbit, would suddenly feel at ease.

There had been a bleakness about unpacking for herself: no one to care whether her stockings and gloves went into the left-hand drawer or the right. Such decisions, if Florrie were here, would be of major importance: there would be a pleasant fuss. Rose's underclothing, unpacked by Rose, fell wanly into swathes — not at all as Florrie would have laid it. Her dresses, hung on hooks, looked curiously lifeless, insulted beyond protest. Even George's photograph had a surprised look, plonked on a crochet mat beside a curly shell. As she laid out her ivory brushes, she had caught a glimpse of her face in the ill-hung looking glass: it stared back at her like a frightened rabbit. "And that's what she is," she had realized, "this Mrs George Pullen, if she exists at all . . ." With fingers that trembled slightly, she had powdered her nose, tilted the mirror out of focus and had taken herself downstairs.

The luncheon room on that first morning had been full of foreigners, jabbering noisily — Italians, Austrians, Swiss and Germans (no English) — and they all seemed very much at home. Not so Rose. She was too used, she realized, to being greeted by name and led with bows to her table. She was suddenly aware, standing on the threshold, of the curious, unplaceable quaintness of her clothes and person which, where she was not known, was apt to make strangers smile. Erculano had come forward, of course, as soon as he perceived her; but her table was a little table, so she was bound to sit at it alone.

For two days she had borne it, keeping herself to herself, sliding inconspicuously from bedroom to dining room, dining room to terrace, terrace to village square; avoiding anyone who might involve her in the maddening local dialect. On the third morning, she had woken up in tears — Whittaker must be out of his mind: this is no way, she decided, to build up confidence — it was far more likely to destroy what little she had. Drying her eyes, she had dressed quickly and had taken out her writing case: this was one anxiety she *could* kill: "Dear Felix," she had scribbled — hurriedly, before she could relent, "it isn't that I do not like the play. Or the part. I do. It grieves me to say "no": the plain truth being (my dear kind friend) that I do not yet feel up to anything the size of Madame S. The responsibility, just at the moment, both on your behalf and mine, is more than I dare contemplate. But I am much better, and later hope to do a little filming. In the meantime, dear Felix, accept

171

my loving gratitude for all your patience and understanding. Forgive me. Rose."

She should have felt more peaceful after that, but she didn't: she had felt more lost than ever and had carried this letter about in her bag, sealed but unstamped, as a saboteur carries a bomb. Sometimes her steps were drawn towards the post-box in the hall; at other times, she hurried past as though that grinning slit were waiting to swallow her life. She had capitulated finally by cabling to Ella: "Heavenly here. Come soonest." So much for Whittaker, she had thought, as she handed the form across the desk. So much for managing alone.

The hall porter looked up at her and, smiling, she met his eyes: sad, wise, monkey eyes, they were, in a shrivelled monkey face. He spoke a little English. His name, she knew, was Giuseppe. "You like it here?" he had asked, having read the message. He had sensed her loneliness, she felt, and seemed surprised. "Very much, very much," she had assured him. (And, indeed, she was aware of the loveliness about her and a growing interest in exploring further. But one should be something, somebody . . . not a walking cypher.) "How does one cross the lake?" she had asked, to prolong the conversation. "I take you," he had replied quickly. "On the other side is my village. I go tomorrow. You would like?" Why not? Of course she would like: she had felt warmed suddenly by the shrivelled, kindly face — a face devoid of guile.

And it was on that morning she had found the bowl of primroses on her luncheon table instead of the vase of privet. "Celestina put them," Erculano explained, as

172

he piled up her plate, "you like?" Rose liked very much. She threw a quick glance round the other tables and was touched to see that no one else had primroses. Later that afternoon, on the quay, the small Austrian boy had lent her his second fishing rod. They had fished happily together for sprat-like shreds of silver and had talked in classroom French. When she came back in through the hall, dishevelled and slightly sunburnt, she had passed the post-box without a qualm. Erculano had cooked the small fish; and had come to her table for coffee after dinner, and had told her about his life . . .

"Of course," said Ella suddenly, breaking the silence, "he's a charming man."

Startled, Rose looked up, "Who is?"

"The proprietor. Hercules — or whatever he's called."

"Erculano," said Rose, "Erculano Orestes Mattino."

"He has a kind of presence," said Ella.

"Yes," said Rose. She glanced across to where he moved, grey-suited, amongst the tables: a large, gentle figure, stooping a little as though under the weight of his constant concern: a word here, a smile there; a plate removed, a dish proffered.

"He could be anybody," Ella pointed out, "if you see what I mean."

"Yes," agreed Rose.

Ella narrowed her eyes. She had noticed the stooped shoulders and a faint drag in the carefully placed footsteps. "He's getting on a bit," she said after a moment. "Would you say as much as seventy?"

"No," exclaimed Rose, rather too sharply.

"Well, very near it," Ella went on equably, "seventy I mean. It won't be long before that great kitchen gets too much for him. And all this waiting at table . . ."

"He enjoys that. It's his thing."

"Yes," agreed Ella, "he certainly has the touch!"

"And in the kitchen, he only deals with his trout. That nice son of his does the game and meat. And the daughter-in-law does the pasta. There *is* some other help: Celestina, for instance . . ."

"Well the place always seems full. And not particularly with tourists." She thought for a moment. "He must be making a packet."

"He isn't. Not enough bedrooms." He had explained this too to Rose: how, the house being built on a promontory, it was impossible to enlarge — he must depend, he had told her, on situation and his cuisine.

The day after he had cooked her tiny catch, he had shown her his kitchen: the great gleaming stove, the ikon above it with the frescoed Virgin, the warming racks, his collection of knives. His son and his son's wife had risen from their well-laid table: she had been introduced to his little grandchild. She had seen the famous salmon trout laid out on old stone slabs and the hose with which he washed them. Again she had been reminded of back-stage, star turns up without make-up, and work behind the scenes. He had taken up a knife and shown her how to gut; had described how the trout was cooked: the light stock, the white wine, the hint of tarragon . . . "Simple, a question of timing . . . when the eye falls out it is ready. It is good luck for me," he had gone on to say, "that the chief dish is quick to make. At all hours people come here, tired from the road — a small hors-d'oeuvre, a glass of wine and — presto! — the fish is done."

"You can't keep it hot?" Rose had asked.

"No, no. It would fall to pieces."

"Can you depend on the supply?"

He had looked puzzled at that: "I do not understand."

"I mean," Rose had tried to explain, "the daily catch. Doesn't it vary?"

"Ah," he had said, "the daily catch?" and had looked at her sideways; there had been mischief in his face and a hint of guilt, "that's another story."

"How do you mean?" asked Rose. She had felt a little startled.

He had smiled then, slyly, laying his knife against the silver scales — lovingly, he laid it, conspiratorially. "It is shy, this fish, and clever. For this fish, I dare not depend on the fishermen. You understand? I must have it every day . . ."

"Then how do you get it?" asked Rose.

He had hesitated a moment, his eyes on her face, as though he were summing her up. "I buy it," he said then, watching her expression, "lightly frozen, from the breeding pools up river."

Rose had been silent, taking this in. "But do you tell this to customers?" she had asked, after a moment.

"Ah, no —" it was his turn to look startled, "God forbid!"

"But you tell me?" There was a breathless catch in Rose's voice.

"Ah, you?" he had said thoughtfully, staring down at the flat of his knife as though he felt surprised. "You, Signora, are different."

"I am a customer."

He had laughed then and shrugged. "All the same — how can I say? — you are . . . well, somehow different . . ."

"But if they ask you outright?"

He laughed: "They do not. They see the lake. They see the nets. They see the fishermen."

"But if they did? I mean, they might — I asked you."

"With rod and line, I would say —" (he flung out an arm towards the lake in a stiff but dramatic gesture: he deepened his voice, acting the part) "very early, I would say — before you are awake."

Rose, still slightly startled, caught his amused eye and began to laugh. Delighted, he joined in her laughter, flinging down the knife which clattered on the slab. "There you have it," he said, "there you have it! That's what I'd say to those people who ask . . ." Suddenly, they were both laughing, almost helplessly without knowing quite why.

Rose wondered later why that laughter had so changed her mood that, in spite of the afternoon and evening becoming cold, wet and windy nothing seemed able to depress her spirits. She had rung for Celestina and had ordered some coat-hangers, and spent a happy evening rearranging her clothes.

Next day, it was fine again and she had climbed the hillside with the Austrian boy's parents — a professor and his wife who lived just over the frontier. They had picked primroses and grape-hyacinths and had drunk white wine under the vines — vines just coming into leaf, spring-pale and silvery thick, tender as carved jade.

The Austrians had joined her for coffee after dinner and Erculano had come too. They had talked of peasant customs, and of peasant songs and witchcraft, and drunk cognac "on the house". At one moment, Rose, opening her bag to take out her compact, had seen her letter to Felix and (so gay had been her mood) she had nearly torn it up. Filled with good wine, she had suddenly seen the part through different eyes and how she might approach it: and there would always be Felix to direct her, to fill the gaps . . . sometimes this worked magic.

Now, Ella, pen in hand, was watching their host, as he moved among the tables. "The personal touch!" she commented, rather too clearly. "Herculano, or whatever he's called. Just look at him. That party of Germans — they've called him back four times: he doesn't turn a hair . . ."

"He's tremendously kind," said Rose.

"Kind?" said Ella and laughed again. "I bet he loathes their guts: he's been up since five and cooked both dinner and lunch. He knows his job, that's all."

Rose was silent a moment. "How do you know," she asked at last, "that he's been up since five?"

"Sometimes earlier," said Ella. "We had a long talk last night. While you were in your bath."

"Oh," said Rose. She had become very still.

"Yes. That's when he showed me the visitors' book. He's had an odd life," Ella went on. She lit a cigarette and fanned out the match. "Did you know," she asked through the first exhalation of smoke, "that this place was once his home ?"

"Yes, he did tell me," said Rose.

"Amazing, what he's done. Have you seen the kitchens?"

"Yes, he did show me," said Rose.

"Twelfth century, that fresco over the stove. And there is another in the bathroom. His wife died while he was a prisoner and he had to call his son back from the university. Politics, of course. He hadn't a penny, he said, when he came out. Just this house and the clothes he stood up in . . ."

Rose ran her hand along the clasp of her handbag: a faint breeze had sprung up from the lake and her finger tips felt numb. "What else did he tell you?" she asked.

"Oh, that he knew about food — always had, but that he'd never actually cooked. He was just beginning on that," said Ella, "— how he learned, I mean — when you came down —"

"I'm sorry," said Rose.

"What for?"

"For interrupting."

Ella looked at her sharply. "Darling, what's the matter?"

"Nothing," said Rose, "I just began to feel a bit cold."

Ella's expression softened: shy, funny Rose . . . such odd things she minded: perhaps, now, that she had been here a week and had not been told this story. She leaned forward impulsively, a hand on Rose's wrist: "Darling," she said, laughing a little, "people always gossip at me: I'm such an old gossip myself." She laughed again, "You should know your old Ella, by now . . ."

"I do," said Rose. She tried to smile.

"Everybody's life histories . . . I'm as bad as a hairdresser. It doesn't mean a thing . . ." She spread out her postcards, flicking one over, "This is for George. A view of Lake Ledro. I've said you look splendid and that you're going to do the play . . ."

Rose clutched her handbag. "No, don't say that —" she whispered.

"But why not?" Ella stared. (Really Rose was the limit — what was the matter now? — she looked quite wild-eyed.)

"I — I —" began Rose — she cleared her throat — "I'd rather tell him myself . . ."

"All right," said Ella, "calm down." Smiling slightly, she tore up the postcard. She piled the pieces in the ashtray. "But I promised I'd write: I'll have to send him another. What about this one — a picture of Juliet's tomb?"

"Yes," said Rose, "send him that."

Ella unscrewed her pen. "Can one get stamps here?" she asked.

"I think so. I hope so," said Rose. She felt in her bag for her letter to Felix: it came quickly under her fingers, crisp, square, reassuring: it only needed a stamp. She sat there dumbly watching Ella write, as the dusk crept over the lake and the distant mountain receded; here and there on the shadowy slopes faint lights sprang up like spangles.

"So you think it's all put on?" she said at last.

Ella laid down her pen. "What's all put on?"

"This thing of Erculano? This manner? You think it's all pretence?"

"Oh, so we're back there," said Ella. She fanned her postcard, back and forth, drying the ink in the breeze.

179

"No, not pretence, exactly. Just part of the job, that's all. You saw him with those Germans? He's got to make each guest feel special. Not only cared for, but somehow singled out. And why not, in heaven's name — it's part of his stock in trade."

"I see what you mean," said Rose, at last.

"Well, it stands to reason."

"Yes —" Rose spoke uncertainly: something else stood to reason; something she needed to know, something she must know. How to put it? "Ella —" she began.

"Yes?"

Rose tried again. "Ella —" She spoke very carefully. "When you went into the kitchen with Erculano," she paused, her eyes on Ella's, "did he show you the salmon trout?"

"Yes, he did. I told you. Out on a slab."

"Oh."

"Why?"

"Did he show you how to gut it?"

"He did, as a matter of fact."

"And how you poach it — with a hint of tarragon, till the eye comes loose?"

"Yes, he did. It sounded rather ghastly . . ."

Rose took a grip on the clasp of her handbag: "And did he tell you —" she paused, still controlling her voice, "how it was caught?"

"Yes, I asked him. I said I hadn't seen it in the boats . . ."

"You asked him? And he told you?"

"Yes," said Ella, surprised.

There was a short silence. Rose ran her tongue across her lips. "How is it caught?" she asked, and held her breath.

"By rod and line, of course."

"He told you that? He used those actual words: 'rod and line'?"

"Yes, that's what he said. And sort of waved his arms. They go out early in the morning. Before we're awake, he said. That's why we don't see it come in. But why do you ask? Why are you so anxious?"

"I wondered," Rose said weakly, sinking back into her chair. She was breathing again . . . "whether it was fresh."

"Of course it's fresh," said Ella sharply. "Darling, it's not like you to care so much about food." She looked slightly worried. "Is that why you left it tonight?"

Rose began to laugh. She lay back in her chair and went on laughing. "Forgive me," she said at last, and took out a handkerchief and began to wipe her eyes, "I'm an awful fool. Just forgive me . . ."

"We all forgive you," Ella said, "far too often. What's the matter now? Are you crying?"

"No," said Rose, blowing her nose, "no, not at all."

She raised a tear-stained face alight, glowing. "Why should I be crying?" Jumping to her feet, she kissed Ella, and with a swift half-hug, ran across to the rail.

"Oh dear," said Ella in an even voice, "don't say you're going to be sick . . ."

"I won't," cried Rose, laughing. Leaning over the water her voice seemed curiously hollow and detached.

"You must try not to mind," went on Ella after a moment. "So much, I mean — about little things . . ."

But she sounded for once, less certain. There was a silence except for the lapping of the lake: she guessed she had not been heard.

After a while, sighing, she rose a trifle stiffly and joined her friend at the rail. They stood together staring out across the darkening water. "What about bed?" suggested Ella.

"Yes," said Rose, "bed. A good idea . . . we can pack tomorrow."

Neither looked down at the water at their feet. There was nothing to see there: the few rather chunky bits of torn white paper had sailed gently away into the dark.

CHAPTER
TWELVE

A House in Portugal

My mother has often described her first sight of it —
white, piled, and, at one end, a tower.

On that hot September day, as she stepped out of the
car, she remembers a strange, sub-tropical smell
breathed up from the garden below — a smell both spicy
and glutinous; a smell indigenous to that place. The
white sand of the terrace seemed to float in the glare of
the sun and under the stone porch was, not coolness, but
a faint, grey abatement of the heat. Silence lay about her,
the silence of the deep country.

My father laid his shoulder to the door, but it would
not open easily; it groaned against his weight and
scraped noisily — when at last it yielded — on the
polished, marble floor. This my mother discovered later
was because, the house being open on all sides to the
garden, the front door was seldom used.

My mother felt herself picked up and set down within;
while the chauffeur stood by, obsequiously tender. Here
was coolness and height, glass and marble and carved
stucco; and another smell, the smell of the house itself.

It was nineteen twenty-seven; and she was twenty-
one.

Through glass doors she saw a long dining room, mirror-lined, and with persiennes, closed against the heat.

My father opened a shutter and the garden leapt into the room, reflected in the mirrors that faced the line of windows. One after another he pinned the shutters back, and my mother saw that shutters and windows were built alike, framed delicately by slender pillars. A fountain played outside on the terrace and again, in reflection, on the mirrored wall.

She felt it then more strange than beautiful, though beautiful it was — and became so to her in memory.

That day she noticed first the gold chairs, the pedestals with palms, the long, red, hideous carpet . . . so assured they looked, and inherent, as though she, not they, had trespassed out of her era. Behind her, glass-enclosed, lay the music room.

My father led her out again to the hall. Up marble steps to another level, where two staircases branched apart, shallow and graceful, with their carved stone balustrades. At the head of each were closed, double doors.

On her left, hung heavy curtains. My father drew one back — it slid easily but with a dim clatter of rings — and my mother peered within: leather benches like railway carriage seats lined a mirrored alcove, lit from above by a cupola of glass; the floor was of patterned marble.

"We call it the smoking-room . . ."

My mother shivered a little in spite of the heat. She saw in her imagination rows of men, very foreign, in tasselled velvet caps, with not even a table on which to place their drinks; a place of banishment, where masculinity withdrew into itself, doubly distilled, almost nefarious . . .

"It leads to the chapel . . ."

The chapel looked derelict. A swarm of bees in the painted ceiling buzzed angrily. They were to stay there, undisturbed, throughout our childhood.

"It's supposed to be haunted," my father told her, "by something called 'the *Psst-Psst da Capella*' . . ."

Psst-Psst!

A cheerful sound, and, to my mother, associated with the Portuguese summoning of waiters or the drawing of attention to a dropped glove; with lights and bustle and crowded places . . . it was only coming in from the garden at grey dusk that she was to remember another interpretation of that warning hiss and to run, like a marked thing, through the watching shadows.

Upstairs, and yet — the house being built on a slope — still part of the ground floor, was the Big Dining Room. It was furnished in pear wood; pale, ornate sideboards reared up into undustable infinity; heavy curtains flowed downwards on to slippery floors; epergnes raised their graceful, silver cups. The pale expanse of table, when fully extended, sat forty people.

Beyond, were the Little Dining Room, the kitchens, rows of bedrooms, and the boudoir. This last adjoined her own room and was filled with chintz. It was the wrong chintz. Or the wrong room — too high, too cool, with a tiled bay window that was almost a winter-garden.

Tea, on that first day, was laid in the boudoir — massive silver on an uncomfortably high table. My mother remembers a small, dark maid escaping shyly as they entered.

"Oh, Conceição!" my father called, using, it seemed to my mother, the vocative case with a downward, nasal swing at the last syllable, "this is your mistress."

My mother took the small, uncertain hand and looked into a smiling face, not young but with all the charm and vitality of youth.

"Conceição has been here — how long? — twenty-two years . . ."

My mother did not understand the graceful phrase of welcome, but she knew it to be well-turned.

"Thank you," she said, shy too, "thank you very much."

They had tea and my mother poured out. There were sandwich cakes, frosted lightly with sugar, and a chafing-dish of hard toast. The bread had a curious taste, slightly sourish, and the massive teapot weighed on her wrist.

There was not time, my father said, to show her the garden. He had to get back to Lisbon. How could she sense, beneath this casual phrase, the first, faint, warning rumble of the Great Depression?

But they found time for the kitchen; vast and light; the great tables scrubbed to whiteness; the copper pans on the walls hotly reflecting the sunlight; the stove like a black city of cells and caves — an old-fashioned horror — but to my mother it appeared modern, so serene it looked and eminently practical in the glow of efficient care.

More handshakes, smiles, and murmured greetings.

How charming they are, thought my mother, how pretty — aprons spotless, heads beautifully combed — little Conceição and big Conceição; Elvira, with her doe's eyes, Madalena, Virginia, Maria-Rita. All wore rope-soled shoes, not whitened, but laundered and bleached in the sunshine. They gazed with delight at my mother in her brief, pale clothes; ladies, in Lisbon, still wore long-sleeved black or blue.

My father went ahead to the balcony. "We can go out this way," he called, and my mother following, with backward smiles, paused when she came to the doorway: two old witches stood there, waiting for alms. They came — she discovered later — every Friday: Tia Maria and Tia Joachina. But this was a special Friday and my father, as he led the way down the steps towards the car, left them croaking and bowing and champing their toothless gums. Blessings followed my mother as she ran down the steps, blessings which half alarmed her, spewed as they were, harshly, into the white sunlight.

The heat.

It had been lying in wait for her and now enveloped her.

"You'd better put on a hat," my father advised.

"I'm all right," she insisted. But the temperature startled her. It seemed, leaving the comparative shade of the kitchen, as though she had walked into something rather than out of something.

The house stood on a terrace and the garden fell away below so that the tree-tops were level with the second-floor windows. My mother waved goodbye to the car and ran down the lichen-encrusted steps to the deep shade. They were strange to her, the trees — judas, oleander, camellia, and tulip. There were clumps of grass palms whose leaves hung like coarse hair. The ground was dusty but sweet-smelling, and there was an old stone tank full of water-lilies. My mother wandered vaguely, touching and smelling. She found a dark spring edged with maidenhair. She saw a praying mantis.

She found a well, and, in the well, a toad. They stared at each other, he with his striped eyes. They were, through the years, to get to know each other very well. My mother made him, but not until much later, a little raft on which he would take the sun.

Once she told me that she had lived in the house a week before she found the upper storey. She had passed and repassed the double doors that hid the stairway. There were so many double doors in that house, high, gracefully proportioned, and very much alike.

They were very plain, those upper rooms. The carpetless floors were yellow scrubbed, and the furniture, though solid, was undistinguished. My mother did not recognize, at the time, the beauty and cleanliness of such austerity; her thoughts flew ahead, almost anguished, to wax polish and bright cretonne.

In one of the box rooms she found a case of saints. It was a long, low box, like a giant's coffin, and the saints lay recumbent, staring up at her with mild painted eyes. Some were of stone, some of plaster; some ancient, some modern. She picked out a Santa Lucia in a pastel gown with silver stars. The drapery swirled with life and the gentle hand held a dish — nonchalantly, almost carelessly — and, on the dish, a pair of eyes. It would have been a feat in itself to balance such round eyes on so flat a dish. There was something faintly shocking in this bland inconsequence. But she's tired, thought my mother — legend had saddled her with eyes, and eyes she must carry till the end of time.

Another case, the same size, symmetrically revealed a stack of bed-pans: a relic of Spanish 'flu.

Those early weeks must have been lonely for my mother. Caught in the first, frenzied struggle against the rising tide of Depression, my father spent all his time at the office and my mother was left to fill her days alone.

She found some half-sewn cushion covers of metal lamé which she dutifully finished, though hating the garish pattern and the scrape of steel on gold. In that house she felt it *de rigueur* for a wife to ply her needle "of an evening" while her husband read beside the lamp; and, with her piled closets and completed trousseau, what else was there to sew?

English books were few and far between and such as the house contained she quickly read. She would wander through the shady garden and out beyond it to the pine-tree slopes. She would lean on hot rocks, watching ant battles among the dried grass stems, or trace the furry, writhing line of processional caterpillars to their doomed tree. She would find heather in bloom, reminding her of England, and, among its dark roots, the burning gas-flame blue of leaning lithospermum.

Sometimes she came face to face with a large, green lizard, the feared *legarto*, and it would bare its sharp teeth in a silent hiss as it straddled the path on bandy legs. My mother, unlike the peasants, only half feared it, not knowing its reputation for attacking women, though it fled from men.

She would watch her oxen ploughing the ground under the orange trees; the men, in their stocking caps, singing directions. "A stone . . . a stone . . . take care . . . a stone . . ." they would chant, and delicately, ears attuned, the great creatures would swing the plough a hand's breath, avoiding the obstacle. Enwrapped and comforted, they seemed, by the voice of their driver, which flowed about them in ceaseless reassurance.

A gong would summon her to meals and she would go obediently, having washed her hands, into the cool and shuttered dining room.

Each meal would be a surprise and a mystery. Perhaps, before he left for the office, my father might find time to issue hurried instructions, but, for the most part, the menu was left to the cook. Some meals my mother found delicious: fried cod-fish balls, light and dry as biscuit, with tomato salad in a deep glass dish; rice dishes of all kinds, tossed and savoury; salads of green peppers, of chick peas, of mottled beans — with their flavour of rainwater; and great dishes of fruit — peaches, nectarines, grapes, melon, and passion fruit. And wine. My mother always drank a light, sweet wine, most delicately flavoured, called Grandjó.

Coffee was brought to her afterwards, in the boudoir, in little round cups of swan-handled Sevres, rudely nicknamed *panicos*, resembling as they did in shape "an enamelled object of the most domestic significance".

There were other meals she found less appetizing — *percebes*, for instance, a dish, it seemed to her, of miniature goats' hooves on rubber stalks. These were starkly and badly presented — a steaming triangle of black obscenity . . . Medusa's hair!

Big Conceição, at length, came to her rescue, showing her how by a skilful twist the hoof was severed from the wrinkled tube, drawing with it — as meat is drawn from a crab's leg — a delicate stalk of quivering flesh. It tasted like shrimp and was quite delicious. When next she saw *percebes* it was on the keel of an up-turned boat, and she knew them to be barnacles.

But mid-day lunch was, after all, a trifling affair and quickly disposed of. Not so dinner. The cook was an artist and nobody worried much, least of all my mother, if the aperitif hour were pleasantly prolonged. The meal, when at length announced, was usually worth waiting for, and it followed the traditional pattern of soup, fish, entre, joint; but its sauces, its soups, its delectable gravies still "live within the sense they quicken". Nor could one forget the headsplitting, aching sweetness of the sweets . . .

These sweets shared a common base of egg yolks and sugar, on which simple theme endless variations were evolved. When other dishes ignominiously were carried away out of sight, the sweet sustained pride of place in the dining-room cupboard (in after years locked against our childish raids — a formality we easily forgave, knowing the mantled top to be removable). It was in one sense a gift from the cook, an unselfish offering from whose excellence the kitchen would reap no share. But if, after two appearances, any still remained, Conceição would receive the plundered dish, on behalf of her

191

colleagues, with a bow, a smile, and a formal speech of thanks.

My mother would sit at dinner on my father's right like a guest: she felt marooned and forlorn if banished, as she would have been, to the end of the table.

Big Conceição — with her grey hair and humorous, wrinkled, almost Mongolian face — was nearly stone-deaf, but a lifted eyebrow would bring her to one's elbow or a sideways glance direct her to a guest. She worked in a silent vacuum of her own professionalism, unhurried, undistractable. For rare condiments or sudden gastronomic whims, a sign language evolved itself. My mother showed me a gesture which described — and that only — a bottle of Worcestershire sauce.

Gradually, my mother began to pick up Portuguese and to take a more active part in the running of the house. Each morning, after breakfast, she would go along to the kitchen, keys in hand, to consult the cook. By this hour the great tables were scrubbed and bare; the zinc shelves wiped down; the stove — anointed while hot with olive oil — a rich glow of lustrous black.

The first gambit was a dramatic throwing open of cupboard doors (there was no refrigerator or ice-box) and the placing on the table of a row of nameless shapes modestly shrouded in linen. Maria-Rita would flick off these napkins and there before my mother's carefully controlled gaze would be half a turkey, the remains of a sea bream, two raw cutlets, a dish of cooked rice, and an unrecognizable mess of brown gravy.

Then began a curious game in which my mother, while seeming to keep the initiative, would — in her broken Portuguese — inveigle Maria-Rita into making decisions. This was achieved mostly by facial expression: a look of profound thought mingled with judicious doubt and the sudden repetition in firm tones of whatever Maria-Rita had said last.

This make-believe over, pencil and pad were produced and my mother would "make the *rol*". The *rol* was a list of necessities to be purchased later by the chauffeur. Petitions came from all sides: "would the Senhora please order this . . . or this . . . or this . . .?" Sometimes they stumped her, and, as she took refuge in phonetic spelling, she would wonder unhappily whether she had ordered a rush fan or fly-paper. Very often the *rol* ended on a strangely philanthropic note with a commodity known in the kitchen as "medicine for the ants".

The *rol* disposed of, my mother would take up her keys and, followed by her flock, lead the way to the *dispensa*. The *dispensa* was a two-storeyed apartment, half store room, half wine cellar. There were bins for flour, for rice, for dried peas and beans, and stone troughs for salting bacon. There were kegs of brandy and *aqua ardente* and, among the wines, my father's favourite — a white wine which had been stored in a Madeira cask. Smoked sausages hung from the ceiling — strong, bacony sausages, almost kippered. Mottled soap, soft from the making, was laid out in bars to dry. There was tea, coffee, sugar, and olive oil — this last, in a great metal container with a fitted tap.

A rough queue would form, and my mother, wielding her scoop, would ladle out provisions sufficient unto the day. In this way, she was somewhat at the mercy of her servants. Virginia, the char — or "woman of days" — kept her household in soap by a regular demand for double the necessary quantity. Bread, too, she would take and *potaça*, a rough, white cleaning powder. Occasionally her caches were discovered and there would be tears and wringing of hands. She would swear strange oaths: "May I be as blind as the little mice if ever again I touch so much as a crumb of rice —" "But, Virginia, you have only to ask —" But Virginia would never ask. She preferred to steal and keep her independence.

But "the young ladies of the house" (as they were called in the village) had no incentive for dishonesty; bottles, bowls, tins, jugs, and earthenware basins were extended pell-mell, and gently, methodically, my mother filled them as directed. There was little demand for metal polish; the great brass pans in the kitchen were cleansed with bitter orange and sand, scoured and re-scoured out of doors in the sunlight.

"Now, have you all got everything? Think."

Yes, they had everything — every single thing they would require to keep her household nourished, clean, and peaceful for the next twenty-four hours. But, as they traipsed out and she locked the door after them, my mother often wondered which one of them it would be (by instinct they could find her in the remotest corner of the loneliest pine-wood), panting and flushed, to demand either her presence or the key for some indispensable commodity inexplicably overlooked.

The house stood in its own grounds — about twelve hundred acres — and between it and Lisbon lay twenty miles of pock-marked, rutted roadways, some almost impassable. A drive to Lisbon was an expedition.

My father, to whom all engines purred and grovelled, took this daily in his stride. Swaying, bumping, bounding behind the wheel, holding (it seemed at times) the car together by sheer will power, he would urge the shuddering vehicle up banks and over pot-holes at what appeared a suicidal speed; a speed which, he would patiently explain to terrified passengers, he could not slacken for fear of losing momentum. His negotiations of the familiar ups and downs had a swing to it, a dash, a rhythm — one could lose oneself in my father's driving; it suspended all thought — like a thundering sonata; it was a headlong battle between him and the road and one which, it seemed to my mother, left the road beaten and a-quiver.

This explained the number of cars parked in garage and stable; seven in all, of varying degrees of respectability. On an average, three of these might be in running order, the rest undergoing some form of internal surgery. Spare parts were manufactured on the premises with much anvil-clanging and bellow-blowing, and, after a short period of trial and convalescence, the invalid — whole but shaky — would be urged once more upon the road.

This also explained the comparative isolation in which my mother lived. Friends who drove out from Lisbon under their own steam were apt to say, "Never again," and on future occasions allow themselves to be marooned at the nearest railway station until rescued, at my father's own risk, in one of his demon cars.

There was a closed sedan for my mother in which she could be driven by the chauffeur. Eugenio's technique was different from my father's (my mother was convinced he passed every second at the wheel in silent prayer) and his responsibilities greater. Once when the car stopped for no ascertainable reason and rather far from home, Eugenio broke down and cried. He cried at his failure to deliver, intact and in time, such an awe-inspiring combination as my father's best car and newly acquired bride. My mother, who could not at that time speak Portuguese, cried too at her inability to comfort Eugenio. There was an emotional scene in which both wrung their hands in their respective languages. I forget how, there being no service stations, they eventually got home.

At first my mother did not attempt to hide her intolerance of local hygiene. As far as personal cleanliness was concerned, she could find no fault. Body-linen, washed in the spring, dried in the sun, and ironed with great charcoal irons, was changed daily: a shirt might well be patched but never, even by the humblest labourer, twice put on. Yet she could not help feeling hen feathers and olive oil to be inadequate treatment for a burn; and that a group of old women, "sewing" furiously on an imaginary ball of string, were unlikely to effect much improvement in a sprain — especially as the sufferer sat glumly by excluded from any part in the operation.

And diagnosis was weak: one man, with a black and swollen ankle, was carefully "sewn" by a group of elderly neighbours, and, not responding to treatment, was "sewn" again. There still being no improvement, the good women in a fever of professional frustration gave him a sewing to end all sewings — all night they went at it and part of the next day. When at last, exhausted, they laid down their needles, the patient still obstinately persisting in his complaints of pain, they gave up. They washed their hands of him. His relations, greatly puzzled and deeply upset, assisted him to a cart, and, at his own urgent request, drove him away to the hills, where he insisted there dwelt a wise man in whom he had true faith. It was a long and tiring journey and the hut of the wise man was hard to locate. When at last they found him and the bandages had been taken off, the wise man stared hard and long at the injured foot. "But this has been sewn," he said irritably; "what ignorance — it's a break, not a sprain!" And he sighed wearily as he dragged up a stool: "Now I've got all that to unpick . . ." According to the patient, his pain lessened with every "stitch" removed, and the final treatment, to my mother's surprise and slight discomfiture, proved miraculously successful.

All the same, she looked up the word "germ" in the dictionary and delivered little lectures. She would have done better to save her breath. They were polite but puzzled, as if by a hint of unexpected weakness in a mind they were beginning to respect. So she learned to compromise, prescribing two aspirins and one Our Father for a headache caused by the Evil Eye; and suggesting that a sufferer from heartburn should bow three times to the moon before tossing back a glass of bicarbonate of soda. As her cures worked, so her prestige increased.

Inflated by her success in the field of medicine, she began to tackle slightly graver problems such as occurred when Manuel, an under-gardener, threatened to shoot two of "the young ladies of the house"; if neither would have him, he was reported to have said, he would shoot them both. Manuel was an underhung, ape-like creature with great arms, and my mother quailed a little inwardly as she sallied forth to tackle him. The "kitchen" was in a flutter and she was conscious, as she made her way down the steps to the garden, of unseen faces peering excitedly from windows in the tower.

As he slowly straightened himself, and she saw, under the brutal brows, the dog-like humility of the long-lashed eyes, all the carefully prepared threats of policemen, arrest, imprisonment for life sank out of her mind. She heard herself saying, with what she was pleased to recognize as a fair degree of sternness, ". . . and if you should shoot even one of them, your master and I would be very angry, very angry indeed."

Manuel, she heard later, had withdrawn his threat; not from compunction, but "out of respect for the house".

Towards the end of summer, when the woods were tinder-dry, there would be fires. The cry would be heard in the valley — a far-carrying wail.

"Hush," my father might say at dinner, laying down his fork. Then clear, but distant, we would hear it —

"*O fogo-o-o-o-*. . . *O fogo-o-o-o*" — a banshee sound, like the baying of wolves.

In a second, all was bustle; one ran to the telephone; others to the tower — "Over towards Fonte Santa . . . coming this way!"

The girl at the telephone exchange acted as liaison. Land feuds and personal animosities were suspended as news flew back and forth between neighbours.

From the tower a glow might be seen or sometimes the blaze itself. My father would pull on some old clothes, and the cars would race out into the darkness. Sometimes my mother would go too, in the oddest assortment of snatched-up garments. She would squeeze into the car with the men and hold on like grim death while it plunged and lurched over rocks and heather. No need for headlights as they approached the blaze; every twig and stone stood in a dancing, quivering clarity of nightmare light.

They would, at length, have to abandon the car and pant along on foot, cutting branches, as they went, with which to beat out the flames. Ahead, outlined sharply against the glow like a string of marionettes, a line of demon figures swayed and rolled in frenzied rhythm as they beat upon the underbrush; my father's men, and every other able-bodied man from within a radius of several miles.

Pine trees, with a rush and a roar, seemed absorbed rather than burned; torpid smoke, crackling with sparks, moved dully across the stars.

Once it was over, the last smouldering gleam stamped out, there was a great darkness. Where to tread? In which direction lay the best route home? The skyline itself had altered. With the fire as a beacon, lighting the countryside, men had run, climbed and jumped across furze, rock and brook — like moths to a candle, heedless of hurt. Few had stayed for lanterns; many did not possess them. Now, sweaty and exhausted, each must find his laboured way home across pathless ground known only to shepherds and swineherds.

My mother often spoke of this sudden aftermath and the anti-climax of the slow trek home. It was then that clothes were ripped, faces torn, and ankles cut; not, as might be imagined, during the excitement of the fire. She always felt it, as she stumbled carwards beside my father, to be vaguely symbolic.

But she could not foresee another fire, one that was to burn for a week; an almost famous fire, achieving for itself a small column in the London *Times*; a fire that was fought day and night by all the men of the locality in order, during his absence abroad, to save my father's house.

It was checked just in time, a question of yards. When my father came back among them, distributing his thanks and largesse, they were proud and happy — and lived for weeks in the satisfying glow of extraordinary achievement.

How could they know that the bottom had fallen out of shipping? That the house, about to pass out of the family anyway, was insured for a sum which at that moment might have saved my father's fortunes? As he distributed gifts he could ill afford, he reflected somewhat ruefully on the faithful servitors who had so loyally struck down the hand of Fate, outstretched for once to help him.

Fate did not try again.

CHAPTER
THIRTEEN

Sailing with Robert

Sailing is not so bad as you might think; it can at times be almost pleasant. No, not pleasant, exactly; but now and again it is possible to be relatively unaware of active discomfort. It is with such moments in mind that I venture to pass on a few hints.

Should, for instance, Robert announce glumly at breakfast that there's hardly enough wind to get out of the harbour, you can safely accept any subsequent invitation, provided that, in the meantime, there is no change in the weather. But should he, after glancing out the window, proclaim, with what one has learned to recognize as sinister satisfaction, that there's "quite a nice sailing breeze", be wary; borrow a sou'wester and take a towel; leave your wrist watch at home and enter the boat shoeless; make sure the boiler is stoked for a bath on your return and there's enough in the bottle for a hot toddy.

If ever you hear him remark, with deceptive casualness, that there's "quite a nice, stiff sailing breeze", neither hesitate nor quibble, simply run: run out of the house, up the garden, into the road. And stay there until Robert, wandering morosely about, has selected another victim to be his crew. The key word, remember, is "stiff". Dreadful things can happen to those who, in their guilelessness, pick on the word "nice" as being in any way descriptive of the experience that is in store for them.

But there's no need to dwell on the harrowing. Forewarned, you will select the happier instance — the day of little wind — and you will voice your first enthusiastic "I'd love to!" In your clean white shoes, with your sweater on your arm, you are prepared to step aboard. Robert, you feel, at his most charming, will help you in, pull on a rope; the white wings will lift; and away you'll float, skimming lightly across the harbour and out beyond the sunlit, distant blue.

It will not be quite like that. To start with you will be disconcerted by the sum of things Robert will make you carry: rolls of canvas, two pairs of oars, a zinc bailer, and a basket of hooks and fishing tackle (on top of which, in an unguarded and long-to-be-regretted moment, you lay your sweater). "Hang on to these," Robert will say, "while I get the pram." Momentarily, you will be relieved to hear that your burden is to be wheeled (somewhat eccentrically) rather than carried, and you must show no dismay when the pram turns out to be a very small boat at the foot of an extremely long, slimy and rusted flight of steps leading to the water. The pram will look very small, like half a walnut shell, and the water under the dank, seaweedy quay wall will look very black and deep. Do not worry. Through long practice, Robert can stow you, himself, twice that amount of gear, and your grandmother (should you care to bring her) into this frail craft. What you have not bargained for is that he, standing at ease and steadying the boat, will keep sending you up and down the dank and dizzy steps to fetch the stuff in relays.

He may or may not warn you, when at length he hands you in, that you will step into several inches of bilge water, although he might suggest, as a casual afterthought, that you should have hitched up your nether garments before you sat down.

Perilously he will then propel this teetering load across the gentle swell of the harbour. All I can say to you now is: Keep still, deadly still. Robert, seated, as one might say, with his back to the engine, may ask you to guide him. This means that when approaching any other vessel, moored or moving, you should cry, "Port" or "Starboard" — either of these words will do, as Robert always looks both ways.

Soon you will be alongside *Edith*. You may be disappointed, if you are expecting something grander, to find that, though strong and seaworthy, she is undecked; that she looks, in other words, like an extremely large rowing boat with a pole stuck in her.

Robert will go aboard first, and you will hand him the gear. This chore is seldom achieved without some personal injury, as the pram is extremely volatile and the gear is heavy; but it is a good idea at this point to show Robert what stuff you are made of: wipe off the blood with the back of your hand and say nothing.

When, finally, you climb aboard, you will scrape some skin from the shin of the leg which, somehow, wants to stay in the pram. Forewarned of this tendency, you will be more likely to control any unguarded verbal exclamation, because Robert would immediately point out that it was your own fault for not "balancing your weight on the boat you are boarding rather than on the one you are leaving".

"Better let down the centreboard," Robert may then say, busy with some ropes for'ard. This you can manage. The key word is "centre" — a little fiddling amidships, and the drop keel will go down. Don't ask Robert why all the water in the harbour doesn't come up through the centreboard hole: he will be busy with the jib.

Later, he may flatteringly suggest (if you have behaved as I have enjoined) that you put in the rudder. This will turn out to be an extremely large and heavy piece of wood, which, as you have been standing on it, you have mistaken for part of the hull.

Somehow you must heave the rudder up and swing it out over the stern. As you gingerly lower it into the water, it will be gripped by a surprisingly strong current. Your fingers will slip, and your wrists will ache; but even you will realize that you must hang on. And not only hang on, but thread against the pull of the current, two large iron pins into two dimly conspicuous eyes, well below the water line (get the top one in first, they say). Keep trying: Robert, from his end of the boat, happily cannot see.

Robert may then ask you to help him unleash the mainsail. Look bright. This is easy — all you have to do is unwind a piece of rope tied round a long bundle of canvas and two poles. If, as he hoists the sail, he says, "Pass that sheet under the thwart, will you?" do not, in your enthusiasm, grab at the mainsail, the only sheet-like thing in sight: he means only, as he could have perfectly well said in the first place, that you should pass a piece of rope under the seat rather than over it.

"Now the tiller," he will exclaim, which means you must look for a thing like a broom handle and stick it into the top of the rudder, where there is a slot for it. When you have done this, it is safer to move away and go for'ard, for anything the boat does when you are in the vicinity of the tiller will be your fault, and whatever it does will be wrong.

Robert will now cast off, and you will find yourself under sail. Robert will be at the tiller, where he will sprawl in lordly comfort and give you warnings to "look out for the boom". You crouch apprehensively on your thwart, contemplating grey, squelchy shoes.

As *Edith* glides forward, with no sound of a boom or kindred loud noise, you find courage to raise your head a little, even to turn it to one side. You may then catch a glimpse from under the mainsail of the quay, where you will see — because he is always there — a stout man with a wooden leg and a dog on a lead. It does not matter if, in your circumscribed view, he becomes gradually decapitated, then detruncated, by the expanse of the mainsail; during the next half hour, you will have many opportunities for observing him.

On the starboard side your view will be less obstructed, and you will realize that the boat is making straight across the harbour for the Sea Gull Café. Just as it seems that you are about to plunge under the orange awning among the startled coffee drinkers, Robert will yell, "Coming about!"

Then everything happens: the boat turns; the boom swings; you slither down your thwart; back *Edith* goes, skimming across the harbour, to the man with the wooden leg.

He stands there unblinking, in a sea-coma, as people do on quays, and his dog, as you approach, sits down: this, the dog seems to say, will be a long business. The dog is right. "Coming about!" yells Robert, and back you go to the Sea Gull Cafe, slightly raising the temperature of the coffee drinkers, and return once more, like a homing pigeon, to the man with the wooden leg.

Do not, after forty minutes of this, suggest to Robert that it might be fun to change direction and sail out of the harbour towards the open sea. On shore the gentlest of creatures, afloat he is likely to be irritable, and there will come a moment, if you will only be patient, when instead of fetching up opposite the man with the wooden leg, you will fetch up just in front of the dog, and Robert will exclaim happily, "Quite a bit of headway that time!"

Soon you, too, will fall into a sea-coma, moving mechanically to Robert's now less strident cries of "Coming about!" and it will come as a bit of a shock when your thwart leaps under you as the wind whips into the sails and *Edith*, suddenly and terrifyingly alive, creaks, as rearing and plunging, she prances into the swell. "Bit fresher out here," Robert will remark complacently. Keep calm. Do not panic.

Quite suddenly, there is a great deal of sea and no harbour to speak of. Spurts of green water hiss away on either side.

Lumps of this come aboard — very cold and surprisingly heavy. *Edith* swings down into the trough and up again to the wind-broken crest. Your untrained innards catch the rhythm just slightly out of step — as you go up, you meet them coming down. But don't, at this point, ask Robert to back-pedal; he is busy getting away from a lee shore, which, minute by bouncing minute, becomes more distant, so you must put out of your mind now, once and for all, that final hope of a courageous swim to land.

Edith tilts to a horrific angle, and rigid with terror, you wedge yourself uphill and cling on for dear life. The bilge water swirls away from your feet in a breaking wave, and the ocean goes thundering past your toes. Robert, dry and exhilarated in the stern, looks pleased. "That's right," he says, "trim the boat!"

The next hour or two need not be nightmare: it is possible to bail, as Robert insists, without disturbing the trim of the boat — just lean over from your perch on the gunwale — and the boat will not sink if you keep bailing, nor will your arm drop off. Your past life swims by in grey, kaleidoscopic undulations before your staring eyes; but it is useless to wonder whether *Edith* can float keel upmost, and to what you should cling or whether, as old fishermen say, you should take three gulps of sea water for ballast and go down quickly.

"Enjoying it?" Robert always asks at this juncture. Your word, here, should be, "Glorious!" but a nod will do. Just keep on bailing, and the mind goes numb.

At his bidding, you achieve the impossible — you crawl, you climb, you tighten, you loosen — while

Robert, still sitting high and dry at the tiller, nods careless approval.

"Want your sweater?" he may suggest thoughtfully some hours later, having stowed it ungettably aft. With chattering teeth, you shake your head, bailing manfully the while. "What about a couple of mackerel lines?" he may add suddenly, as though inspired. No, this is not — as for one wild moment you hope — some form of lifesaving device. He actually means you to fish. When he throws you the spools, you must unwind them, and toss the spinners overboard, and make the lines fast to a cleat. Not that you will ever have the satisfaction of catching a fish. As you pull in a line, Robert, from his vantage point in the stern, will see the spinner long before you do. "Nothing," he'll say. "Let her go." Or, "That's right. Wind her in." You, under his direction, will still be a machine — a puller-in, a de-hooker, and a thrower-out.

Nothing is said about going back; only Robert hears the Lorelei call, which, at long last, turns *Edith* towards shore. But the moment does come when, light as a gull's feather, she sails homeward along the path of the setting sun. The bar of the harbour will slide past on your left, and there, on your right, will be the Sea Gull Café, its tables stripped of cloths and customers, its awning furled. The water will have risen part way up the slimy steps; the man with the dog will long since have gone home, and the harbour will be dreaming softly in a golden evening light.

But do not relax too soon. "Go right for'ard, will you," Robert says casually, "and stand by to grab." If you glance towards him, as you are bound to do, in apprehension or bewilderment, you will notice an expression of strain about his mouth and eyes, a set tenseness about his jaw: some imminent or unknown danger seems impending. And so it is. If you fail him now, no amount of charm, no amount of powder on the nose, no amount of sympathetic listening will avail you anything: you will go down in history forever as "the girl who made me miss my moorings". All you have to do is lean over the bow and catch the pram as you pass close. Just grab it and hang on.

It sounds easy, but I must tell you that on this trifling operation depends, for some obscure and extraordinary reason, Robert's whole reputation as one who can handle a boat. As far as you are concerned, the quay seems empty and the sunlit windows sleepy and indifferent; but to a yachtsman, this peaceful picture has other implications: every house front has its watcher, every watcher has his telescope, and every telescope is trained maliciously, at just this moment, on Robert's humble craft. So roll up your sleeves, brace your diaphragm, and lean well over.

You won't have much hope of recognizing the pram — the harbour seems alive with them, bobbing up and down, as like as thimbles. But if you do succeed in seizing the right one at the right moment, you must be prepared to have your arm torn slowly out of its socket by the pull. Try not to mind. Just hang on. *Edith* always gives way in the end. She flaps her sails like a caught bird and, quite suddenly, sits still.

Robert will then roar up beside you, breathing hard. "Good girl," he'll say as he pulls aboard slimy ropes and slabs of dripping cork. "Good girl!" He may say it several times. In his relief, he will become extravagant. Then he'll invite you to fold up the jib, and praise you for doing it wrong. He'll be amazed when, of your own accord, you pull up the centreboard (you know that one, having let it down) and almost ecstatic when you remember to extract the bar of the tiller from the slot where you placed it. But don't rest on your laurels. Go right ahead. Dazzle him. Take out the rudder — it's much easier than putting it in. Give him a hand with lashing the mainsail. You don't have to do anything but hold on to one end of it and look stern.

Then he'll hand you into the pram, and there you'll sit while he passes you the gear. Make a show of stowing it — a push here and there and a slight frown do the trick.

Then Robert will perilously climb in. Hold tight! The pram will go down and the harbour rush up. There will be a sway and a wobble and a few seconds of sickening uncertainty. *Edith*, so big, so strong, so stable, slides away to the end of her mooring rope, leaving you marooned in this teetering cockleshell with, waist high on all sides, an impatient, brimming flood. Keep quiet. Don't move. All will be well. Gratefully, happily, Robert will get you back across the harbour.

There'll be sloshing and splashing, grazing and bumping, as you unload; but because it is now high tide, not so many steps to climb with the gear. Plunk it all down on the wet stones for Robert to sort out. He'll load you up later, like a pack horse, methodically but fairly humanely (he'll stop before your thigh bones buckle), and then, giving you a slight, helpful push, he'll set you off walking unsteadily on a straight course for home.

When, finally, you stagger in through the front door — weighted down, soaked to the skin, itching with salt, smarting with cuts, burning with blisters — someone is sure to look up and ask casually, "Have a good sail?" As you stiffly and painfully let the heavier parts of your burden slide to the floor, you'll be surprised to hear yourself say, in a breathless but cheerful voice, "Yes. Glorious!" And oddly enough — this is the most mysterious part of the whole business — suddenly you find you mean it.

CHAPTER
FOURTEEN

The Fish Tank

Emma sat silent while he gave the order, staring blankly at the tablecloth: she still felt breathless and Paul seemed too close now, sitting there beside her.

"Extraordinary, isn't it?" she heard him say and, when she did not answer, he went on slowly in the same dazed voice, "we're poles apart, you know that, don't you?"

She nodded, moving her knife slightly on the tablecloth to hide the coffee stain. Raising her head she saw again the plate glass window, opaque now against the darkened street . . . the spinning brightness of the neon lighting. "I've been in this place all afternoon," she said.

He looked round quickly at the crowded tables: "Here — why?"

"I don't know, I still get lost in Paris. I walked and walked. In the end you have to sit down somewhere . . ." She moved her hands along the plush-covered bench. "I think I left my glasses here." He lifted a flap of coarse linen and leaning sideways stared at the shadowed space below the table. "They're not there," he told her, shuffling his feet.

"It doesn't matter. Let's not bother. I'll ask later — at the desk . . ." He let the cloth fall and she leaned back in sudden lassitude against the padded bench. "What did you order?" she asked.

"Oysters, that's what you have here. And Muscadet. I — we can't afford champagne."

"We?" She smiled, her eyes closed. "Can't we?" she murmured, just above her breath. And aware of secret scrutiny added quickly, "Don't look at my hair — there's nothing I can do."

"There's nothing you need do," he said after a moment.

"I cut it myself," she explained, smiling a little, "this afternoon, with the nail scissors."

"And this?" he asked, his hands on the sleeve of her jersey, "where did you get this?"

"The wrong end of the rue de Rivoli. Off a clothes stall."

"It's like mine . . ." he remarked.

"And like Simone's, and like Nana's — and like Jean-Marie's . . ." she shrugged. "It's the uniform."

"You got it to take away? As a souvenir?"

"Of you. Not of them."

"Don't be against them. There's no need, not any more."

"It's different for you. You've always lived here. You're half-French —"

"It isn't really a question of nationality. And I haven't always lived here. Darling Emma, look at me. Open your eyes . . ."

She opened them suddenly, blinking a little against the brightness: two men were staring straight at their table — blobs of faces, expressionless to Emma: we must look idiotic, she thought vaguely, sitting side by side, dressed like twins in fishermen's jerseys, and she turned to look at Paul. Seeing his face so close, she felt breathless again. "Oh, Paul —" she murmured, a little scared, again incredulous.

"It's all right," he told her quickly.

"I was crazy," she whispered, and her eyes filled with tears.

The waiter came up with wine glasses; he straightened the cutlery and removed the service plates: and there was the coffee stain, grimly accusing — dead circular and copper dark. Emma touched it wonderingly, tracing an outer circle. "I did that," she confessed.

"When? This afternoon?"

"Yes. They should have changed the cloth."

"You recognize it?'he asked, surprised.

"Yes. I stared at it for so long." after a moment she added, thinking back, "It was a drop off the end of the spoon."

"How long were you here?" asked Paul after a short silence.

"I don't know — hours and hours. I kept on thinking," she went on in sudden embarrassment, dragging her finger, "that if I made another little blob just beside this bigger one, it would look like a penny-farthing."

"Oh, Emma —" he murmured, amused and anguished.

"Yes," she said, "what time is it now?"

"About six-thirty."

"It feels like something I went through years ago. Or in a dream. Or in some other life . . ."

"What were you trying to do?" he asked after a moment, "get up courage?"

"No. I wasn't trying to do anything. I'd given up. I just sat."

"Drinking coffee?"

"Yes. Drinking coffee . . . drowning in coffee."

She looked up: a third man now was staring at her table — she wished she could see his expression; her hand strayed uncertainly past her shorn nape to the few sparse feathered fronds above her ear.

"You mean," Paul was saying, "that after sitting here for hours you just sprang up — in cold blood, like that —" he snapped his fingers, "and called a taxi?"

Emma looked pensive. "Not exactly," she said slowly, "there was a reason . . ." She hesitated then, as though changing her mind, turned quickly towards him: "If you hadn't been at the Martinique I wasn't going to look anywhere else. But if I did see you there, sitting outside in your usual place, that was to be my sign. I —" she coloured slightly, "then I'd say my piece. Otherwise —"

"You'd have called it a day?"

"Yes. I told the man to drive on past . . ."

"But there we were."

"Yes. There you were." Emma hesitated. "Then suddenly you looked up and saw me."

"Yes," he said, and made a sharp, half-painful roll of the head upon his hand. "It was extraordinary . . ."

"You didn't recognize me, did you — at first?"

"No."

"You did a sort of double-take . . ."

He glanced up quickly and away again.

"It was extraordinary," he repeated lamely; he picked up a fork and swung it slightly like a pendulum.

"I can't remember what I said even."

"You said —" he began to smile, "something like —"

"No, no!" she cried, and put her hands to her ears. "Don't tell me. What I said doesn't matter. Except that if I hadn't said it," and her voice became panic-stricken, "you'd have let me go away tomorrow. Back to Connecticut. You'd have let me do it, Paul."

"Please, Emma," he said.

"You wouldn't even have said goodbye."

He caught at her forearm. "It's all right now. Everything's all right. Don't worry. Just be quiet."

"But not even to say goodbye —"

"We did say goodbye. Last night."

"Yes, so we did. In the public lounge of the Plaza Athenee, with all the relations gaping, and poor old Randall with his snapshots! You said: 'Goodbye, Emma, good luck,'" her voice hardened, "'It's been fun,' you said, 'Hasn't it?'"

"No, no, I didn't say 'fun'. I couldn't have said that — not 'fun'."

"Yes, you did. And you stood there backed away from me gripped on to the back of that hideous gilt chair, as though it was a weapon to ward me off with or something, and you said, 'It's been fun, hasn't it?' with a terrible look on your face, 'goodbye and good luck' you said. And all the time you knew —" without warning, her voice broke and a flood of deeper colour ran into her cheeks and brow, "that I had one more day in Paris — one more evening."

There was a long silence. "Yes," he said at last; he did not look at her.

"Only, 'yes'?"

He rubbed his hand in his hair: he almost groaned, "What's the good of talking?"

"Better to talk now — just once."

"Well, for one thing," he said, "I didn't dream you'd be free tonight. I mean, there they all were — your aunt, uncle, your pimply cousin — I thought you'd be packing or . . . having to be with them." He frowned, swinging his fork. "Anyway, right up to yesterday, you were as gay as a cricket — 'home the day after tomorrow', you kept saying, and going on about the boat trip."

"Don't be silly, Paul. My aunt was paying for it. I had to seem grateful." She leaned towards him, pleading a little. "They'd stood me the whole trip, don't forget — Stamford Conn to Paris."

"Parked you here, you mean, while they galloped off to Sweden."

"There was never any thought of taking me on to Sweden. I was always going to be dropped off in Paris: that was the whole point." She hesitated. "There was one thing, though, I didn't quite bargain for —"

"Meeting me?"

"I was going to say — feeling lonesome."

"Lonesome?" —he put down the fork.

"Of course, Paul. Being dumped suddenly in a strange city, in a strange house, with a strange woman — yes, I know she's your mother but she's French-born and strange to me — and when you come down to it there's more to understand between foreigners than just

217

language. For a girl like me — coming from a large, untidy, hard-up family — at first she did seem a bit — not cold exactly," Emma hesitated, "— a bit formal."

"Formidable?"

"No, just formal. And there was never anywhere to *be*, when we weren't sight-seeing — except my bedroom or that stiff little salon with an electric light plunk in the middle of the ceiling. And never letting me utter one word of English. Of course, I was lonesome. You might have guessed it," she added.

"Emma," he said, and drew a long breath, "be reasonable — I hardly knew you. And my mother's always having these girls, English and American; it isn't my place to comfort them."

"But, this time, there weren't any others — this time, there was only me."

"But, good Lord, I didn't even live there . . ."

"You were just across the courtyard —"

"But a separate apartment."

"You were always in and out — to borrow an egg or something."

"Maybe. But I lived quite separately — I had my own life . . . my own friends."

"Your own friends. Yes, that was it, I suppose . . ." She paused. "I remember one night," she spoke slowly, thinking back, "when you gave a party . . ."

He picked up a spent match and pressed it lightly against the cloth, leaving a charcoal indent. "I didn't know you then," he said.

"We'd been introduced."

"I didn't know you," he repeated.

"You never tried to. If ever you came to your mother's apartment and I was there, you did a bolt — ran like a hare. I might have had the plague."

"I was polite, surely?"

"You bowed from the waist and glared at me, if that's what you mean. 'Mademoiselle!' you'd say," she copied him, "like that. I never even knew you were English!"

"I'm not, really."

"You have a British passport."

"Never mind. Go on."

"And that first time we met in the Martinique."

"What about it?"

"Well, I guessed at once that these were the people that had been at the party . . . There you all were — a closed circle."

"Who was there?"

"Simone, Nana, Jean-Marie . . . the whole crowd. And a red-haired boy with his head on the table . . ."

"Fritz. He was asleep."

"Or drunk."

"Fritz doesn't drink. He'd been working all night, that's all."

"At what?"

"Swotting out his weekly column — the one I illustrate."

"Fritz writes that — the thing you call your comic strip?"

"Yes, thanks be. He's very clever."

"Well, I didn't know what any of you did. I thought you were just —"

"No-good tramps?"

"Art students . . . I don't know — the girls looked sulky, and as though they never combed their hair. But chic, somehow, all the same. Jean-Marie was picking his teeth, I remember. And you were all wearing those black jerseys — except Simone: and she wore a white one — dead plain —" Emma broke off. "I never knew that Simone was a cellist; nor that she has a blind husband . . ."

Thoughtfully he looked down at her hand, spreading his fingers along hers, as though to measure them. "There was quite a lot you didn't know," he said.

"And you all looked so at home," Emma went on, "almost insultingly at home, if you see what I mean; and somehow — superior, as though —" she hesitated, "as though it was your sidewalk . . ."

"So it is, in a way — that bit of it."

". . . your chairs, your tables, your waiters. As though people like us were intruders."

"By 'us' you mean your aunt and uncle and this famous cousin Randall?"

"And myself. When you saw me you looked caught out, I thought." Emma gave a short laugh.

Paul sat silent, jabbing at the tablecloth. "It wasn't like that," he said, at last.

"What was it like then?"

"I did come over to your table but, on that occasion, I didn't introduce the others because —"

"Because we embarrassed you in some way?"

He hesitated. "Yes," he said, "frankly, you did a bit. But that wasn't it. There were six or seven of us — most of them pretty broke; either we'd have to cash in and sponge or —"

220

"Yes," said Emma, "I see." She was silent a moment and then she asked, "In what way, specially, did we embarrass you?"

"Oh, I don't know. The whole set-up. Your aunt's mink cape with the tails round the bottom — like bobbles round a lamp-shade. And tell me, Emma — that pimply cousin of yours, hung with cameras — why must he have so many? Could he get by, say, on three?"

"It's his hobby," explained Emma. She thought a moment: "So it was Randall?" she said.

"Not entirely, no. You see . . . most of us had been working all day and there was your uncle ordering expensive drinks and going on in that voice of his about 'student' Paris, JeanPaul Sartre and what-not . . ." He broke off, leaning back in his chair. "Oh, I don't know. I suppose I was prejudiced. And that first day when you all arrived —"

"Go on. Say it. Let's say everything. Just once," she added quickly with sudden caution.

"Well, that great grinning brute of a car, champing its metal teeth, too big even to get in the courtyard —"

"You were watching — that day we arrived?"

"Of course I was watching. Most of the rue de Seine was watching. I was up in my room trying to draw."

Emma looked thoughtful. "I was happy that day," she said after a moment, "happier, I think, than I've ever been since in Paris. I was enchanted with the whole place — the narrow street, the glimpse of the river — and then your gate with this sudden turn into the courtyard: the vine, the broken shutters . . . I suppose I was —" she broke off suddenly. "And so you were there, all the time, sulking behind the curtains — spying down on us?"

"I wasn't spying," explained Paul patiently. "And I don't have curtains. You were making the hell of a row."

"We were?" exclaimed Emma. "You mean the police were. And the concierge. And that wall-eyed man with the long loaves. We just sat there, quiet as mice, stuck in the gateway. And even *that* wasn't our fault, the woman had said — drive in."

"And so you could have," he retorted quickly, "with a normal-sized car!"

Emma laughed.

"And it wasn't my car," Emma went on, "there was no need, afterwards, to take it out on me. I mean, once you heard I was only a poor relation —"

"I don't know what you mean," said Paul.

"A student teacher — that sort of thing: I mean even then you went on being pretty unfriendly. Until that day —" Emma smiled suddenly, thinking back, "the day I broke a heel off my shoe. Do you remember? And Jean-Marie brought me home in a taxi . . ." she hesitated, watching his face.

"What about it?" asked Paul, expressionless.

"You were better after that. Much better. He must have started a rumour that I was human or something."

"He didn't rave, if that's what you think."

"What did he say?" asked Emma curiously.

Paul smiled. "'*Pas mal*', I think, were the exact words."

Emma flushed: "Why does anyone ever try to make out that the French are fulsome?"

"Do they?" he asked, laughing.

"But," she went on, a slight edge to her voice, "even after that, if ever I happened to come alone to the Martinique . . ."

"You shouldn't ever have come alone to the Martinique."

"Paul, I had to go somewhere . . . sometimes. But even then, as I say, there was still a kind of atmosphere . . . I couldn't get past your politeness. And after a bit, the talk would die off; people would wander away — and I knew perfectly well you would all meet up again later, somewhere else . . . somewhere safer from me."

"No, Emma, you're wrong: it wasn't like that, at all."

"What was it, then?"

"You were so obviously a bird of passage; we felt laid-on, somehow, like local colour — as though you were slumming, or sight-seeing, or something. You belonged to a different world — a neutral observer — and we knew you were going back: to report there most likely."

"What kind of world? Why was it so different? You knew I was working my way through college? That's not luxury, you know . . ."

"But those were just words . . . I mean, words don't always register. People go by —" he broke off suddenly. "Oh, I don't know."

"You do know," said Emma, watching him as he leaned over the table, drawing with his matchstick. "I mean, the first time you saw me, somehow . . . for some reason, you just took against me."

"Not exactly," he said, without looking up and, after a moment, he laughed.

"Go on," urged Emma, "you long to say it."

He raised his head and looked at her, cocking an eyebrow: "You were so damnably overdressed," he said slowly.

Emma blinked, the barest hurt flicker. "Was I?" she said evenly. After a moment, she went on. "They were only the kind of clothes that any girl — I mean, a girl like me who hasn't been to Paris — thinks of wearing in Paris. And, even then, they were nothing out of the ordinary — I mean, some of them were quite cheap."

"You're angry."

"Not very."

"I'm just saying it," he interrupted, "— once." He laughed, a trifle uncertainly, watching her face. "Well, that was the idea, wasn't it?"

"Yes," agreed Emma without conviction and, after a moment, she went on, "it's a pity in one way, that you didn't say it earlier."

"Why, Emma?"

"It's funny, " she explained, "now I look back on it: the more dull and touristy you made me feel, the more trouble I took with my clothes; glamour at all costs, sort of thing. I used to put on all my dresses one after another — in a kind of desperate rotation. Didn't you notice?"

"Yes," he said. "That was a mistake."

"Didn't you like any of my clothes?"

"On a garden-party level, yes — all of them. Drink up your wine."

Emma took a sip: it was ice-cold, a little too dry — not comforting. She set aside the glass. After a while she said hopefully, "But you took to me all the same?"

"Yes, darling Emma, I took to you."

"Why?"

"I can't tell you now in a fish restaurant."

"Couldn't you try?"

"No, Emma," he said, "why don't you eat?"

Emma took up her fork and touched an oyster; then, unhappily, she laid down the fork. She buttered a piece of bread and, biting into it, she remarked: "And I know the exact day and the exact moment when you decided to give me up."

He paused at his third oyster. "I decided? When?" He seemed amazed.

"It was that night we came home late," said Emma, "the night we walked along the river."

"But we often walked along the river."

"Not after dark. It was the night you showed me Notre Dame upside down, floodlit in the black water — and when we got back you climbed the gate, not to wake the concierge . . . Don't you remember?"

"Oh, that night," he said; and seemed shaken a little; he swallowed two more oysters and took a gulp of wine. "What did I say?"

"You didn't say anything. I just stood beside you in the darkness and I knew. After that night, wherever we went or whatever we did, you always brought Simone."

"Sounds a bit obvious," he remarked.

"It was obvious," said Emma.

225

He pushed his plate away — suddenly impatient. "I was in love with you," he explained angrily.

Emma caught her breath: "But what had you got against me? Why was that so wrong?"

"I don't know — I couldn't make you out. I — I thought you might just go to town on it for the moment — somebody-I-met-in-Paris — Notre Dame-in-the-moonlight — that sort of thing. And — I wasn't going to wear it. I knew, when this uncle and aunt of yours turned up from Sweden, you were going back with them. And that would be that. Better back-pedal, I thought — and make a wide loop — while the going was good."

"The going wasn't good — for me. I sensed you were back-pedalling as you call it. And I didn't know why. I sensed it that night, when we got back, and stood in the dark hall. We had taken off our shoes you remember — because it was so late and you didn't want your mother to grumble — and we couldn't find the light switch. Do you remember, Paul?"

"Yes, I remember."

"Suddenly, as I stood beside you in the darkness, I felt you make that decision. I remember everything about that evening . . . the front door half open, the smell of lime flowers from the river . . . we stood there quite a moment without speaking, with our shoes in our hands, and it was as though I could hear your thoughts as well as your breathing. And suddenly —" she paused as though to control her voice, "I — I felt them change . . ."

"What happened?"

"Nothing happened." She gave a short laugh. "After a moment, you switched on the light . . ."

He was silent, looking down; after a while he said slowly, "If, say, just before that — you'd have put out your hand —"

"Oh, no, Paul —" she cried sharply.

He turned, surprised by the panic in her voice: and she stared back at him, rigid-faced: it was as though she were trying not to tremble. "You'd have repulsed me," she said, slowly — keeping her eyes steady.

"No, Emma. Never —"

"You stood there with your hand on the light switch and watched me go upstairs. And when I turned and smiled at you from the half-landing —" she hesitated, "I saw your face."

"Don't, Emma —"

"It was . . . closed, cold . . . but sort of amused: you smiled —" she turned her head sharply as though to flick off the memory. "No wonder, after that, I began to talk about the trip home. No wonder, no wonder. And going about with you and Simone . . . *dragging* about with you and Simone . . . trying to laugh, trying to make conversation, trying to look as though I did not care . . ."

"I thought you didn't," he said.

"I did it as well as that?"

He threw her a glance: "You did it very well."

"You minded?"

There was a small movement in his face, a flicker: "Don't be silly, Emma —" he said quietly.

She was silent, watching his expression. "Then you did it very well," she remarked after a moment.

He turned towards her: "Need we go on with this?"

"No, we needn't. I was just thinking —" she began to smile, "about this back-pedalling of yours; you were trying so hard to make a 'wide loop' as you call it, but what you really got us into was a 'vicious circle'. And there we'd still be — going round and round: I mean, one of us had to break out, somehow."

He laughed, a trifle grimly. "And I suppose it had to be me."

Emma smiled lightly. "I suppose it ought to have been, really."

He looked surprised: "Well, it was, wasn't it?"

"I don't understand," said Emma bewildered.

"I came round to the hotel this morning. Didn't you get my message. Asking you to telephone before twelve?"

"No," said Emma blankly.

"I waited in until about three-thirty. You mean to say they never told you?"

"No, when I came in, some Brazilians were arriving: they were all round the desk — and I rather rushed through the foyer . . . And the next time I came downstairs —" her hand strayed to her hair, "I must have looked quite different." She turned an amused face towards him: "They didn't recognize me!" she said.

Paul frowned, leaning forward. "One moment, Emma, let's get this straight: when you came just now to the Martinique and said what you did say, you hadn't had my message? You came without knowing — without knowing whether . . ."

"Yes," said Emma, "I came without knowing."

"Oh, Emma —" said Paul, and reached out his hand.

"Don't make me cry," she implored, blinking hard and trying to smile.

He took hold of her wrist. "You swear you didn't know? You swear you didn't get the message?"

"Of course I didn't. If only I *had* got it! After that ghastly goodbye business last night — I mean, Paul that was a brush-off if ever there was one — to hear that you had come round this morning: that you were waiting for me to telephone — that would have been —" she broke off. "Oh, don't you see, Paul?"

"Of course, I see." After a moment, he asked bluntly, "Why did you cut your hair?"

"Just to see."

"See what?"

"What it looked like with this jersey. That long hair looked wrong somehow — with this great jersey. I meant to cut it only a little. But I couldn't get it straight. I kind of just went on cutting —" she laughed uncertainly. "Well, you see the result."

"Yes, it's —" he broke off, leaning back to look at her.

"It's what? Do say —"

"Perfect. As well you know."

"I didn't know," exclaimed Emma angrily, "I thought it looked hideous. Before I came in here, I — I could have jumped in the Seine."

"Why, Emma? — what do you mean — before you came in here?"

"You see —" said Emma more gently, "I had a kind of reason for buying this jersey."

"What kind of reason?"

She gave a slight laugh. "I wanted to see, just once, what I looked like dressed like — Nana or Simone or any of that Martinique lot. Whether I really was so different. I mean, Paul, I'm just as young, just as struggling —"

"I know, I know," he said quickly.

"Then when I looked in the glass, I wished suddenly that *you* could see me too, just once — dressed like this. I felt almost bold enough to try it — to walk down to the Martinique, and see if you were there — it was as though this jersey was a kind of disguise or armour, or something. But, after I'd cut my hair —" her voice became tragic suddenly — "I hadn't the courage. No, let me finish . . ." placatingly, she touched his face. "I didn't dare even to face my aunt . . . let alone you! That's why I ran out of the hotel — to put off meeting her. Then I didn't know where to go: I just walked and walked and ended up here."

"And you haven't been back?"

"Not yet."

"Did you telephone?"

"Once. They'd gone out to lunch."

"What are you going to say to your aunt about us?"

Emma looked down at her plate. After a moment, she said in a tentative voice, "She knows."

"knows?" repealed Paul incredulously.

"Oh, Paul —" cried Emma suddenly, in anguished impatience, "I was very upset last night."

"Of course," said Paul. "I was, too. I —"

"What did you do?" she asked curiously.

"I walked about. I don't know what I did."

"Well, I behaved like an idiot — I did a kind of faint in the hallway. They got the hotel doctor. I think it was rather a bad kind of faint. He gave me an injection. He asked if I'd ever had rheumatic fever . . ."

"Have you?"

"No. Then he asked my aunt if I'd had any kind of emotional shock lately . . ."

"Oh, Emma —" exclaimed Paul.

"It's all right," said Emma, "it was a good thing really because afterwards, when they'd put me to bed, and I was sniffling rather, my aunt came in. I — you have to tell somebody: so I told her."

"What did she say?"

"She wanted to call you up: she wanted to get you to come round."

"Good lord!"

"Her heart's in the right place, Paul — even if she does wear bobbles round the bottom of her cape. But I wouldn't let her call you — I'd had enough by then: I just wanted to get on the boat to get away," she turned towards him. "Did you mind my telling her?"

"No, no. I —" Paul looked down; there was a strange expression on his face.

"Well," prompted Emma.

"I told my mother," he said.

"Oh, no —"

"Yes. She's got a key to my apartment and there she was in the kitchen this morning — making coffee."

"Why?" asked Emma. "Does she often do that?"

"No, never. But the concierge let me in at God knows what hour and she must have gone gossiping to my mother, said I was ill or drunk — or something . . ."

"And what happened? What did she say?"

"She suggested we took a trip to the Midi."

"You and I?" asked Emma, amazed.

Paul laughed. "No, darling, she and I." He ran a hand through his hair, "For me to get over it, I imagine."

"You told her it was me?"

"No, I just said — a girl."

Emma smiled. "They're very romantic, aren't they? I mean far more than we are?"

"My mother isn't: she's French."

"I'm terrified of your mother."

"It's me you're going to marry," he reminded her.

"Oh —" began Emma and caught back her breath.

"Well, aren't you?"

"I didn't quite know —" said Emma, but at the look on his face she added hurriedly, "Yes, yes, of course I am —"

"But just now —" he seemed bewildered, "when you came down to the Martinique, you said —"

"I don't remember what I said," cried Emma interrupting.

(But she did remember; staring now at the questioning, anxious eyes, she remembered the whole scene: the incredulous look on his face as she marched up to the table, the stunned slow way he had risen from his chair. And the words she had learned by heart: short and to the point, a bald announcement, one he might take or leave: "I can't go tomorrow. I want to stay here. And live with you or marry you or —" here she had dried up for a moment and had concluded lamely, "or whatever you want."

Then for the first time she had become aware of the ring of startled faces, unrecognizable individually, blurred as much by panic as by her lack of glasses; and that Paul had seized her roughly by the elbow and, with his other hand had signalled a taxi; she remembered the taxi drawing up, Jean-Marie diving across the pavement to open the door; she remembered scrambling in with Paul behind her (the cab door swinging to on his calf, as is the way with Paris taxis); she remembered Simone's white jersey detaching itself from the darker ones around the table, and Simone's face at the car's closed window; she remembered trying to hear what Simone was saying; Simone laughing suddenly and blowing a hurried kiss from her two cupped hands. She remembered the sudden, awful moment of shyness alone with Paul in the taxi; the livid flicker of the street lights across his face as he leaned towards her, saying "Where now?" And how, stammering a little, she had asked to be brought back here, to this fish restaurant where some minutes before she had left her glasses.)

Paul had been watching her face: "Let's go now," he said, breaking a silence.

Emma came back from her dream. "Yes," she said gently on a long breath.

"What I still don't see," he persisted in a puzzled voice, pushing aside his plate, "is why you went on sitting here, for hours and hours. I mean, once you'd decided to come and find me."

"I hadn't decided. Quite the contrary. I just sat here. Feeling hideous and drinking coffee. You were the last person I wanted to see . . ."

"But something changed your mind."

"Yes," said Emma.

"What?"

Emma looked thoughtful. "I think . . ." she began to smile, "it was a little man in a toupé, eating whelks. Whelks or snails — something you pick out with a chromium thing like a crochet-hook. He gave me confidence."

"Now, Emma —" Paul begged, in a voice which sounded both patient and despairing, "don't let's start being symbolical."

"He kept looking at me," Emma explained.

"But men always look at girls in Paris."

"Not like this," she assured him seriously, "he seemed positively entranced; it was extraordinary — I actually put on my glasses to make sure."

"Of what?"

"His expression: it might have been horror."

"But you don't put on your glasses. Darling Emma, that isn't the technique, at all."

"I had to *know*. At first I thought I must have a smut on the end of my nose, or something. But I hadn't. And after I'd put my glasses on, I saw that quite a number of other people were staring, too — with the same kind of expression. And what's more," she told him, her eyes widening, "two of them were women."

"What kind of expression?"

"Serious, terribly interested. You couldn't feel embarrassed or offended by it: it wasn't quite a personal look — it was more the kind of look you'd give a picture."

Paul laughed: "Honestly, Emma —"

"Well, it was most impressive. People would eat a little and then look up again. You may laugh, but I'm not exaggerating: nobody has ever looked at me quite like that before — not in my whole life! And there you have it," she went on, as Paul signalled a waiter, "the whole story: I suppose, that is what changed my mind. And I might never have noticed," she went on, feeling in her pocket for a lipstick, "except for the little man eating whelks."

Glancing up, she saw again the blur of faces of which only the waiter's swam into focus as he hurried towards their table. She ran a smoothing hand across her wisps of hair. "Where are we going?" she asked.

"Anywhere," he said, "away from here."

The waiter pulled aside the table as Emma, half-rising, slid her way along the bench. "I'll ask about my glasses," she explained, "and meet you at the door."

He watched her as she crossed the room, childish-looking in her bulky sweater, picking her way among the crowded tables, her smooth hair shining through the smoke haze. And he watched, too, the heads which turned as she passed. Barely turned, he noticed with surprise: the casual approving glance — that was all; the usual Gallic tribute to a pretty face — no more, no less. He took out his wallet, chose a note and, suddenly thoughtful, laid it on the table.

The waiter took no notice; and Paul, looking up, saw the glassy brightness of a pair of eyes staring blankly into space. Blankly? No, not quite — the man was watching something, his expression rapt and serious, his gaze absorbed, held and directed past Paul's head and slightly above Paul's left shoulder.

It is not easy to turn on a high-backed bench: it involves a conspicuous and awkward movement of the whole body. Paul, throwing a preliminary glance round the nearest tables noticed, with some bewilderment, several similar stares converging on his table. So this was what Emma had spoken of. But Emma was not here!

And then he saw.

Behind Emma's seat and obliquely behind his own, stood a brightly-lighted, glass-fronted aquarium — larger than most; it had to be for (Paul saw) it contained — in sluggish motion — one fair-sized octopus, two large conger eels and an indeterminate number of blue-black lobsters, weaving a curiously sinister pattern of deep-sea life as they crawled, poured, folded and unfolded in penned, frustrated passion. There was slow menace and cold fury in that tank — an awe-inspiring glimpse of sullen savagery incongruous to find in such surroundings.

No wonder, he thought, that it caught the eye and held the fascinated attention.

Paul gazed a moment — who would not? — and then, turning away, an uneasy thought seemed to strike him: a thought which, from the scared way he whipped round on the bench, had suddenly assumed a shade of panic. Staring across the room, he saw Emma at last, partially obscured by a group of new arrivals: she was standing beside the cash desk and was shaking hands with the proprietress; both were smiling in some genial glow of mutual congratulation; and in Emma's free hand, as she raised her wrist in a laughing gesture, he saw the glint of glass. As he waited impatiently, tapping his foot, for the waiter to dole out his change, he saw with something like terror Emma turn and gaze short-sightedly across the room straight towards his table; he watched her take out her handkerchief and — with what, then, seemed like sadistic deliberation — begin to polish her glasses.

Paul marvelled afterwards, thinking it over, at the speed at which he must have shot from his bench and the precision with which he skidded out his lightning, zig-zag course across the room, scattering in his wake a trail of careless, backthrown apologies.

"Oh, there you are," said Emma, with mild surprise as he hurtled into focus.

He seized her two hands in his — glasses, handkerchief and all, and dragged her hurriedly towards the door: "Come on," he stammered, "quick!"

"But what's the hurry?" she asked, looking (he noted in spite of his panic) suddenly like a very odd boy-angel.

"We've got to get a taxi," he explained, and hit by chance on a tone of voice so blandly reasonable, that for the short moment, it deflected opposition. Once through the swing doors, he breathed again. "There!" he said, releasing her hands suddenly. And they faced each other on the lighted pavement.

"Paul —" began Emma, with a backward glance at the still moving swing door, "I rather wanted to —"

Quickly he took her in his arms, firmly he kissed her: "Promise me something —" he begged.

"What?" asked Emma.

"Promise me that never, in your whole life, will you ever enter that place again. Ever, you hear? On any account whatsoever."

"But why?" she asked, very bewildered.

"Never mind why. Promise."

"All right — I promise. But what's the hurry? Why are you pulling me?"

"Across the road — to get a taxi."

"Where are we going?"

"Somewhere. Anywhere you like —"

"I don't know . . ." Suddenly, she laughed and twisted round to face him. Their eyes met. Both stared for a moment, both questioning. Then Emma turned away. "Oh well," she said with seeming carelessness, "what about the Martinique . . . ?"

CHAPTER
FIFTEEN

Beauty Bar

Mum heard the words first.

With metallic clarity, they clove through the babble of the bargain basement.

"Stand a little closer, please, ladies! You needn't be afraid of me; I'm not selling anything and we must leave the gangway free. A little closer, please, madam, and then I needn't shout . . ."

There was an uneasy shuffling of feet; shopping bags were gripped closer and slipping parcels adjusted as, obediently, the ring of tired faces moved inwards towards the chromium-plated shrine.

Mum joined on, behind.

"Now, I want you all to watch me carefully while I apply the powder . . ."

Mum pushed a little. Her feet were hurting her and she let her ankles sag so that the outer edge of her soles took the weight of her body. She forgot, for a moment, the haunting, Lorelei-call of the straw hat with its twist of mauve veiling. Something was happening here and Mum had never been one to miss a sight. The stolid faces about her expressed a defensive curiosity; avoiding each other's eyes they gazed on the high-priestess whose

239

hands and tongue, in ceaseless movement, wove the charm that held the circle spellbound.

"In this palette, I have mixed a special powder for madam — a little peach, a little coral, a touch of 'suntan', and a dash of green; of green, yes, ladies!" Mum blinked before the brightness of that dazzling smile. "Why green — you ask me?" they had asked her nothing. "Well, ladies, I reply with another question. Why do you use Dolly Blue bluing in your washing tubs?"

Expressionless and still, they looked back at her. It was not what she said that drew their interest, but how she said it, the lift-girl accent, the hair-thin eyebrows and the flashing pinktipped hands.

Mum edged a little nearer. Now, she could see the victim — a grey-blue, tweed coat; flesh-coloured stockings; uncleaned brown shoes and a pair of red hands gripping a purse and gloves; but the face — head turned back, with closed eyes, the throat exposed — was sculptured, gleaming, almost beautiful.

"Now, watch carefully, ladies, because it is most important to apply your powder in the right way. Be lavish!" The face of the victim disappeared in a floury haze and emerged at last lifeless, still, unearthly pale. A death mask.

"Goodness!" ejaculated Mum, under her breath.

"She doesn't look too healthy, does she, ladies? But she feels grand; don't you, madam? Your skin feels ever so fresh, doesn't it now?" The victim's lips twisted a little; they mumbled assent and went on smiling, painfully self-conscious.

"Now we wipe off the surplus . . . I must remind you ladies that this is only a slight demonstration of what you get inside for the three shillings and sixpence. Three-and-sixpence, ladies, the price of one packet of cigarettes! Miss Lorimer, have you room for one more lady? Two? There, ladies, two of you can go inside and get just what I'm giving this lady, for three-and-sixpence each. Only takes ten minutes and you just won't know yourself when you come out. There, madam, I thought so. You won't regret it."

With morbid fascination, Mum watched two bashful women edge their way towards the curtained alcove; she was enjoying herself; if only she could sit down, her cup would be full. She leaned her hip against a pillar and adjusted her parcels to relieve her aching arm.

Mum was little and brown. She had a sweet, sallow, rather shiny face and quick, dark eyes; patient as a monkey's. Her shoes were down at heel because they were her old ones. She had not dressed up. She had just popped out: "I'll just pop out and match that sweater of Ernie's." She had cooked the dinner. She had washed up. She had damped and folded the clothes and would run an iron over them before supper and then, in the evening, she would have a nice sit-down with the paper.

It had been lovely outdoors today. Spring. You felt, somehow, you wanted to get out: I'll just slip my coat on and run round to the bargain basement. The sun was so hot that she had walked on the shady side of the street; some girls were wearing sleeveless frocks and Mum would have taken her coat off if her old skirt had met the blouse at the back. The hats in the shop windows were trimmed with flowers and gay with wisps of coloured tulle.

That dark straw with its twist of lilac veil — it was on the twelve-and-sixpenny counter — she had held it on her hand, twisting it about. It would look really silly on me with me old navy coat, she had told herself, but it would sort of suit me. She meant that she had had, when she was a young girl, just such a hat as this — perched on the head — and that Dad had liked it. Courting, they were then. But the sight of her older face in the mirror had disillusioned her, almost grey it looked, with a wisp of falling hair. "No, it would look really silly on me" — and, without self-pity or regret, completely matter-of-fact, she had placed it back upon the stand. Anyway, she had only eleven shillings to last her until the end of the week.

Just as well, she thought, craning her neck. The demonstrator — oh, so lightly — was brushing the client's brows with a little black brush. Well I never, thought Mum, feeling to see if her purse was safe (there was that pound note in the inner pocket to be paid into her post office savings account) — so that's how they do it. Yes, she had her purse all right and she ought really to be getting along. Soon the children would be home from school and Ernie was going out and would want his supper early. But she lingered still and watched, absorbed. The victim was standing up now, shaking down her coat, straightening her hair. Well, she was a pretty girl — she was, really — except for her hands and feet. She didn't look too painted up, either.

". . . for three shillings and sixpence. But I can do one more lady free. Don't all speak at once." Some people turned to go so Mum edged to the front; she would like to see it right from the beginning — it took only ten minutes, after all. "What shy ladies you all are! Come along . . . it's not often you'd get a treatment like this free. Why, in Bond Street a treatment like this would cost you a guinea. Or perhaps you're all beautiful enough already!"

Mum smiled sheepishly with the others, and the demonstrator caught her eye. "What about you, madam?"

Mum went weak at the knees. She had the drawn feeling she felt in a lift when it overshot the mark. There were a few desperate seconds while she calculated whether to turn and walk away — so rude to this smart smiling young lady, whose own manners were impeccable — or to shake her head firmly and say, "no" (ungrateful, after all this free entertainment). She hesitated, smiling uncomfortably, clutching her parcels more tightly.

"Come along, madam: be a sport. You look the sort of lady who'd be game for anything. You'll feel ever so fresh and rested afterwards. It's quite free."

The other women were looking at her, half-smiling, willing her to go: urging her, it seemed, to be their sacrifice. Mum knew she must accept: she wanted to stop herself while there was yet time, but she had hesitated for too long; she felt herself nod and heard her own voice mumble, "All right".

Then it all became a dream, or like being in a stage play; or a bride again, with everybody staring at her outside the church. The assistant took her parcels; the demonstrator took her hat, laying it with such care on the shelf (as if it were a Paris model instead of her old felt) and her gloves beside it. How worn they looked, and cracked! It was a comfort to sit down; to take her weight off her aching feet. She felt a lot better, sitting — more at ease. She could even give a shy glance at the ring of sheepish women. They looked so awkward, somehow, standing up. She was the queen now and they, as it were, the courtiers. She laid her head back, as she had seen the other woman do, and closed her eyes. A band of cool linen was pinned round her brow and they had tied something below her chin. Eyes closed, the crowd shut out, a blessed peace enfolded her — a suave sense of bland irresponsibility.

Something cold was lightly slapped upon her cheeks. Dreamily she heard the patter; ". . . liquefying cleansing cream . . . always the upward movement . . . lift the sagging muscles . . ." Lightly-tapping, cool fingers, curiously hypnotic and comforting. She felt the tiredness being worked from her face, being lifted off and flicked away by a flip of those nimble fingers. It could not hurt her, after all. When she was young, she had had a pretty skin — like ivory, they said it was. Young? Well, she still wasn't so old — only forty-nine and not a grey hair.

"Our special astringent lotion."

Ah! This was cold and stinging, like the spray on her cheeks that day at Lulworth Cove — on her honeymoon, it was. Her cheeks had felt just like this — cold as slabs of meat and wet with spray. Spring . . . just this time of year, but colder.

"Now, ladies, I am about to apply our Oil-of-Turtle-Skin-Food-and-Powder-Foundation combined. Just a dab on forehead, chin and cheeks. Work it in . . . always the upward movement."

Velvet-smooth her face felt now, thick and soft, no longer wet and slippery.

"Now, ladies, for the rouge . . ."

Mum opened her eyes at that. She saw the ring of faces, the glaring bulb of light and, beyond, the kaleidoscopic aisles of the shop, a dim, humming accompaniment of sound and colour. She realized again just where she was. Rouge. She thought of Dad and Ernie, and of Flo, her sister-in-law; she thought of the younger ones, Rosie and Lionel, arriving home from school: she thought of tea, of ironing, and of supper; and here she was, on this chair, making a fool of herself in front of all these people. But there was no escape. She was a prisoner . . . bound in bands of linen stronger than fetters of steel . . . she dared not move a muscle of her face, much less get up and walk away. Well, what does it matter, for once; she told herself; I slave for them, don't I? — And the more I do, the more they expect. Look at Ernie bringing me his shoes to clean. He really oughtn't to bring me his shoes to clean. (But it was Mum who said, "Give them here, Ernie. I'll do them twice as well in half the time.") Well, let them get their own tea for once; it wouldn't hurt them; Flo was there, wasn't she? She could look after things for a change. But she'd always something to say, Flo had, and an eye on the clock — proper spinster, as you might say; critical: not that she'd any right to be — they'd taken her in, hadn't they, she and Dad — and given her a home? But when she closed her eyes again, repose had fled.

"On the cheekbones . . . blend it carefully . . . no hard edges . . . always the upward movement. Never forget the upward movement. The colour I have chosen for madam is Rose-geranium . . ."

Rose-geranium! Mum opened panic-stricken eyes meeting those of the demonstrator (stiff-lashed with mascara) as the latter leaned above. The carmine smile responded gaily to the anguish of that inarticulate appeal: "Very discreet, madam. Don't be alarmed. I am giving you what we call our Back-to-Nature make-up."

Slightly reassured, Mum sat quiet for the powder and lipstick. ". . . follow the line of the upper lip; take it right into the corners. And now, ladies, I am going to give you a tip — a really valuable tip — free! When you kiss a friend, don't want (do you) to leave a big red mark on her cheek . . ." Mum had a startled vision of Flo's lean jowl branded shrilly with a scarlet bow. "And you know how embarrassing it is to leave a rim of lipstick on a cup . . . " Mum saw Dad's thick breakfast cup with the coloured birds.

"Or on the end of your cigarette . . ." For this Mum had no picture. "Well, all you have to do is to take a piece of tissue — so; and lay it between the lips — so. Now, lightly press together — press the lips together, madam — and all superfluous colour is removed — so!"

It was like a dance. It was like a ritual. Mum was caught up again in the metallic, scented rhythm. She suffered her eyebrows to be brushed and her lashes to be darkened. She even consented to "the teeniest, weepiest, little soupcon of eye shadow."

When they removed the head bandage, Mum looked at her face in the hand glass.

It was not her face at all.

But it was a nice face. She rather liked it, with those brown eyes — sort of neat and bright and tidy. But it was not her face. She couldn't just stare at it like that. She'd have to take it somewhere and get used to it first. "Yes," she said. "Very good. Very good, I call it."

They were brushing down her coat. She smiled at the crowd, no longer afraid of them — a humorous little smile, almost a wink; it said: "A lot of nonsense, but I've done it. I've got it over . . ." The demonstrator was saying, "Another lady. I can do one other lady free. Don't all speak at once. Stand a little closer, please, ladies, we must leave the gangway clear. You needn't be frightened of me . . ."

Mum gathered up her parcels, laying her hat on top of them. No, they needn't be frightened. She'd done it. Mum had done it. It's all right really, nothing much to be frightened of.

She elbowed her way out of the ring. The shop looked different, somehow. She felt rested, almost gay and there, a little way along on the left-hand side, were the mirrors of the hat counter. She'd just have another look at that face.

People brushed by her; perhaps they thought she always looked like this because they did not stare at her; they looked through her with the anxious, searching eyes of shoppers — the wandering, dazzled eyes, people in a dream, clasping their parcels, dragging their children, lost in a world of fancy blouse fronts and satin-covered coat-hangers. Above and through the shrubbery of hatstands. Mum saw her face. It seemed, now, more like herself but brighter and younger. She turned away: Mum never thought it was right to stare too long into a looking glass. It was as bad as sitting down with a book in the morning or going to the pictures more than twice a week. And then, once more, she saw the dark, straw hat with its cunning twist of lilac veil. Irresistibly attracted, she laid her parcels on the counter. Her "old felt" rolled to the floor. She did not even notice. The straw hat was in her hand and then, as if by magic, on her head.

Well!

And it had looked so plain, but they made them in a kind of way . . . "artistic" you might say, but it was more like . . . more like a trick, done by a conjurer, more like a miracle . . .

"Nice, madam, isn't it? A copy of a model. We don't often get hats like that down here."

Mum looked sideways at the lounging attendant. "How much is it?"

"Twelve-and-six, madam, reduced from six guineas upstairs."

"It sort of suits me," said Mum, staring, spellbound, at her reflection.

She'd seen people looking like that. Yes, she'd seen them in the street and in buses, but she had never dreamed that she, Mum, could look like that. It didn't seem to matter that she wasn't really good-looking. Below the hat, her face was softly glowing, neat, alive.

She looked — well, she looked "smart", sort of; she looked nice. But barely articulate, struggling up from the deep well of her sound common sense, came the thought: "Not with my own face, I wouldn't —" But just to walk down the street, in that hat and with that face, once! That glowing face, that curving hat brim swathed in lilac mist! "I could", thought Mum, "just buy myself a little box of Rose-geranium if it makes all that difference . . ."

"Twelve-and-six," said Mum aloud. "I don't call that so cheap."

"Oh, it is, madam. For that hat."

Somehow Mum could not bring herself to take it off. She noticed her old felt and stooped to pick it up. It was dusty from the floor. Absentmindedly, she beat it against her coat, staring into the glass. She was losing her reason, that's what was happening to her. Eleven shillings to last until the end of the week and here she was, with her face all painted up and a twelve-and-sixpenny hat on her head! But on the other hand, she *did* work — and she never bought anything for herself. Why, even this old navy coat had been Flo's. Dad wouldn't mind. Dad often said, "Go and buy yourself a nice hat. Go and get yourself a decent pair of shoes."

But there were the grocer and the butcher, and the rent, and the rates, and the light, and the coal . . . and come rain or shine, putting a little by. Yes, she had that pound note for the post office savings bank. Ah — physically, Mum felt the impact — that pound note! It was all very well, and quite safe, to try on a twelve-and-sixpenny hat with only eleven shillings in your purse — but thirty-one shillings was another story. A pound note, to Mum a symbol of her life's security . . . never, each month, had she failed to save it — never failed to put it in; with it she held at bay those lurking shadows — illness, accident, loss of work — which haunted the darker corners of her mind.

No, she couldn't break into that pound note. Sheer wickedness, that would be! But, she reminded herself, an extra five shillings a month would, in four months, make up a pound. A pound? The hat was only twelve-and-six.

"All right," said Mum aloud, "I'll take it."

The attendant was waiting. What for? For her to take off the hat? The idea! — As if she were going to take it off now! "Put my felt in a bag, will you?" she said hurriedly and took out her pound note. Well, she'd done it and no mistake; and there was Flo, her sister-in-law, to face.

It was not what Flo said, thought Mum, so much as how she said it: the venomous patience and the steady eye: "Rosie needs new shoes, Alice, — her toes are all cramped . . ." — that's all it would take, said right.

But she doesn't, Mum told herself, fighting her way up towards the ground floor, I looked this morning . . . they're plenty big enough — she can't say that, not about Rosie. Nor about Ernie's sweater . . . I've got the wool, haven't I? And the rubber mat she asked for, and her prescription. And she's got that beige beret she's so proud of . . .

Outdoors, spring glittered on the pavements; it was there waiting for her as she emerged from the heated department; she stepped into it and it flowed over her; it refreshed and excited her; her face felt lovely; it really did in this light air and the misty lavender veil just stirred against her cheek. I wish, she thought, that I hadn't got to go straight home. I feel as if I'd like — her mind hesitated, searching for acceptable dissipation — to go to the pictures.

But she couldn't. That would never do, not on her own like that, without the others. "And anyway", she told herself, "here's my bus . . ."

As she climbed the stairs to the flat, compunction assailed her. ". . . spending all that money. I ought to have brought something home for Dad — a nice bit of liver sausage." She stood on the murky landing outside the front door. She heard the children arguing and Flo's sharp whine, "Now, that's enough!"

At last she moved. Piling her parcels upon the mat, she took off the new hat; armed with her "old felt", she rang the bell.

"So there you are!" said Flo, looking, in the dark passage, more like a bird of prey than ever. "I've done the ironing," she added. The first phrase was a rebuke; the second a complaint. Suddenly, Mum felt very tired.

"You needn't of," she said crossly.

"Wherever've you been?"

"Out," said Mum.

She laid her parcels on the hall table, except the bag that held the hat.

"Ernie wanted his tea early. I had to make it special. We didn't know where on earth you'd got to. And Rosie's hurt her hand."

Mum pushed past Flo towards the bathroom. "Is the table laid?" she asked, without turning her head.

"How could the table be laid? I've been ironing on it."

"All right," said Mum. "I won't be a jiff," and she locked the bathroom door.

There at the mirror, she put on the hat. Under the curved brim her new face looked at her, forlorn and anxious-eyed but, somehow, "nice" — smooth and softly tinted, with shadowed eyes and accentuated lips; it was Mum and it wasn't Mum. As she looked, the brown eyes filled with tears. Wise eyes they were, sad, monkey eyes.

"Come on, Mum," called Dad, from the sitting room. "We all want our tea."

Mum's hand felt blindly for the tap. No, it wasn't any good. Who did she think she was, anyway — Marlene Dietrich? But she couldn't look away from the glass; she saw, surprised, the tears on her cheeks — not her cheeks: those other cheeks.

"All right," she called, "I'm coming. Give us a chance."

Give us a chance? She took her hand from the tap . . . that's what those eyes said — Give us a chance . . . Shakily, a little clumsily, she pulled down the veil: "I'm coming," she called again and unlocked the door.

"Look, Dad," she said, upon the threshold of the sitting room, "got myself a hat."

Dad took the pipe out of his mouth. He was collarless, and his waistcoat sagged in wrinkles above his stomach; but, over the fierce grey moustache, his eyes were round and blue, like a child's. He did not speak at once, and then he said, "You have — and no mistake."

"Like it, Dad?" she asked.

"It's all right." He spoke in a hesitating, careful voice. He sat quite still, his square fingers gripping his pipe, looking back at her as she stood, shyly, in the doorway. A rattle of cups from the kitchen announced that Flo had begun to lay the table. "Makes you look sort of powdered up," Dad added after a moment, but there was no criticism in his voice.

"Well, I am, sort of," said Mum.

Slowly Dad knocked out his pipe, his eyes still on her face. There was a silence in the room, except for the kitchen clatter. Awkwardly Mum touched her hair. "Well," she said, "I'd better be getting this tea," and she turned away as if seeking cover.

Dad sat quite still, looking past the empty doorway.

Mum bustled into the kitchen and flung open the doors of the china cupboard; she began to collect the plates.

Flo laid down the bread knife, her eyes staring.

"Got yourself a new hat, I see."

Mum did not look round. "Any objection?" she asked tartly.

Flo did not reply, and Mum's sharp words vibrated in the silence until at last she turned, plates in hand. "Like it?" she asked, more gently.

The two children, at the table by the window, looked up from their exercise books. "Oh, Mum," Rosie said warmly, "it's ever so nice!"

Still Flo was silent. She stood by the breadboard, the lines in her face and neck cruelly accentuated by the pale, fading light.

"Well," said Mum, putting the plates on the table. "Just thought I'd show you. I'll go and take it off now."

"How much did it cost?" asked Flo.

"Seven-and-six," said Mum, without hesitation.

"Doesn't look to me like a seven-and-sixpenny hat."

"No, it doesn't, does it?" said Mum, edging her way towards the door.

"And your face. You've been and done something to your face!" The incredulous amazement nearly swamped the venom.

Where was Dad? There he was standing in the open doorway of their bedroom; she quickly came beside him and, as if it were a lifeline, she clutched his watch chain.

"What do you want, dear?" she gasped.

Dad's blue eyes looked past her, over her head. He was gazing at a corner cupboard. "My blue suit," he said.

"Yes, dear, of course . . ." and then she stared: "Your blue suit! Whatever do you want with your blue suit?" Slowly she turned to face him.

"To put it on," said Dad.

"Your blue suit! Where are you going?"

"I thought we might go out and get something to eat."

"Who?"

"You and me. Flo'll see to the kids."

In her amazement, Mum's face went blank: "Have you had a raise?" she asked, stupefied.

"A raise? I don't need a raise for a bit of sausage and mash and a seat at the Empire."

Mum glanced quickly at Flo's frozen face; she looked back at Dad. "We've got plenty to eat — you know — the rest of that corned beef we had on Thursday."

"I feel like a bit of something hot tonight," said Dad.

Flo stood quite still, holding the breadknife. There was wonder in her face, a kind of awe.

"Flo wouldn't mind — would you, Flo?" And Flo stared back at him. "No," she said slowly; then, "I wouldn't mind." She spoke automatically, still staring.

"There's a girl," said Dad awkwardly and Flo dropped her head; stooped, she stood, and very still, her chin pressed inwards, as though she held her breath.

As Mum opened the corner cupboard and lifted out the blue suit . . . she saw in its shape the gentle imprint of his personality; human, it looked as it hung from the hanger — the pockets bagged by his hands, the shiny patch where he sat, the stretched cloth at the knees. Eight years old, this suit, and still his best. As gently she laid it on the bed, a feeling of safety and deep gratitude swept over her.

"There you are," she said as he came beside her. They looked down at it as it lay on the quilt, standing together. Neither spoke; then, hesitantly, Mum touched a cuff — very gently — as she might have his hand. "Let's take Flo," she whispered.

ISIS publish a wide range of books in large print, from fiction to biography. A full list of titles is available free of charge from the address below. Alternatively, contact your local library for details of their collection of ISIS large print books.

Details of ISIS complete and unabridged audio books are also available.

Any suggestions for books you would like to see in large print or audio are always welcome.

ISIS

7 Centremead
Osney Mead
Oxford OX2 0ES
(01865) 250333